SCRIBNER REPRINT EDITIONS

THE AMBASSADORS

VOLUME I

HENRY JAMES

AUGUSTUS M. KELLEY • PUBLISHERS
NEW YORK 1971

First Published 1909
(New York: Charles Scribner's Sons.)
Copyright 1909 by Henry James
Renewal Copyright 1937 by Henry James

RE-ISSUED 1971 BY
AUGUSTUS M. KELLEY · PUBLISHERS
New York New York 10001
By Arrangement with CHARLES SCRIBNER'S SONS

· · · · · · · · · · · · · · · · ·

I S B N 0 6 7 8 0 2 8 2 1 4
L C N 7 5 1 5 8 8 0 0

· · · · · · · · · · · · · · · · ·

PRINTED IN THE UNITED STATES OF AMERICA
by THE MURRAY PRINTING COMPANY, FORGE VILLAGE, MASS.

PREFACE

NOTHING is more easy than to state the subject of " The Ambassadors," which first appeared in twelve numbers of *The North American Review* (1903) and was published as a whole the same year. The situation involved is gathered up betimes, that is in the second chapter of Book Fifth, for the reader's benefit, into as few words as possible — planted or " sunk," stiffly and saliently, in the centre of the current, almost perhaps to the obstruction of traffic. Never can a composition of this sort have sprung straighter from a dropped grain of suggestion, and never can that grain, developed, overgrown and smothered, have yet lurked more in the mass as an independent particle. The whole case, in fine, is in Lambert Strether's irrepressible outbreak to little Bilham on the Sunday afternoon in Gloriani's garden, the candour with which he yields, for his young friend's enlightenment, to the charming admonition of that crisis. The idea of the tale resides indeed in the very fact that an hour of such unprecedented ease should have been felt by him *as* a crisis, and he is at pains to express it for us as neatly as we could desire. The remarks to which he thus gives utterance contain the essence of " The Ambassadors," his fingers close, before he has done, round the stem of the full-blown flower ; which, after that fashion, he continues officiously to present to us. " Live all you can ; it 's a mistake not to. It does n't so much matter what you do in particular so long as you have your life. If you have n't had that what *have* you had ? I 'm too old — too old at any rate for what I see. What one loses one loses ; make no mistake about that. Still, we have the illusion of freedom ; therefore don't, like me to-day, be without the memory of that illusion. I was either, at the right time, too stupid or too intelligent to have it, and now I 'm a case of reaction against the mistake. Do what you like so long

as you don't make it. For it *was* a mistake. Live, live!"
Such is the gist of Strether's appeal to the impressed youth,
whom he likes and whom he desires to befriend; the word
" mistake " occurs several times, it will be seen, in the course
of his remarks — which gives the measure of the signal
warning he feels attached to his case. He has accordingly
missed too much, though perhaps after all constitutionally
qualified for a better part, and he wakes up to it in conditions that press the spring of a terrible question. *Would*
there yet perhaps be time for reparation? — reparation, that
is, for the injury done his character; for the affront, he is
quite ready to say, so stupidly put upon it and in which he
has even himself had so clumsy a hand? The answer to
which is that he now at all events *sees*; so that the business
of my tale and the march of my action, not to say the
precious moral of everything, is just my demonstration of
this process of vision.

Nothing can exceed the closeness with which the whole
fits again into its germ. That had been given me bodily, as
usual, by the spoken word, for I was to take the image over
exactly as I happened to have met it. A friend had repeated
to me, with great appreciation, a thing or two said to him
by a man of distinction, much his senior, and to which a
sense akin to that of Strether's melancholy eloquence might
be imputed — said as chance would have, and so easily
might, in Paris, and in a charming old garden attached to a
house of art, and on a Sunday afternoon of summer, many
persons of great interest being present. The observation
there listened to and gathered up had contained part of the
" note " that I was to recognise on the spot as to my purpose — had contained in fact the greater part; the rest was
in the place and the time and the scene they sketched: these
constituents clustered and combined to give me further support, to give me what I may call the note absolute. There
it stands, accordingly, full in the tideway; driven in, with
hard taps, like some strong stake for the noose of a cable,
the swirl of the current roundabout it. What amplified the
hint to more than the bulk of hints in general was the gift

with it of the old Paris garden, for in that token were sealed up values infinitely precious. There was of course the seal to break and each item of the packet to count over and handle and estimate; but somehow, in the light of the hint, all the elements of a situation of the sort most to my taste were there. I could even remember no occasion on which, so confronted, I had found it of a livelier interest to take stock, in this fashion, of suggested wealth. For I think, verily, that there are degrees of merit in subjects — in spite of the fact that to treat even one of the most ambiguous with due decency we must for the time, for the feverish and prejudiced hour, at least figure its merit and its dignity as *possibly* absolute. What it comes to, doubtless, is that even among the supremely good — since with such alone is it one's theory of one's honour to be concerned — there is an ideal *beauty* of goodness the invoked action of which is to raise the artistic faith to its maximum. Then truly, I hold, one's theme may be said to shine, and that of " The Ambassadors," I confess, wore this glow for me from beginning to end. Fortunately thus I am able to estimate this as, frankly, quite the best, " all round," of all my productions; any failure of that justification would have made such an extreme of complacency publicly fatuous.

I recall then in this connexion no moment of subjective intermittence, never one of those alarms as for a suspected hollow beneath one's feet, a felt ingratitude in the scheme adopted, under which confidence fails and opportunity seems but to mock. If the motive of " The Wings of the Dove," as I have noted, was to worry me at moments by a sealing-up of its face — though without prejudice to its again, of a sudden, fairly grimacing with expression — so in this other business I had absolute conviction and constant clearness to deal with; it had been a frank proposition, the whole bunch of data, installed on my premises like a monotony of fine weather. (The order of composition, in these things, I may mention, was reversed by the order of publication; the earlier written of the two books having appeared as the later.) Even under the weight of my hero's years I could feel

PREFACE

my postulate firm; even under the strain of the difference between those of Madame de Vionnet and those of Chad Newsome, a difference liable to be denounced as shocking, I could still feel it serene. Nothing resisted, nothing betrayed, I seem to make out, in this full and sound sense of the matter; it shed from any side I could turn it to the same golden glow. I rejoiced in the promise of a hero so mature, who would give me thereby the more to bite into — since it's only into thickened motive and accumulated character, I think, that the painter of life bites more than a little. My poor friend should have accumulated character, certainly; or rather would be quite naturally and handsomely possessed of it, in the sense that he would have, and would always have felt he had, imagination galore, and that this yet would n't have wrecked him. It was immeasurable, the opportunity to "do" a man of imagination, for if *there* might n't be a chance to "bite," where in the world might it be? This personage of course, so enriched, would n't give me, for his type, imagination in *predominance* or as his prime faculty, nor should I, in view of other matters, have found that convenient. So particular a luxury — some occasion, that is, for study of the high gift in *supreme* command of a case or of a career — would still doubtless come on the day I should be ready to pay for it; and till then might, as from far back, remain hung up well in view and just out of reach. The comparative case meanwhile would serve — it was only on the minor scale that I had treated myself even to comparative cases.

I was to hasten to add however that, happy stopgaps as the minor scale had thus yielded, the instance in hand should enjoy the advantage of the full range of the major; since most immediately to the point was the question of that *supplement* of situation logically involved in our gentleman's impulse to deliver himself in the Paris garden on the Sunday afternoon — or if not involved by strict logic then all ideally and enchantingly implied in it. (I say "ideally," because I need scarce mention that for development, for expression of its maximum, my glimmering story was, at the earliest stage, to have nipped the thread of connexion with the possibilities of the actual reported speaker. *He* remains but the happiest of accidents; his actualities, all too definite, precluded any range of possibilities; it had only been his charming office to project upon that wide field of the artist's vision — which hangs there ever in place like the white sheet suspended for the figures of a child's magic-lantern — a more fantastic and more moveable shadow.) No privilege of the teller of tales and the handler of puppets is more delightful, or has more of the suspense and the thrill of a game of difficulty breathlessly played, than just this business of looking for the unseen and the occult, in a scheme half-grasped, by the light or, so to speak, by the clinging scent, of the gage already in hand. No dreadful old pursuit of the hidden slave with bloodhounds and the rag of association can ever, for " excitement," I judge, have bettered it at its best. For the dramatist always, by the very law of his genius, believes not only in a possible right issue from the rightly-conceived tight place; he does much more than this — he believes, irresistibly, in the necessary, the precious "tightness" of the place (whatever the issue) on the strength of any respectable hint. It being thus the respectable hint that I had with such avidity picked up, what would be the story to which it would most inevitably form the centre? It is part of the charm attendant on such questions that the " story," with the omens true, as I say, puts on from this stage the authenticity of concrete existence. It then *is*, essentially — it begins to be, though it may more or less obscurely lurk; so that the point is not in the least what to make of it, but only, very delightfully and very damnably, where to put one's hand on it.

In which truth resides surely much of the interest of that admirable mixture for salutary application which we know as art. Art deals with what we see, it must first contribute full-handed that ingredient; it plucks its material, otherwise expressed, in the garden of life — which material elsewhere grown is stale and uneatable. But it has no sooner done this than it has to take account of a *process* — from which only when it 's the basest of the servants of man, incurring ignominious dismissal with no " character, " does it, and whether under some muddled pretext of morality or on any other, pusillanimously edge away. The process, that of the expression, the literal squeezing-out, of value is another affair — with which the happy luck of mere finding has little to do. The joys of finding, at this stage, are pretty well over; that quest of the subject as a whole by " matching, " as the ladies say at the shops, the big piece with the snippet, having ended, we assume, with a capture. The subject is found, and if the problem is then transferred to the ground of what to do with it the field opens out for any amount of doing. This is precisely the infusion that, as I submit, completes the strong mixture. It is on the other hand the part of the business that can least be likened to the chase with horn and hound. It 's all a sedentary part — involves as much ciphering, of sorts, as would merit the highest salary paid to a chief accountant. Not, however, that the chief accountant has n't *his* gleams of bliss; for the felicity, or at least the equilibrium, of the artist's state dwells less, surely, in the further delightful complications he can smuggle in than in those he succeeds in keeping out. He sows his seed at the risk of too thick a crop; wherefore yet again, like the gentlemen who audit ledgers, he must keep his head at any price. In consequence of all which, for the interest of the matter, I might seem here to have my choice of narrating my " hunt " for Lambert Strether, of describing the capture of the shadow projected by my friend's anecdote, or of reporting on the occurrences subsequent to that triumph. But I had probably best attempt a little to glance in each direction; since it comes to me again and again, over this licentious record, that one's bag of adventures, conceived or conceivable, has been only half-emptied by the mere telling of one's story. It depends so on what one means by that equivocal quantity. There is the story of one's hero, and then, thanks to the intimate connexion of things, the story of one's story itself. I blush to confess it, but if one 's a dramatist one 's a dramatist, and the latter imbroglio is liable on occasion to strike me as really the more objective of the two.

The philosophy imputed to him in that beautiful outbreak, the hour there, amid such happy provision, striking for him, would have been then, on behalf of my man of imagination, to be logically and, as the artless craft of comedy has it, " led up " to ; the probable course to such a goal, the goal of so conscious a predicament, would have in short to be finely calculated. Where has he come from and why has he come, what is he doing (as we Anglo-Saxons, and we only, say, in our foredoomed clutch of exotic aids to expression) in that *galère?* To answer these questions plausibly, to answer them as under cross-examination in the witness-box by counsel for the prosecution, in other words satisfactorily to account for Strether and for his " peculiar tone," was to possess myself of the entire fabric. At the same time the clue to its whereabouts would lie in a certain *principle* of probability : he would n't have indulged in his peculiar tone without a reason ; it would take a felt predicament or a false position to give him so ironic an accent. One had n't been noting " tones " all one's life without recognising when one heard it the voice of the false position. The dear man in the Paris garden was then admirably and unmistakeably *in* one — which was no small point gained ; what next accordingly concerned us was the determination of *this* identity. One could only go by probabilities, but there was the advantage that the most general of the probabilities were virtual certainties. Possessed of our friend's nationality, to start with, there was a general probability in his narrower localism ; which, for that matter, one had really but to keep under the lens for an hour to see it give up its secrets. He would have issued, our rueful worthy, from the very heart of New England — at the heels of which matter of course a perfect train of secrets tumbled for me into the light. They had to be sifted and sorted, and I shall not reproduce the detail of that process ; but unmistakeably they were all there, and it was but a question, auspiciously, of picking among them. What the

" position " would infallibly be, and why, on his hands, it had turned " false "— these inductive steps could only be as rapid as they were distinct. I accounted for everything — and " everything " had by this time become the most promising quantity — by the view that he had come to Paris in some state of mind which was literally undergoing, as a result of new and unexpected assaults and infusions, a change almost from hour to hour. He had come with a view that might have been figured by a clear green liquid, say, in a neat glass phial ; and the liquid, once poured into the open cup of *application*, once exposed to the action of another air, had begun to turn from green to red, or whatever, and might, for all he knew, be on its way to purple, to black, to yellow. At the still wilder extremes represented perhaps, for all he could say to the contrary, by a variability so violent, he would at first, naturally, but have gazed in surprise and alarm ; whereby the *situation* clearly would spring from the play of wildness and the development of extremes. I saw in a moment that, should this development proceed both with force and logic, my " story " would leave nothing to be desired. There is always, of course, for the story-teller, the irresistible determinant and the incalculable advantage of his interest in the story *as such* ; it is ever, obviously, overwhelmingly, the prime and precious thing (as other than this I have never been able to see it) ; as to which what makes for it, with whatever headlong energy, may be said to pale before the energy with which it simply makes for itself. It rejoices, none the less, at its best, to seem to offer itself in a light, to seem to know, and with the very last knowledge, what it 's about — liable as it yet is at moments to be caught by us with its tongue in its cheek and absolutely no warrant but its splendid impudence. Let us grant then that the impudence is always there — there, so to speak, for grace and effect and *allure ;* there, above all, because the Story is just the spoiled child of art, and because, as we are always disappointed when the pampered don't " play up," we like it, to that extent, to look all its character. It probably does so, in truth, even when we most flatter ourselves that we negotiate with it by treaty.

All of which, again, is but to say that the *steps*, for my fable, placed themselves with a prompt and, as it were, functional assurance — an air quite as of readiness to have dispensed with logic had I been in fact too stupid for my clue. Never, positively, none the less, as the links multiplied, had I felt less stupid than for the determination of poor Strether's errand and for the apprehension of his issue. These things continued to fall together, as by the neat action of their own weight and form, even while their commentator scratched his head about them; he easily sees now that they were always well in advance of him. As the case completed itself he had in fact, from a good way behind, to catch up with them, breathless and a little flurried, as he best could. *The* false position, for our belated man of the world — belated because he had endeavoured so long to escape being one, and now at last had really to face his doom — the false position for him, I say, was obviously to have presented himself at the gate of that boundless menagerie primed with a moral scheme of the most approved pattern which was yet framed to break down on any approach to vivid facts ; that is to any at all liberal appreciation of them. There would have been of course the case of the Strether prepared, wherever presenting himself, only to judge and to feel meanly; but *he* would have moved for me, I confess, enveloped in no legend whatever. The actual man's note, from the first of our seeing it struck, is the note of discrimination, just as his drama is to become, under stress, the drama of discrimination. It would have been his blest imagination, we have seen, that had already helped him to discriminate; the element that was for so much of the pleasure of my cutting thick, as I have intimated, into his intellectual, into his moral substance. Yet here it was, at the same time, just here, that a shade for a moment fell across the scene.

There was the dreadful little old tradition, one of the platitudes of the human comedy, that people's moral scheme

PREFACE

does break down in Paris; that nothing is more frequently
observed; that hundreds of thousands of more or less hypo-
critical or more or less cynical persons annually visit the
place for the sake of the probable catastrophe, and that I
came late in the day to work myself up about it. There
was in fine the *trivial* association, one of the vulgarest in
the world; but which gave me pause no longer, I think,
simply because its vulgarity is so advertised. The revolution
performed by Strether under the influence of the most interesting of great cities was to have nothing to do with any
bêtise of the imputably "tempted" state; he was to be
thrown forward, rather, thrown quite with violence, upon
his lifelong trick of intense reflexion: which friendly test
indeed was to bring him out, through winding passages,
through alternations of darkness and light, very much *in*
Paris, but with the surrounding scene itself a minor matter,
a mere symbol for more things than had been dreamt of in
the philosophy of Woollett. Another surrounding scene
would have done as well for our show could it have represented a place in which Strether's errand was likely to lie
and his crisis to await him. The *likely* place had the great
merit of sparing me preparations; there would have been
too many involved — not at all impossibilities, only rather
worrying and delaying difficulties — in positing elsewhere
Chad Newsome's interesting relation, his so interesting
complexity of relations. Strether's appointed stage, in fine,
could be but Chad's most luckily selected one. The young
man had gone in, as they say, for circumjacent charm; and
where he would have found it, by the turn of his mind,
most "authentic," was where his earnest friend's analysis
would most find *him;* as well as where, for that matter, the
former's whole analytic faculty would be led such a wonderful dance.

"The Ambassadors" had been, all conveniently, "arranged for"; its first appearance was from month to month,
in the *North American Review* during 1903, and I had been
open from far back to any pleasant provocation for ingenuity that might reside in one's actively adopting — so as to

xiv

make it, in its way, a small compositional law — recurrent breaks and resumptions. I had made up my mind here regularly to exploit and enjoy these often rather rude jolts —having found, as I believed, an admirable way to it; yet every question of form and pressure, I easily remember, paled in the light of the major propriety, recognised as soon as really weighed; that of employing but one centre and keeping it all within my hero's compass. The thing was to be so much this worthy's intimate adventure that even the projection of his consciousness upon it from beginning to end without intermission or deviation would probably still leave a part of its value for him, and *a fortiori* for ourselves, unexpressed. I might, however, express every grain of it that there would be room for — on condition of contriving a splendid particular economy. Other persons in no small number were to people the scene, and each with his or her axe to grind, his or her situation to treat, his or her coherency not to fail of, his or her relation to my leading motive, in a word, to establish and carry on. But Strether's sense of these things, and Strether's only, should avail me for showing them; I should know them but through his more or less groping knowledge of them, since his very gropings would figure among his most interesting motions, and a full observance of the rich rigour I speak of would give me more of the effect I should be most "after" than all other possible observances together. It would give me a large unity, and that in turn would crown me with the grace to which the enlightened story-teller will at any time, for his interest, sacrifice if need be all other graces whatever. I refer of course to the grace of intensity, which there are ways of signally achieving and ways of signally missing — as we see it, all round us, helplessly and woefully missed. Not that it is n't, on the other hand, a virtue eminently subject to appreciation — there being no strict, no absolute measure of it; so that one may hear it acclaimed where it has quite escaped one's perception, and see it unnoticed where one has gratefully hailed it. After all of which I am not sure, either, that the immense amusement of the whole cluster of difficulties so arrayed may not operate, for the fond fabulist, when judicious not less than fond, as his best of determinants. That charming principle is always there, at all events, to keep interest fresh: it is a principle, we remember, essentially ravenous, without scruple and without mercy, appeased with no cheap nor easy nourishment. It enjoys the costly sacrifice and rejoices thereby in the very odour of difficulty—even as ogres, with their "Fee-faw-fum!" rejoice in the smell of the blood of Englishmen.

Thus it was, at all events, that the ultimate, though after all so speedy, definition of my gentleman's job—his coming out, all solemnly appointed and deputed, to "save" Chad, and his then finding the young man so disobligingly and, at first, so bewilderingly not lost that a new issue altogether, in the connexion, prodigiously faces them, which has to be dealt with in a new light—promised as many calls on ingenuity and on the higher branches of the compositional art as one could possibly desire. Again and yet again, as, from book to book, I proceed with my survey, I find no source of interest equal to this verification after the fact, as I may call it, and the more in detail the better, of the scheme of consistency "gone in" for. As always— since the charm never fails—the retracing of the process from point to point brings back the old illusion. The old intentions bloom again and flower—in spite of all the blossoms they were to have dropped by the way. This is the charm, as I say, of adventure *transposed*—the thrilling ups and downs, the intricate ins and outs of the compositional problem, made after such a fashion admirably objective, becoming the question at issue and keeping the author's heart in his mouth. Such an element, for instance, as his intention that Mrs. Newsome, away off with her finger on the pulse of Massachusetts, should yet be no less intensely than circuitously present through the whole thing, should be no less felt as to be reckoned with than the most direct exhibition, the finest portrayal at first hand could make her, such a sign of artistic good faith, I say, once it's unmistakeably there, takes on again an actuality not too much impaired by the comparative dimness of the particular success. Cherished intention too inevitably acts and operates, in the book, about fifty times as little as I had fondly dreamt it might; but that scarce spoils for me the pleasure of recognising the fifty ways in which I had sought to provide for it. The mere charm of seeing such an idea constituent, in its degree; the fineness of the measures taken — a real extension, if successful, of the very terms and possibilities of representation and figuration — such things alone were, after this fashion, inspiring, such things alone were a gage of the probable success of that dissimulated calculation with which the whole effort was to square. But oh the cares begotten, none the less, of that same "judicious" sacrifice to a particular form of interest! One's work should have composition, because composition alone is positive beauty; but all the while — apart from one's inevitable consciousness too of the dire paucity of readers ever recognising or ever missing positive beauty — how, as to the cheap and easy, at every turn, how, as to immediacy and facility, and even as to the commoner vivacity, positive beauty might have to be sweated for and paid for! Once achieved and installed it may always be trusted to make the poor seeker feel he would have blushed to the roots of his hair for failing of it; yet, how, as its virtue can be essentially but the virtue of the whole, the wayside traps set in the interest of muddlement and pleading but the cause of the moment, of the particular bit in itself, have to be kicked out of the path! All the sophistications in life, for example, might have appeared to muster on behalf of the menace — the menace to a bright variety — involved in Strether's having all the subjective "say," as it were, to himself.

Had I, meanwhile, made him at once hero and historian, endowed him with the romantic privilege of the "first person" — the darkest abyss of romance this, inveterately, when enjoyed on the grand scale — variety, and many other queer matters as well, might have been smuggled in by a back door. Suffice it, to be brief, that the first person, in the long piece, is a form foredoomed to looseness, and that

PREFACE

looseness, never much my affair, had never been so little so as on this particular occasion. All of which reflexions flocked to the standard from the moment — a very early one — the question of how to keep my form amusing while sticking so close to my central figure and constantly taking its pattern from him had to be faced. He arrives (arrives at Chester) as for the dreadful purpose of giving his creator " no end " to tell about him — before which rigorous mission the serenest of creators might well have quailed. I was far from the serenest; I was more than agitated enough to reflect that, grimly deprived of one alternative or one substitute for " telling," I must address myself tooth and nail to another. I could n't, save by implication, make other persons tell *each other* about him — blest resource, blest necessity, of the drama, which reaches its effects of unity, all remarkably, by paths absolutely opposite to the paths of the novel : with other persons, save as they were primarily *his* persons (not he primarily but one of theirs), I had simply nothing to do. I had relations for him none the less, by the mercy of Providence, quite as much as if my exhibition *was* to be a muddle ; if I could only by implication and a show of consequence make other persons tell each other about him, I could at least make him tell *them* whatever in the world he must ; and could so, by the same token — which was a further luxury thrown in — see straight into the deep differences between what that could do for me, or at all events for *him*, and the large ease of " autobiography." It may be asked why, if one so keeps to one's hero, one should n't make a single mouthful of " method," should n't throw the reins on his neck and, letting them flap there as free as in " Gil Blas " or in " David Copperfield," equip him with the double privilege of subject and object — a course that has at least the merit of brushing away questions at a sweep. The answer to which is, I think, that one makes that surrender only if one is prepared *not* to make certain precious discriminations.

The " first person " then, so employed, is addressed by the author directly to ourselves, his possible readers, whom

xviii

PREFACE

he has to reckon with, at the best, by our English tradition, so loosely and vaguely after all, so little respectfully, on so scant a presumption of exposure to criticism. Strether, on the other hand, encaged and provided for as "The Ambassadors" encages and provides, has to keep in view proprieties much stiffer and more salutary than any our straight and credulous gape are likely to bring home to him, has exhibitional conditions to meet, in a word, that forbid the terrible *fluidity* of self-revelation. I may seem not to better the case for my discrimination if I say that, for my first care, I had thus inevitably to set him up a confidant or two, to wave away with energy the custom of the seated mass of explanation after the fact, the inserted block of merely referential narrative, which flourishes so, to the shame of the modern impatience, on the serried page of Balzac, but which seems simply to appal our actual, our general weaker, digestion. "Harking back to make up" took at any rate more doing, as the phrase is, not only than the reader of to-day demands, but than he will tolerate at any price any call upon him either to understand or remotely to measure; and for the beauty of the thing when done the current editorial mind in particular appears wholly without sense. It is not, however, primarily for either of these reasons, whatever their weight, that Strether's friend Waymarsh is so keenly clutched at, on the threshold of the book, or that no less a pounce is made on Maria Gostrey — without even the pretext, either, of *her* being, in essence, Strether's friend. She is the reader's friend much rather — in consequence of dispositions that make him so eminently require one; and she acts in that capacity, and *really* in that capacity alone, with exemplary devotion, from beginning to end of the book. She is an enrolled, a direct, aid to lucidity; she is in fine, to tear off her mask, the most unmitigated and abandoned of *ficelles*. Half the dramatist's art, as we well know — since if we don't it's not the fault of the proofs that lie scattered about us — is in the use of *ficelles*; by which I mean in a deep dissimulation of his dependence on them. Waymarsh only to a slighter degree belongs, in the whole business, less to my subject than to my treatment of it; the interesting proof, in these connexions, being that one has but to take one's subject for the stuff of drama to interweave with enthusiasm as many Gostreys as need be.

The material of "The Ambassadors," conforming in this respect exactly to that of "The Wings of the Dove," published just before it, is taken absolutely for the stuff of drama; so that, availing myself of the opportunity given me by this edition for some prefatory remarks on the latter work, I had mainly to make on its behalf the point of its scenic consistency. It disguises that virtue, in the oddest way in the world, by just *looking*, as we turn its pages, as little scenic as possible; but it sharply divides itself, just as the composition before us does, into the parts that prepare, that tend in fact to over-prepare, for scenes, and the parts, or otherwise into the scenes, that justify and crown the preparation. It may definitely be said, I think, that everything in it that is not scene (not, I of course mean, complete and functional scene, treating *all* the submitted matter, as by logical start, logical turn, and logical finish) is discriminated preparation, is the fusion and synthesis of picture. These alternations propose themselves all recogniseably, I think, from an early stage, as the very form and figure of "The Ambassadors"; so that, to repeat, such an agent as Miss Gostrey, pre-engaged at a high salary, but waits in the draughty wing with her shawl and her smelling-salts. Her function speaks at once for itself, and by the time she has dined with Strether in London and gone to a play with him her intervention as a *ficelle* is, I hold, expertly justified. Thanks to it we have treated scenically, and scenically alone, the whole lumpish question of Strether's "past," which has seen us more happily on the way than anything else could have done; we have strained to a high lucidity and vivacity (or at least we hope we have) certain indispensable facts; we have seen our two or three immediate friends all conveniently and profitably in "action"; to say nothing of our beginning to descry others, of a remoter intensity, getting into motion, even if a bit vaguely as yet, for our further enrichment. Let my first point be here that the scene in question, that in which the whole situation at Woollett and the complex forces that have propelled my hero to where this lively extractor of his value and distiller of his essence awaits him, is normal and entire, is really an excellent *standard* scene; copious, comprehensive, and accordingly never short, but with its office as definite as that of the hammer on the gong of the clock, the office of expressing *all that is in* the hour.

The "*ficelle*" character of the subordinate party is as artfully dissimulated, throughout, as may be, and to that extent that, with the seams or joints of Maria Gostrey's ostensible connectedness taken particular care of, duly smoothed over, that is, and anxiously kept from showing as "pieced on," this figure doubtless achieves, after a fashion, something of the dignity of a prime idea: which circumstance but shows us afresh how many quite incalculable but none the less clear sources of enjoyment for the infatuated artist, how many copious springs of our never-to-be-slighted "fun" for the reader and critic susceptible of contagion, may sound their incidental plash as soon as an artistic process begins to enjoy free development. Exquisite — in illustration of this — the mere interest and amusement of such at once "creative" and critical questions as how and where and why to make Miss Gostrey's false connexion carry itself, under a due high polish, as a real one. Nowhere is it more of an artful expedient for mere consistency of form, to mention a case, than in the last "scene" of the book, where its function is to give or to add nothing whatever, but only to express as vividly as possible certain things quite other than itself and that are of the already fixed and appointed measure. Since, however, all art is *expression*, and is thereby vividness, one was to find the door open here to any amount of delightful dissimulation. These verily are the refinements and ecstasies of method — amid which, or certainly under the influence of any exhilarated demonstration of which, one must keep one's head and not lose one's way. To cultivate an adequate intelligence for them and to make that sense

PREFACE

operative is positively to find a charm in any produced ambiguity of appearance that is not by the same stroke, and all helplessly, an ambiguity of sense. To project imaginatively, for my hero, a relation that has nothing to do with the matter (the matter of my subject) but has everything to do with the manner (the manner of my presentation of the same) and yet to treat it, at close quarters and for fully economic expression's possible sake, as if it were important and essential — to do that sort of thing and yet muddle nothing may easily become, as one goes, a signally attaching proposition; even though it all remains but part and parcel, I hasten to recognise, of the merely general and related question of expressional curiosity and expressional decency.

I am moved to add after so much insistence on the scenic side of my labour that I have found the steps of re-perusal almost as much waylaid here by quite another style of effort in the same signal interest — or have in other words not failed to note how, even so associated and so discriminated, the finest proprieties and charms of the non-scenic may, under the right hand for them, still keep their intelligibility and assert their office. Infinitely suggestive such an observation as this last on the whole delightful head, where representation is concerned, of possible variety, of effective expressional change and contrast. One would like, at such an hour as this, for critical licence, to go into the matter of the noted inevitable deviation (from too-fond an original vision) that the exquisite treachery even of the straightest execution may ever be trusted to inflict even on the most mature plan — the case being that, though one's last reconsidered production always seems to bristle with that particular evidence, " The Ambassadors " would place a flood of such light at my service. I must attach to my final remark here a different import ; noting in the other connexion I just glanced at that such passages as that of my hero's first encounter with Chad Newsome, absolute attestations of the non-scenic form though they be, yet lay the firmest hand too — so far at least as intention goes — on representational

PREFACE

effect. To report at all closely and completely of what " passes " on a given occasion is inevitably to become more or less scenic; and yet in the instance I allude to, *with* the conveyance, expressional curiosity and expressional decency are sought and arrived at under quite another law. The true inwardness of this may be at bottom but that one of the suffered treacheries has consisted precisely, for Chad's whole figure and presence, of a direct presentability diminished and compromised — despoiled, that is, of its *proportional* advantage ; so that, in a word, the whole economy of his author's relation to him has at important points to be redetermined. The book, however, critically viewed, is touchingly full of these disguised and repaired losses, these insidious recoveries, these intensely redemptive consistencies. The pages in which Mamie Pocock gives her appointed and, I can't but think, duly felt lift to the whole action by the so inscrutably-applied side-stroke or short-cut of our just watching, and as quite at an angle of vision as yet untried, her single hour of suspense in the hotel salon, in our partaking of her concentrated study of the sense of matters bearing on her own case, all the bright warm Paris afternoon, from the balcony that overlooks the Tuileries garden — these are as marked an example of the representational virtue that insists here and there on being, for the charm of opposition and renewal, other than the scenic. It would n't take much to make me further argue that from an equal play of such oppositions the book gathers an intensity that fairly adds to the dramatic — though the latter is supposed to be the sum of all intensities ; or that has at any rate nothing to fear from juxtaposition with it. I consciously fail to shrink in fact from that extravagance — I risk it, rather, for the sake of the moral involved ; which is not that the particular production before us exhausts the interesting questions it raises, but that the Novel remains still, under the right persuasion, the most independent, most elastic, most prodigious of literary forms.

HENRY JAMES.

THE AMBASSADORS
VOLUME I

BOOK FIRST

THE AMBASSADORS

I

STRETHER'S first question, when he reached the hotel, was about his friend; yet on his learning that Waymarsh was apparently not to arrive till evening he was not wholly disconcerted. A telegram from him bespeaking a room "only if not noisy," reply paid, was produced for the enquirer at the office, so that the understanding they should meet at Chester rather than at Liverpool remained to that extent sound. The same secret principle, however, that had prompted Strether not absolutely to desire Waymarsh's presence at the dock, that had led him thus to postpone for a few hours his enjoyment of it, now operated to make him feel he could still wait without disappointment. They would dine together at the worst, and, with all respect to dear old Waymarsh — if not even, for that matter, to himself — there was little fear that in the sequel they should n't see enough of each other. The principle I have just mentioned as operating had been, with the most newly disembarked of the two men, wholly instinctive — the fruit of a sharp sense that, delightful as it would be to find himself looking, after so much separation, into his comrade's face, his business would be a trifle bungled should he simply arrange for this countenance to present itself to the nearing steamer as the first "note," of Europe. Mixed with everything was the apprehension, already, on Strether's part, that it would, at best, throughout, prove the note of Europe in quite a sufficient degree.

That note had been meanwhile — since the previous afternoon, thanks to this happier device — such a consciousness of personal freedom as he had n't known for years; such a deep taste of change and of having above all for the moment nobody and nothing to consider, as promised already, if headlong hope were not too foolish, to colour his adventure with cool success. There were people on the ship with whom he had easily consorted — so far as ease could up to now be imputed to him — and who for the most part plunged straight into the current that set from the landing-stage to London; there were others who had invited him to a tryst at the inn and had even invoked his aid for a "look round" at the beauties of Liverpool; but he had stolen away from every one alike, had kept no appointment and renewed no acquaintance, had been indifferently aware of the number of persons who esteemed themselves fortunate in being, unlike himself, "met," and had even independently, unsociably, alone, without encounter or relapse and by mere quiet evasion, given his afternoon and evening to the immediate and the sensible. They formed a qualified draught of Europe, an afternoon and an evening on the banks of the Mersey, but such as it was he took his potion at least undiluted. He winced a little, truly, at the thought that Waymarsh might be already at Chester; he reflected that, should he have to describe himself there as having "got in" so early, it would be difficult to make the interval

BOOK FIRST

look particularly eager; but he was like a man who,
elatedly finding in his pocket more money than usual,
handles it a while and idly and pleasantly chinks it
before addressing himself to the business of spending.
That he was prepared to be vague to Waymarsh about
the hour of the ship's touching, and that he both wanted
extremely to see him and enjoyed extremely the duration of delay — these things, it is to be conceived, were
early signs in him that his relation to his actual errand
might prove none of the simplest. He was burdened,
poor Strether — it had better be confessed at the
outset — with the oddity of a double consciousness.
There was detachment in his zeal and curiosity in his
indifference.

After the young woman in the glass cage had held
up to him across her counter the pale-pink leaflet
bearing his friend's name, which she neatly pronounced, he turned away to find himself, in the hall,
facing a lady who met his eyes as with an intention
suddenly determined, and whose features — not
freshly young, not markedly fine, but on happy terms
with each other — came back to him as from a recent
vision. For a moment they stood confronted; then the
moment placed her: he had noticed her the day before, noticed her at his previous inn, where — again
in the hall — she had been briefly engaged with some
people of his own ship's company. Nothing had actually passed between them, and he would as little have
been able to say what had been the sign of her face
for him on the first occasion as to name the ground
of his present recognition. Recognition at any rate
appeared to prevail on her own side as well — which

would only have added to the mystery. All she now began by saying to him nevertheless was that, having chanced to catch his enquiry, she was moved to ask, by his leave, if it were possibly a question of Mr. Waymarsh of Milrose Connecticut — Mr. Waymarsh the American lawyer.

"Oh yes," he replied, "my very well-known friend. He's to meet me here, coming up from Malvern, and I supposed he'd already have arrived. But he does n't come till later, and I'm relieved not to have kept him. Do you know him?" Strether wound up.

It was n't till after he had spoken that he became aware of how much there had been in him of response; when the tone of her own rejoinder, as well as the play of something more in her face — something more, that is, than its apparently usual restless light — seemed to notify him. "I've met him at Milrose — where I used sometimes, a good while ago, to stay; I had friends there who were friends of his, and I've been at his house. I won't answer for it that he would know me," Strether's new acquaintance pursued; "but I should be delighted to see him. Perhaps," she added, "I shall — for I'm staying over." She paused while our friend took in these things, and it was as if a good deal of talk had already passed. They even vaguely smiled at it, and Strether presently observed that Mr. Waymarsh would, no doubt, be easily to be seen. This, however, appeared to affect the lady as if she might have advanced too far. She appeared to have no reserves about anything. "Oh," she said, "he won't care!" — and she immediately thereupon remarked that she believed Strether knew

6

the Munsters; the Munsters being the people he had seen her with at Liverpool.

But he did n't, it happened, know the Munsters well enough to give the case much of a lift; so that they were left together as if over the mere laid table of conversation. Her qualification of the mentioned connexion had rather removed than placed a dish, and there seemed nothing else to serve. Their attitude remained, none the less, that of not forsaking the board; and the effect of this in turn was to give them the appearance of having accepted each other with an absence of preliminaries practically complete. They moved along the hall together, and Strether's companion threw off that the hotel had the advantage of a garden. He was aware by this time of his strange inconsequence: he had shirked the intimacies of the steamer and had muffled the shock of Waymarsh only to find himself forsaken, in this sudden case, both of avoidance and of caution. He passed, under this unsought protection and before he had so much as gone up to his room, into the garden of the hotel, and at the end of ten minutes had agreed to meet there again, as soon as he should have made himself tidy, the dispenser of such good assurances. He wanted to look at the town, and they would forthwith look together. It was almost as if she had been in possession and received him as a guest. Her acquaintance with the place presented her in a manner as a hostess, and Strether had a rueful glance for the lady in the glass cage. It was as if this personage had seen herself instantly superseded.

When in a quarter of an hour he came down, what

7

his hostess saw, what she might have taken in with a vision kindly adjusted, was the lean, the slightly loose figure of a man of the middle height and something more perhaps than the middle age — a man of five-and-fifty, whose most immediate signs were a marked bloodless brownness of face, a thick dark moustache, of characteristically American cut, growing strong and falling low, a head of hair still abundant but irregularly streaked with grey, and a nose of bold free prominence, the even line, the high finish, as it might have been called, of which, had a certain effect of mitigation. A perpetual pair of glasses astride of this fine ridge, and a line, unusually deep and drawn, the prolonged pen-stroke of time, accompanying the curve of the moustache from nostril to chin, did something to complete the facial furniture that an attentive observer would have seen catalogued, on the spot, in the vision of the other party to Strether's appointment. She waited for him in the garden, the other party, drawing on a pair of singularly fresh soft and elastic light gloves and presenting herself with a superficial readiness which, as he approached her over the small smooth lawn and in the watery English sunshine, he might, with his rougher preparation, have marked as the model for such an occasion. She had, this lady, a perfect plain propriety, an expensive subdued suitability, that her companion was not free to analyse, but that struck him, so that his consciousness of it was instantly acute, as a quality quite new to him. Before reaching her he stopped on the grass and went through the form of feeling for something, possibly forgotten, in the light overcoat he carried on his arm; yet the essence of the act was no more than the impulse to gain time. Nothing could have been odder than Strether's sense of himself as at that moment launched in something of which the sense would be quite disconnected from the sense of his past and which was literally beginning there and then. It had begun in fact already upstairs and before the dressing-glass that struck him as blocking further, so strangely, the dimness of the window of his dull bedroom; begun with a sharper survey of the elements of Appearance than he had for a long time been moved to make. He had during those moments felt these elements to be not so much to his hand as he should have liked, and then had fallen back on the thought that they were precisely a matter as to which help was supposed to come from what he was about to do. He was about to go up to London, so that hat and necktie might wait. What had come as straight to him as a ball in a well-played game — and caught moreover not less neatly — was just the air, in the person of his friend, of having seen and chosen, the air of achieved possession of those vague qualities and quantities that collectively figured to him as the advantage snatched from lucky chances. Without pomp or circumstance, certainly, as her original address to him, equally with his own response, had been, he would have sketched to himself his impression of her as: "Well, she's more thoroughly civilized—!" If "More thoroughly than *whom?*" would not have been for him a sequel to this remark, that was just by reason of his deep consciousness of the bearing of his comparison.

9

The amusement, at all events, of a civilisation intenser was what — familiar compatriot as she was, with the full tone of the compatriot and the rattling link not with mystery but only with dear dyspeptic Waymarsh — she appeared distinctly to promise. His pause while he felt in his overcoat was positively the pause of confidence, and it enabled his eyes to make out as much of a case for her, in proportion, as her own made out for himself. She affected him as almost insolently young; but an easily carried five-and-thirty could still do that. She was, however, like himself, marked and wan; only it naturally could n't have been known to him how much a spectator looking from one to the other might have discerned that they had in common. It would n't for such a spectator have been altogether insupposable that, each so finely brown and so sharply spare, each confessing so to dents of surface and aids to sight, to a disproportionate nose and a head delicately or grossly grizzled, they might have been brother and sister. On this ground indeed there would have been a residuum of difference; such a sister having surely known in respect to such a brother the extremity of separation, and such a brother now feeling in respect to such a sister the extremity of surprise. Surprise, it was true, was not on the other hand what the eyes of Strether's friend most showed him while she gave him, stroking her gloves smoother, the time he appreciated. They had taken hold of him straightway, measuring him up and down as if they knew how; as if he were human material they had already in some sort handled. Their possessor was in truth, it may be communicated, the mistress of a hundred cases or categories, receptacles of the mind, subdivisions for convenience, in which, from a full experience, she pigeon-holed her fellow mortals with a hand as free as that of a compositor scattering type. She was as equipped in this particular as Strether was the reverse, and it made an opposition between them which he might well have shrunk from submitting to if he had fully suspected it. So far as he did suspect it he was on the contrary, after a short shake of his consciousness, as pleasantly passive as might be. He really had a sort of sense of what she knew. He had quite the sense that she knew things he did n't, and though this was a concession that in general he found not easy to make to women, he made it now as good-humouredly as if it lifted a burden. His eyes were so quiet behind his eternal nippers that they might almost have been absent without changing his face, which took its expression mainly, and not least its stamp of sensibility, from other sources, surface and grain and form. He joined his guide in an instant, and then felt she had profited still better than he by his having been, for the moments just mentioned, so at the disposal of her intelligence. She knew even intimate things about him that he had n't yet told her and perhaps never would. He was n't unaware that he had told her rather remarkably many for the time, but these were not the real ones. Some of the real ones, however, precisely, were what she knew.

They were to pass again through the hall of the inn to get into the street, and it was here she presently checked him with a question. "Have you looked up my name?"

He could only stop with a laugh. "Have you looked up mine?"

"Oh dear, yes — as soon as you left me. I went to the office and asked. Had n't *you* better do the same?"

He wondered. "Find out who you are? — after the uplifted young woman there has seen us thus scrape acquaintance!"

She laughed on her side now at the shade of alarm in his amusement. "Is n't it a reason the more? If what you 're afraid of is the injury for me — my being seen to walk off with a gentleman who has to ask who I am — I assure you I don't in the least mind. Here, however," she continued, "is my card, and as I find there 's something else again I have to say at the office, you can just study it during the moment I leave you."

She left him after he had taken from her the small pasteboard she had extracted from her pocket-book, and he had extracted another from his own, to exchange with it, before she came back. He read thus the simple designation "Maria Gostrey," to which was attached, in a corner of the card, with a number, the name of a street, presumably in Paris, without other appreciable identity than its foreignness. He put the card into his waistcoat pocket, keeping his own meanwhile in evidence; and as he leaned against the door-post he met with the smile of a straying thought what the expanse before the hotel offered to his view. It was positively droll to him that he should already have Maria Gostrey, whoever she was — of which he had n't really the least idea — in a place of safe keeping. He had somehow an assurance that he should carefully preserve the little token he had just tucked in. He gazed with unseeing lingering eyes as he followed some of the implications of his act, asking himself if he really felt admonished to qualify it as disloyal. It was prompt, it was possibly even premature, and there was little doubt of the expression of face the sight of it would have produced in a certain person. But if it was "wrong" — why then he had better not have come out at all. At this, poor man, had he already — and even before meeting Waymarsh — arrived. He had believed he had a limit, but the limit had been transcended within thirty-six hours. By how long a space on the plane of manners, or even of morals, moreover, he felt still more sharply after Maria Gostrey had come back to him and with a gay decisive "So now —!" led him forth into the world. This counted, it struck him as he walked beside her with his overcoat on an arm, his umbrella under another and his personal pasteboard a little stiffly retained between forefinger and thumb, this struck him as really, in comparison, his introduction to things. It had n't been "Europe" at Liverpool, no — not even in the dreadful delightful impressive streets the night before — to the extent his present companion made it so. She had n't yet done that so much as when, after their walk had lasted a few minutes and he had had time to wonder if a couple of sidelong glances from her meant that he had best have put on gloves, she almost pulled him up with an amused challenge. "But why — fondly as it's so easy to imagine your clinging to it — don't you put it away? Or if it's an inconvenience to you to carry it, one's often glad to have one's card back. The fortune one spends in them!"

Then he saw both that his way of marching with his own prepared tribute had affected her as a deviation in one of those directions he could n't yet measure, and that she supposed this emblem to be still the one he had received from her. He accordingly handed her the card as if in restitution, but as soon as she had it she felt the difference and, with her eyes on it, stopped short for apology. "I like," she observed, "your name."

"Oh," he answered, "you won't have heard of it!" Yet he had his reasons for not being sure but that she perhaps might.

Ah it was but too visible! She read it over again as one who had never seen it. "'Mr. Lewis Lambert Strether'" — she sounded it almost as freely as for any stranger. She repeated however that she liked it — "particularly the Lewis Lambert. It's the name of a novel of Balzac's."

"Oh I know that!" said Strether.

"But the novel's an awfully bad one."

"I know that too," Strether smiled. To which he added with an irrelevance that was only superficial: "I come from Woollett Massachusetts." It made her for some reason — the irrelevance or whatever — laugh. Balzac had described many cities, but had n't described Woollett Massachusetts. "You say that," she returned, "as if you wanted one immediately to know the worst."

BOOK FIRST

"Oh I think it's a thing," he said, "that you must already have made out. I feel it so that I certainly must look it, speak it, and, as people say there, 'act' it. It sticks out of me, and you knew surely for yourself as soon as you looked at me."

"The worst, you mean?"

"Well, the fact of where I come from. There at any rate it *is;* so that you won't be able, if anything happens, to say I've not been straight with you."

"I see" — and Miss Gostrey looked really interested in the point he had made. "But what do you think of as happening?"

Though he wasn't shy — which was rather anomalous — Strether gazed about without meeting her eyes; a motion that was frequent with him in talk, yet of which his words often seemed not at all the effect. "Why that you should find me too hopeless." With which they walked on again together while she answered, as they went, that the most "hopeless" of her countryfolk were in general precisely those she liked best. All sorts of other pleasant small things — small things that were yet large for him — flowered in the air of the occasion; but the bearing of the occasion itself on matters still remote concerns us too closely to permit us to multiply our illustrations. Two or three, however, in truth, we should perhaps regret to lose. The tortuous wall — girdle, long since snapped, of the little swollen city, half held in place by careful civic hands — wanders in narrow file between parapets smoothed by peaceful generations, pausing here and there for a dismantled gate or a bridged gap, with rises and drops, steps up and steps

15

down, queer twists, queer contacts, peeps into homely streets and under the brows of gables, views of cathedral tower and waterside fields, of huddled English town and ordered English country. Too deep almost for words was the delight of these things to Strether; yet as deeply mixed with it were certain images of his inward picture. He had trod this walk in the far-off time, at twenty-five; but that, instead of spoiling it, only enriched it for present feeling and marked his renewal as a thing substantial enough to share. It was with Waymarsh he should have shared it, and he was now accordingly taking from him something that was his due. He looked repeatedly at his watch, and when he had done so for the fifth time Miss Gostrey took him up.

"You're doing something that you think not right."

It so touched the place that he quite changed colour and his laugh grew almost awkward. "Am I enjoying it as much as *that?*"

"You're not enjoying it, I think, so much as you ought."

"I see" — he appeared thoughtfully to agree. "Great is my privilege."

"Oh it's not your privilege! It has nothing to do with *me*. It has to do with yourself. Your failure's general."

"Ah there you are!" he laughed. "It's the failure of Woollett. *That's* general."

"The failure to enjoy," Miss Gostrey explained, "is what I mean."

"Precisely. Woollett is n't sure it ought to enjoy. If it were it would. But it has n't, poor thing,"

Strether continued, "any one to show it how. It's not like me. I have somebody."

They had stopped, in the afternoon sunshine — constantly pausing, in their stroll, for the sharper sense of what they saw — and Strether rested on one of the high sides of the old stony groove of the little rampart. He leaned back on this support with his face to the tower of the cathedral, now admirably commanded by their station, the high red-brown mass, square and subordinately spired and crocketed, retouched and restored, but charming to his long-sealed eyes and with the first swallows of the year weaving their flight all round it. Miss Gostrey lingered near him, full of an air, to which she more and more justified her right, of understanding the effect of things. She quite concurred. "You've indeed somebody." And she added: "I wish you *would* let me show you how!"

"Oh I'm afraid of you!" he cheerfully pleaded.

She kept on him a moment, through her glasses and through his own, a certain pleasant pointedness. "Ah no, you're not! You're not in the least, thank goodness! If you had been we shouldn't so soon have found ourselves here together. I think," she comfortably concluded, "you trust me."

"I think I do! — but that's exactly what I'm afraid of. I shouldn't mind if I didn't. It's falling thus in twenty minutes so utterly into your hands. I dare say," Strether continued, "it's a sort of thing you're thoroughly familiar with; but nothing more extraordinary has ever happened to me."

She watched him with all her kindness. "That

means simply that you've recognised me — which
is rather beautiful and rare. You see what I am."
As on this, however, he protested, with a good-humoured headshake, a resignation of any such claim, she
had a moment of explanation. "If you'll only come
on further as you *have* come you'll at any rate make
out. My own fate has been too many for me, and I've
succumbed to it. I'm a general guide — to 'Europe,'
don't you know? I wait for people — I put them
through. I pick them up — I set them down. I'm
a sort of superior 'courier-maid.' I'm a companion
at large. I take people, as I've told you, about. I
never sought it — it has come to me. It has been my
fate, and one's fate one accepts. It's a dreadful thing
to have to say, in so wicked a world, but I verily believe that, such as you see me, there's nothing I don't
know. I know all the shops and the prices — but I
know worse things still. I bear on my back the huge
load of our national consciousness, or, in other words
— for it comes to that — of our nation itself. Of what
is our nation composed but of the men and women
individually on my shoulders? I don't do it, you
know, for any particular advantage. I don't do it,
for instance — some people do, you know — for
money."

Strether could only listen and wonder and weigh his
chance. "And yet, affected as you are then to so many
of your clients, you can scarcely be said to do it for love."
He waited a moment. "How do we reward you?"

She had her own hesitation, but "You don't!" she
finally returned, setting him again in motion. They
went on, but in a few minutes, though while still

thinking over what she had said, he once more took out his watch; mechanically, unconsciously and as if made nervous by the mere exhilaration of what struck him as her strange and cynical wit. He looked at the hour without seeing it, and then, on something again said by his companion, had another pause. "You're really in terror of him."

He smiled a smile that he almost felt to be sickly. "Now you can see why I'm afraid of you."

"Because I've such illuminations? Why they're all for your help! It's what I told you," she added, "just now. You feel as if this were wrong."

He fell back once more, settling himself against the parapet as if to hear more about it. "Then get me out!"

Her face fairly brightened for the joy of the appeal, but, as if it were a question of immediate action, she visibly considered. "Out of waiting for him? — of seeing him at all?"

"Oh no — not that," said poor Strether, looking grave. "I've got to wait for him — and I want very much to see him. But out of the terror. You did put your finger on it a few minutes ago. It's general, but it avails itself of particular occasions. That's what it's doing for me now. I'm always considering something else; something else, I mean, than the thing of the moment. The obsession of the other thing is the terror. I'm considering at present for instance something else than *you*."

She listened with charming earnestness. "Oh you ought n't to do that!"

"It's what I admit. Make it then impossible."

She continued to think. "Is it really an 'order' from you? — that I shall take the job? *Will* you give yourself up?"

Poor Strether heaved his sigh. "If I only could! But that's the deuce of it — that I never can. No— I can't."

She was n't, however, discouraged. "But you want to at least?"

"Oh unspeakably!"

"Ah then, if you'll try!" — and she took over the job, as she had called it, on the spot. "Trust me!" she exclaimed; and the action of this, as they retraced their steps, was presently to make him pass his hand into her arm in the manner of a benign dependent paternal old person who wishes to be "nice" to a younger one. If he drew it out again indeed as they approached the inn this may have been because, after more talk had passed between them, the relation of age, or at least of experience — which, for that matter, had already played to and fro with some freedom — affected him as incurring a readjustment. It was at all events perhaps lucky that they arrived in sufficiently separate fashion within range of the hotel-door. The young lady they had left in the glass cage watched as if she had come to await them on the threshold. At her side stood a person equally interested, by his attitude, in their return, and the effect of the sight of whom was instantly to determine for Strether another of those responsive arrests that we have had so repeatedly to note. He left it to Miss Gostrey to name, with the fine full bravado, as it almost struck him, of her "Mr. Waymarsh!" what

BOOK FIRST

was to have been, what—he more than ever felt as his short stare of suspended welcome took things in — would have been, but for herself, his doom. It was already upon him even at that distance — Mr. Waymarsh was for *his* part joyless.

II

HE had none the less to confess to this friend that evening that he knew almost nothing about her, and it was a deficiency that Waymarsh, even with his memory refreshed by contact, by her own prompt and lucid allusions and enquiries, by their having publicly partaken of dinner in her company, and by another stroll, to which she was not a stranger, out into the town to look at the cathedral by moonlight — it was a blank that the resident of Milrose, though admitting acquaintance with the Munsters, professed himself unable to fill. He had no recollection of Miss Gostrey, and two or three questions that she put to him about those members of his circle had, to Strether's observation, the same effect he himself had already more directly felt — the effect of appearing to place all knowledge, for the time, on this original woman's side. It interested him indeed to mark the limits of any such relation for her with his friend as there could possibly be a question of, and it particularly struck him that they were to be marked altogether in Waymarsh's quarter. This added to his own sense of having gone far with her — gave him an early illustration of a much shorter course. There was a certitude he immediately grasped — a conviction that Waymarsh would quite fail, as it were, and on whatever degree of acquaintance, to profit by her.

There had been after the first interchange among

the three a talk of some five minutes in the hall, and then the two men had adjourned to the garden, Miss Gostrey for the time disappearing. Strether in due course accompanied his friend to the room he had bespoken and had, before going out, scrupulously visited; where at the end of another half-hour he had no less discreetly left him. On leaving him he repaired straight to his own room, but with the prompt effect of feeling the compass of that chamber resented by his condition. There he enjoyed at once the first consequence of their reunion. A place was too small for him after it that had seemed large enough before. He had awaited it with something he would have been sorry, have been almost ashamed not to recognise as emotion, yet with a tacit assumption at the same time that emotion would in the event find itself relieved. The actual oddity was that he was only more excited; and his excitement — to which indeed he would have found it difficult instantly to give a name — brought him once more downstairs and caused him for some minutes vaguely to wander. He went once more to the garden; he looked into the public room, found Miss Gostrey writing letters and backed out; he roamed, fidgeted and wasted time; but he was to have his more intimate session with his friend before the evening closed.

It was late — not till Strether had spent an hour upstairs with him — that this subject consented to betake himself to doubtful rest. Dinner and the subsequent stroll by moonlight — a dream, on Strether's part, of romantic effects rather prosaically merged in a mere missing of thicker coats — had measurably

23

intervened, and this midnight conference was the result of Waymarsh's having (when they were free, as he put it, of their fashionable friend) found the smoking-room not quite what he wanted, and yet bed what he wanted less. His most frequent form of words was that he knew himself, and they were applied on this occasion to his certainty of not sleeping. He knew himself well enough to know that he should have a night of prowling unless he should succeed, as a preliminary, in getting prodigiously tired. If the effort directed to this end involved till a late hour the presence of Strether — consisted, that is, in the detention of the latter for full discourse — there was yet an impression of minor discipline involved for our friend in the picture Waymarsh made as he sat in trousers and shirt on the edge of his couch. With his long legs extended and his large back much bent, he nursed alternately, for an almost incredible time, his elbows and his beard. He struck his visitor as extremely, as almost wilfully uncomfortable; yet what had this been for Strether, from that first glimpse of him disconcerted in the porch of the hotel, but the predominant note? The discomfort was in a manner contagious, as well as also in a manner inconsequent and unfounded; the visitor felt that unless he should get used to it — or unless Waymarsh himself should — it would constitute a menace for his own prepared, his own already confirmed, consciousness of the agreeable. On their first going up together to the room Strether had selected for him Waymarsh had looked it over in silence and with a sigh that represented for his companion, if not the habit of disapprobation, at least the despair

24

of felicity; and this look had recurred to Strether as the key of much he had since observed. "Europe," he had begun to gather from these things, had up to now rather failed of its message to him; he had n't got into tune with it and had at the end of three months almost renounced any such expectation.

He really appeared at present to insist on that by just perching there with the gas in his eyes. This of itself somehow conveyed the futility of single rectifications in a multiform failure. He had a large handsome head and a large sallow seamed face — a striking significant physiognomic total, the upper range of which, the great political brow, the thick loose hair, the dark fuliginous eyes, recalled even to a generation whose standard had dreadfully deviated the impressive image, familiar by engravings and busts, of some great national worthy of the earlier part of the mid-century. He was of the personal type — and it was an element in the power and promise that in their early time Strether had found in him — of the American statesman, the statesman trained in "Congressional halls," of an elder day. The legend had been in later years that as the lower part of his face, which was weak, and slightly crooked, spoiled the likeness, this was the real reason for the growth of his beard, which might have seemed to spoil it for those not in the secret. He shook his mane; he fixed, with his admirable eyes, his auditor or his observer; he wore no glasses and had a way, partly formidable, yet also partly encouraging, as from a representative to a constituent, of looking very hard at those who approached him. He met you as if you had knocked and he had bidden you enter. Strether, who had n't seen him for so long an interval, apprehended him now with a freshness of taste, and had perhaps never done him such ideal justice. The head was bigger, the eyes finer, than they need have been for the career; but that only meant, after all, that the career was itself expressive. What it expressed at midnight in the gas-glaring bedroom at Chester was that the subject of it had, at the end of years, barely escaped, by flight in time, a general nervous collapse. But this very proof of the full life, as the full life was understood at Milrose, would have made to Strether's imagination an element in which Waymarsh could have floated easily had he only consented to float. Alas nothing so little resembled floating as the rigour with which, on the edge of his bed, he hugged his posture of prolonged impermanence. It suggested to his comrade something that always, when kept up, worried him — a person established in a railway-coach with a forward inclination. It represented the angle at which poor Waymarsh was to sit through the ordeal of Europe.

Thanks to the stress of occupation, the strain of professions, the absorption and embarrassment of each, they had not, at home, during years before this sudden brief and almost bewildering reign of comparative ease, found so much as a day for a meeting; a fact that was in some degree an explanation of the sharpness with which most of his friend's features stood out to Strether. Those he had lost sight of since the early time came back to him; others that it was never possible to forget struck him now as sitting,

BOOK FIRST

clustered and expectant, like a somewhat defiant family-group, on the door-step of their residence. The room was narrow for its length, and the occupant of the bed thrust so far a pair of slippered feet that the visitor had almost to step over them in his recurrent rebounds from his chair to fidget back and forth. There were marks the friends made on things to talk about, and on things not to, and one of the latter in particular fell like the tap of chalk on the blackboard. Married at thirty, Waymarsh had not lived with his wife for fifteen years, and it came up vividly between them in the glare of the gas that Strether was n't to ask about her. He knew they were still separate and that she lived at hotels, travelled in Europe, painted her face and wrote her husband abusive letters, of not one of which, to a certainty, that sufferer spared himself the perusal; but he respected without difficulty the cold twilight that had settled on this side of his companion's life. It was a province in which mystery reigned and as to which Waymarsh had never spoken the informing word. Strether, who wanted to do him the highest justice wherever he *could* do it, singularly admired him for the dignity of this reserve, and even counted it as one of the grounds — grounds all handled and numbered — for ranking him, in the range of their acquaintance, as a success. He *was* a success, Waymarsh, in spite of overwork, or prostration, of sensible shrinkage, of his wife's letters and of his not liking Europe. Strether would have reckoned his own career less futile had he been able to put into it anything so handsome as so much fine silence. One might one's self easily have left Mrs. Waymarsh; and

one would assuredly have paid one's tribute to the
ideal in covering with that attitude the derision of
having been left by her. Her husband had held his
tongue and had made a large income; and these were
in especial the achievements as to which Strether
envied him. Our friend had had indeed on his side
too a subject for silence, which he fully appreciated;
but it was a matter of a different sort, and the figure
of the income he had arrived at had never been high
enough to look any one in the face.

"I don't know as I quite see what you require it for.
You don't appear sick to speak of." It was of Europe
Waymarsh thus finally spoke.

"Well," said Strether, who fell as much as possible
into step, "I guess I don't *feel* sick now that I've
started. But I had pretty well run down before I did
start."

Waymarsh raised his melancholy look. "Ain't you
about up to your usual average?"

It was not quite pointedly sceptical, but it seemed
somehow a plea for the purest veracity, and it thereby
affected our friend as the very voice of Milrose. He
had long since made a mental distinction — though
never in truth daring to betray it — between the voice
of Milrose and the voice even of Woollett. It was
the former, he felt, that was most in the real tradition.
There had been occasions in his past when the sound
of it had reduced him to temporary confusion, and
the present, for some reason, suddenly became such
another. It was nevertheless no light matter that the
very effect of his confusion should be to make him
again prevaricate. "That description hardly does

28

justice to a man to whom it has done such a lot of good to see *you*."

Waymarsh fixed on his washing-stand the silent detached stare with which Milrose in person, as it were, might have marked the unexpectedness of a compliment from Woollett; and Strether, for his part, felt once more like Woollett in person. "I mean," his friend presently continued, "that your appearance is n't as bad as I've seen it: it compares favourably with what it was when I last noticed it." On this appearance Waymarsh's eyes yet failed to rest; it was almost as if they obeyed an instinct of propriety, and the effect was still stronger when, always considering the basin and jug, he added: "You've filled out some since then."

"I'm afraid I have," Strether laughed: "one does fill out some with all one takes in, and I've taken in, I dare say, more than I've natural room for. I was dog-tired when I sailed." It had the oddest sound of cheerfulness.

"*I* was dog-tired," his companion returned, "when I arrived, and it's this wild hunt for rest that takes all the life out of me. The fact is, Strether — and it's a comfort to have you here at last to say it to; though I don't know, after all, that I've really waited; I've told it to people I've met in the cars — the fact is, such a country as this ain't my *kind* of country anyway. There ain't a country I've seen over here that *does* seem my kind. Oh I don't say but what there are plenty of pretty places and remarkable old things; but the trouble is that I don't seem to feel anywhere in tune. That's one of the reasons why I suppose

29

I've gained so little. I have n't had the first sign of that lift I was led to expect." With this he broke out more earnestly. "Look here — I want to go back." His eyes were all attached to Strether's now, for he was one of the men who fully face you when they talk of themselves. This enabled his friend to look at him hard and immediately to appear to the highest advantage in his eyes by doing so. "That's a genial thing to say to a fellow who has come out on purpose to meet you!"

Nothing could have been finer, on this, than Waymarsh's sombre glow. "*Have* you come out on purpose?"

"Well — very largely."

"I thought from the way you wrote there was something back of it."

Strether hesitated. "Back of my desire to be with you?"

"Back of your prostration."

Strether, with a smile made more dim by a certain consciousness, shook his head. "There are all the causes of it!"

"And no particular cause that seemed most to drive you?"

Our friend could at last conscientiously answer. "Yes. One. There *is* a matter that has had much to do with my coming out."

Waymarsh waited a little. "Too private to mention?"

"No, not too private — for *you*. Only rather complicated."

"Well," said Waymarsh, who had waited again,

BOOK FIRST

"I *may* lose my mind over here, but I don't know as I've done so yet."

"Oh you shall have the whole thing. But not to-night."

Waymarsh seemed to sit stiffer and to hold his elbows tighter. "Why not — if I can't sleep?"

"Because, my dear man, I *can!*"

"Then where's your prostration?"

"Just in that — that I can put in eight hours." And Strether brought it out that if Waymarsh did n't "gain" it was because he did n't go to bed : the result of which was, in its order, that, to do the latter justice, he permitted his friend to insist on his really getting settled. Strether, with a kind coercive hand for it, assisted him to this consummation, and again found his own part in their relation auspiciously enlarged by the smaller touches of lowering the lamp and seeing to a sufficiency of blanket. It somehow ministered for him to indulgence to feel Waymarsh, who looked unnaturally big and black in bed, as much tucked in as a patient in a hospital and, with his covering up to his chin, as much simplified by it. He hovered in vague pity, to be brief, while his companion challenged him out of the bedclothes. "Is she really after you? Is that what's behind?"

Strether felt an uneasiness at the direction taken by his companion's insight, but he played a little at uncertainty. "Behind my coming out?"

"Behind your prostration or whatever. It's generally felt, you know, that she follows you up pretty close."

Strether's candour was never very far off. "Oh

it has occurred to you that I'm literally running away from Mrs. Newsome?"

"Well, I have n't *known* but what you are. You're a very attractive man, Strether. You've seen for yourself," said Waymarsh, "what that lady downstairs makes of it. Unless indeed," he rambled on with an effect between the ironic and the anxious, "it's you who are after *her*. Is Mrs. Newsome *over* here?" He spoke as with a droll dread of her.

It made his friend — though rather dimly — smile. "Dear no; she's safe, thank goodness — as I think I more and more feel — at home. She thought of coming, but she gave it up. I've come in a manner instead of her; and come to that extent — for you're right in your inference — on her business. So you see there *is* plenty of connexion."

Waymarsh continued to see at least all there was. "Involving accordingly the particular one I've referred to?"

Strether took another turn about the room, giving a twitch to his companion's blanket and finally gaining the door. His feeling was that of a nurse who had earned personal rest by having made everything straight. "Involving more things than I can think of breaking ground on now. But don't be afraid — you shall have them from me: you'll probably find yourself having quite as much of them as you can do with. I shall — if we keep together — very much depend on your impression of some of them."

Waymarsh's acknowledgement of this tribute was characteristically indirect. "You mean to say you don't believe we *will* keep together?"

BOOK FIRST

"I only glance at the danger," Strether paternally said, "because when I hear you wail to go back I seem to see you open up such possibilities of folly."

Waymarsh took it — silent a little — like a large snubbed child. "What are you going to do with me?"

It was the very question Strether himself had put to Miss Gostrey, and he wondered if he had sounded like that. But *he* at least could be more definite. "I'm going to take you right down to London."

"Oh I've *been* down to London!" Waymarsh more softly moaned. "I've no use, Strether, for anything down there."

"Well," said Strether, good-humouredly, "I guess you've some use for *me*."

"So I've got to go?"

"Oh you've got to go further yet."

"Well," Waymarsh sighed, "do your damnedest! Only you *will* tell me before you lead me on all the way — ?"

Our friend had again so lost himself, both for amusement and for contrition, in the wonder of whether he had made, in his own challenge that afternoon, such another figure, that he for an instant missed the thread. "Tell you — ?"

"Why what you've got on hand."

Strether hesitated. "Why it's such a matter as that even if I positively wanted I should n't be able to keep it from you."

Waymarsh gloomily gazed. "What does that mean then but that your trip is just *for* her?"

"For Mrs. Newsome? Oh it certainly is, as I say. Very much."

33

"Then why do you also say it's for me?"

Strether, in impatience, violently played with his latch. "It's simple enough. It's for both of you."

Waymarsh at last turned over with a groan. "Well, *I* won't marry you!"

"Neither, when it comes to that —!" But the visitor had already laughed and escaped.

III

HE had told Miss Gostrey he should probably take, for departure with Waymarsh, some afternoon train, and it thereupon in the morning appeared that this lady had made her own plan for an earlier one. She had breakfasted when Strether came into the coffee-room; but, Waymarsh not having yet emerged, he was in time to recall her to the terms of their understanding and to pronounce her discretion overdone. She was surely not to break away at the very moment she had created a want. He had met her as she rose from her little table in a window, where, with the morning papers beside her, she reminded him, as he let her know, of Major Pendennis breakfasting at his club — a compliment of which she professed a deep appreciation; and he detained her as pleadingly as if he had already — and notably under pressure of the visions of the night — learned to be unable to do without her. She must teach him at all events, before she went, to order breakfast as breakfast was ordered in Europe, and she must especially sustain him in the problem of ordering for Waymarsh. The latter had laid upon his friend, by desperate sounds through the door of his room, dreadful divined responsibilities in respect to beefsteak and oranges — responsibilities which Miss Gostrey took over with an alertness of action that matched her quick intelligence. She had before this weaned the expatriated from traditions

35

compared with which the matutinal beefsteak was but the creature of an hour, and it was not for her, with some of her memories, to falter in the path; though she freely enough declared, on reflexion, that there was always in such cases a choice of opposed policies. "There are times when to give them their head, you know —!"

They had gone to wait together in the garden for the dressing of the meal, and Strether found her more suggestive than ever. "Well, what?"

"Is to bring about for them such a complexity of relations — unless indeed we call it a simplicity! — that the situation *has* to wind itself up. They want to go back."

"And you want them to go!" Strether gaily concluded.

"I always want them to go, and I send them as fast as I can."

"Oh I know — you take them to Liverpool."

"Any port will serve in a storm. I'm — with all my other functions — an agent for repatriation. I want to re-people our stricken country. What will become of it else? I want to discourage others."

The ordered English garden, in the freshness of the day, was delightful to Strether, who liked the sound, under his feet, of the tight fine gravel, packed with the chronic damp, and who had the idlest eye for the deep smoothness of turf and the clean curves of paths. "Other people?"

"Other countries. Other people — yes. I want to encourage our own."

Strether wondered. "Not to come? Why then do

you 'meet' them? — since it does n't appear to be
to stop them?"

"Oh that they should n't come is as yet too much to
ask. What I attend to is that they come quickly and
return still more so. I meet them to help it to be over
as soon as possible, and though I don't stop them I 've
my way of putting them through. That's my little
system; and, if you want to know," said Maria Gostrey, "it's my real secret, my innermost mission and
use. I only seem, you see, to beguile and approve;
but I 've thought it all out and I 'm working all the
while underground. I can't perhaps quite give you
my formula, but I think that practically I succeed.
I send you back spent. So you stay back. Passed
through my hands —"

"We don't turn up again?" The further she went
the further he always saw himself able to follow. "I
don't want your formula — I feel quite enough, as I
hinted yesterday, your abysses. Spent!" he echoed.
"If that's how you're arranging so subtly to send me
I thank you for the warning."

For a minute, amid the pleasantness — poetry in
tariffed items, but all the more, for guests already
convicted, a challenge to consumption — they smiled
at each other in confirmed fellowship. "Do you call
it subtly? It's a plain poor tale. Besides, you're a
special case."

"Oh special cases — that's weak!" She was weak
enough, further still, to defer her journey and agree
to accompany the gentlemen on their own, might a
separate carriage mark her independence; though it
was in spite of this to befall after luncheon that she

37

went off alone and that, with a tryst taken for a day of her company in London, they lingered another night. She had, during the morning — spent in a way that he was to remember later on as the very climax of his foretaste, as warm with presentiments, with what he would have called collapses — had all sorts of things out with Strether; and among them the fact that though there was never a moment of her life when she was n't "due" somewhere, there was yet scarce a perfidy to others of which she was n't capable for his sake. She explained moreover that wherever she happened to be she found a dropped thread to pick up, a ragged edge to repair, some familiar appetite in ambush, jumping out as she approached, yet appeasable with a temporary biscuit. It became, on her taking the risk of the deviation imposed on him by her insidious arrangement of his morning meal, a point of honour for her not to fail with Waymarsh of the larger success too; and her subsequent boast to Strether was that she had made their friend fare — and quite without his knowing what was the matter — as Major Pendennis would have fared at the Megatherium. She had made him breakfast like a gentleman, and it was nothing, she forcibly asserted, to what she would yet make him do. She made him participate in the slow reiterated ramble with which, for Strether, the new day amply filled itself; and it was by her art that he somehow had the air, on the ramparts and in the Rows, of carrying a point of his own.

The three strolled and stared and gossiped, or at least the two did; the case really yielding for their comrade, if analysed, but the element of stricken

BOOK FIRST

silence. This element indeed affected Strether as charged with audible rumblings, but he was conscious of the care of taking it explicitly as a sign of pleasant peace. He would n't appeal too much, for that provoked stiffness; yet he would n't be too freely tacit, for that suggested giving up. Waymarsh himself adhered to an ambiguous dumbness that might have represented either the growth of a perception or the despair of one; and at times and in places — where the low-browed galleries were darkest, the opposite gables queerest, the solicitations of every kind densest — the others caught him fixing hard some object of minor interest, fixing even at moments nothing discernible, as if he were indulging it with a truce. When he met Strether's eye on such occasions he looked guilty and furtive, fell the next minute into some attitude of retractation. Our friend could n't show him the right things for fear of provoking some total renouncement, and was tempted even to show him the wrong in order to make him differ with triumph. There were moments when he himself felt shy of professing the full sweetness of the taste of leisure, and there were others when he found himself feeling as if his passages of interchange with the lady at his side might fall upon the third member of their party very much as Mr. Burchell, at Dr. Primrose's fireside, was influenced by the high flights of the visitors from London. The smallest things so arrested and amused him that he repeatedly almost apologised — brought up afresh in explanation his plea of a previous grind. He was aware at the same time that his grind had been as nothing to Waymarsh's, and he repeatedly confessed that, to cover his frivolity, he was doing his best for his previous virtue. Do what he might, in any case, his previous virtue was still there, and it seemed fairly to stare at him out of the windows of shops that were not as the shops of Woollett, fairly to make him want things that he should n't know what to do with. It was by the oddest, the least admissible of laws demoralising him now; and the way it boldly took was to make him want more wants. These first walks in Europe were in fact a kind of finely lurid intimation of what one might find at the end of that process. Had he come back after long years, in something already so like the evening of life, only to be exposed to it? It was at all events over the shop-windows that he made, with Waymarsh, most free; though it would have been easier had not the latter most sensibly yielded to the appeal of the merely useful trades. He pierced with his sombre detachment the plate-glass of ironmongers and saddlers, while Strether flaunted an affinity with the dealers in stamped letter-paper and in smart neckties. Strether was in fact recurrently shameless in the presence of the tailors, though it was just over the heads of the tailors that his countryman most loftily looked. This gave Miss Gostrey a grasped opportunity to back up Waymarsh at his expense. The weary lawyer — it was unmistakeable — had a conception of dress; but that, in view of some of the features of the effect produced, was just what made the danger of insistence on it. Strether wondered if he by this time thought Miss Gostrey less fashionable or Lambert Strether more so; and it appeared probable that most of the remarks ex-

changed between this latter pair about passers, figures, faces, personal types, exemplified in their degree
the disposition to talk as "society" talked.

Was what was happening to himself then, was what
already *had* happened, really that a woman of fashion
was floating him into society and that an old friend
deserted on the brink was watching the force of the
current? When the woman of fashion permitted
Strether — as she permitted him at the most — the
purchase of a pair of gloves, the terms she made about
it, the prohibition of neckties and other items till she
should be able to guide him through the Burlington
Arcade, were such as to fall upon a sensitive ear as a
challenge to just imputations. Miss Gostrey was such
a woman of fashion as could make without a symptom of vulgar blinking an appointment for the Burlington Arcade. Mere discriminations about a pair of
gloves could thus at any rate represent — always for
such sensitive ears as were in question — possibilities of something that Strether could make a mark
against only as the peril of apparent wantonness. He
had quite the consciousness of his new friend, for
their companion, that he might have had of a Jesuit
in petticoats, a representative of the recruiting interests of the Catholic Church. The Catholic Church,
for Waymarsh — that was to say the enemy, the
monster of bulging eyes and far-reaching quivering
groping tentacles — was exactly society, exactly the
multiplication of shibboleths, exactly the discrimination of types and tones, exactly the wicked old Rows
of Chester, rank with feudalism; exactly in short
Europe.

There was light for observation, however, in an incident that occurred just before they turned back to luncheon. Waymarsh had been for a quarter of an hour exceptionally mute and distant, and something, or other — Strether was never to make out exactly what — proved, as it were, too much for him after his comrades had stood for three minutes taking in, while they leaned on an old balustrade that guarded the edge of the Row, a particularly crooked and huddled street-view. "He thinks us sophisticated, he thinks us worldly, he thinks us wicked, he thinks us all sorts of queer things," Strether reflected; for wondrous were the vague quantities our friend had within a couple of short days acquired the habit of conveniently and conclusively lumping together. There seemed moreover a direct connexion between some such inference and a sudden grim dash taken by Waymarsh to the opposite side. This movement was startlingly sudden, and his companions at first supposed him to have espied, to be pursuing, the glimpse of an acquaintance. They next made out, however, that an open door had instantly received him, and they then recognised him as engulfed in the establishment of a jeweller, behind whose glittering front he was lost to view. The act had somehow the note of a demonstration, and it left each of the others to show a face almost of fear. But Miss Gostrey broke into a laugh. "What's the matter with him?"

"Well," said Strether, "he can't stand it."

"But can't stand what?"

"Anything. Europe."

"Then how will that jeweller help him?"

BOOK FIRST

Strether seemed to make it out, from their position, between the interstices of arrayed watches, of close-hung dangling gewgaws. "You'll see."

"Ah that's just what — if he buys anything — I'm afraid of: that I shall see something rather dreadful."

Strether studied the finer appearances. "He may buy everything."

"Then don't you think we ought to follow him?"

"Not for worlds. Besides we can't. We're paralysed. We exchange a long scared look, we publicly tremble. The thing is, you see, we 'realise.' He has struck for freedom."

She wondered but she laughed. "Ah what a price to pay! And I was preparing some for him so cheap."

"No, no," Strether went on, frankly amused now; "don't call it that: the kind of freedom *you* deal in is dear." Then as to justify himself: "Am I not in *my* way trying it? It's this."

"Being here, you mean, with me?"

"Yes, and talking to you as I do. I've known you a few hours, and I've known *him* all my life; so that if the ease I thus take with you about him is n't magnificent" — and the thought of it held him a moment — "why it's rather base."

"It's magnificent!" said Miss Gostrey to make an end of it. "And you should hear," she added, "the ease *I* take — and I above all intend to take — with Mr. Waymarsh."

Strether thought. "About *me?* Ah that's no equivalent. The equivalent would be Waymarsh's himself serving me up—his remorseless analysis of me. And he'll never do that" — he was sadly clear. "He'll never remorselessly analyse me." He quite held her with the authority of this. "He'll never say a word to you about me."

She took it in; she did it justice; yet after an instant her reason, her restless irony, disposed of it. "Of course he won't. For what do you take people, that they're able to say words about anything, able remorselessly to analyse? There are not many like you and me. It will be only because he's too stupid."

It stirred in her friend a sceptical echo which was at the same time the protest of the faith of years. "Waymarsh stupid?"

"Compared with you."

Strether had still his eyes on the jeweller's front, and he waited a moment to answer. "He's a success of a kind that I haven't approached."

"Do you mean he has made money?"

"He makes it — to my belief. And I," said Strether, "though with a back quite as bent, have never made anything. I'm a perfectly equipped failure."

He feared an instant she'd ask him if he meant he was poor; and he was glad she did n't, for he really did n't know to what the truth on this unpleasant point might n't have prompted her. She only, however, confirmed his assertion. "Thank goodness you're a failure — it's why I so distinguish you! Anything else to-day is too hideous. Look about you — look at the successes. Would you *be* one, on your honour? Look, moreover," she continued, "at me."

For a little accordingly their eyes met. "I see," Strether returned. "You too are out of it."

BOOK FIRST

"The superiority you discern in me," she concurred, "announces my futility. If you knew," she
sighed, "the dreams of my youth! But our realities
are what has brought us together. We're beaten
brothers in arms."

He smiled at her kindly enough, but he shook his
head. "It does n't alter the fact that you're expensive. You've cost me already —!"

But he had hung fire. "Cost you what?"

"Well, my past — in one great lump. But no matter," he laughed: "I'll pay with my last penny."

Her attention had unfortunately now been engaged
by their comrade's return, for Waymarsh met their
view as he came out of his shop. "I hope he has n't
paid," she said, "with *his* last; though I'm convinced
he has been splendid, and has been so for you."

"Ah no — not that!"

"Then for me?"

"Quite as little." Waymarsh was by this time near
enough to show signs his friend could read, though he
seemed to look almost carefully at nothing in particular.

"Then for himself?"

"For nobody. For nothing. For freedom."

"But what has freedom to do with it?"

Strether's answer was indirect. "To be as good as
you and me. But different."

She had had time to take in their companion's face;
and with it, as such things were easy for her, she took
in all. "Different — yes. But better!"

If Waymarsh was sombre he was also indeed almost
sublime. He told them nothing, left his absence unex-

45

plained, and though they were convinced he had made some extraordinary purchase they were never to learn its nature. He only glowered grandly at the tops of the old gables. "It's the sacred rage," Strether had had further time to say; and this sacred rage was to become between them, for convenient comprehension, the description of one of his periodical necessities. It was Strether who eventually contended that it did make him better than they. But by that time Miss Gostrey was convinced that she did n't want to be better than Strether.

BOOK SECOND

I

Those occasions on which Strether was, in association with the exile from Milrose, to see the sacred rage glimmer through would doubtless have their due periodicity; but our friend had meanwhile to find names for many other matters. On no evening of his life perhaps, as he reflected, had he had to supply so many as on the third of his short stay in London; an evening spent by Miss Gostrey's side at one of the theatres, to which he had found himself transported, without his own hand raised, on the mere expression of a conscientious wonder. She knew her theatre, she knew her play, as she had triumphantly known, three days running, everything else, and the moment filled to the brim, for her companion, that apprehension of the interesting which, whether or no the interesting happened to filter through his guide, strained now to its limits his brief opportunity. Waymarsh had n't come with them; he had seen plays enough, he signified, before Strether had joined him—an affirmation that had its full force when his friend ascertained by questions that he had seen two and a circus. Questions as to what he had seen had on him indeed an effect only less favourable than questions as to what he had n't. He liked the former to be discriminated; but how could it be done, Strether asked of their constant counsellor, without discriminating the latter?

49

THE AMBASSADORS

Miss Gostrey had dined with him at his hotel, face to face over a small table on which the lighted candles had rose-coloured shades; and the rose-coloured shades and the small table and the soft fragrance of the lady — had anything to his mere sense ever been so soft? — were so many touches in he scarce knew what positive high picture. He had been to the theatre, even to the opera, in Boston, with Mrs. Newsome, more than once acting as her only escort; but there had been no little confronted dinner, no pink lights, no whiff of vague sweetness, as a preliminary: one of the results of which was that at present, mildly rueful, though with a sharpish accent, he actually asked himself *why* there had n't. There was much the same difference in his impression of the noticed state of his companion, whose dress was "cut down," as he believed the term to be, in respect to shoulders and bosom, in a manner quite other than Mrs. Newsome's, and who wore round her throat a broad red velvet band with an antique jewel — he was rather complacently sure it was antique — attached to it in front. Mrs. Newsome's dress was never in any degree "cut down," and she never wore round her throat a broad red velvet band: if she had, moreover, would it ever have served so to carry on and complicate, as he now almost felt, his vision?

It would have been absurd of him to trace into ramifications the effect of the ribbon from which Miss Gostrey's trinket depended, had he not for the hour, at the best, been so given over to uncontrolled perceptions. What was it but an uncontrolled perception that his friend's velvet band somehow added, in her appearance, to the value of every other item — to that of her smile and of the way she carried her head, to that of her complexion, of her lips, her teeth, her eyes, her hair ? What, certainly, had a man conscious of a man's work in the world to do with red velvet bands ? He would n't for anything have so exposed himself as to tell Miss Gostrey how much he liked hers, yet he *had* none the less not only caught himself in the act — frivolous, no doubt, idiotic, and above all un-expected—of liking it: he had in addition taken it as a starting-point for fresh backward, fresh forward, fresh lateral flights. The manner in which Mrs. Newsome's throat *was* encircled suddenly represented for him, in an alien order, almost as many things as the man-ner in which Miss Gostrey's was. Mrs. Newsome wore, at operatic hours, a black silk dress—very hand-some, he knew it was "handsome" — and an orna-ment that his memory was able further to identify as a ruche. He had his association indeed with the ruche, but it was rather imperfectly romantic. He had once said to the wearer — and it was as "free" a remark as he had ever made to her — that she looked, with her ruff and other matters, like Queen Elizabeth; and it had after this in truth been his fancy that, as a consequence of that tenderness and an accept-ance of the idea, the form of this special tribute to the "frill" had grown slightly more marked. The con-nexion, as he sat there and let his imagination roam, was to strike him as vaguely pathetic; but there it all was, and pathetic was doubtless in the conditions the best thing it could possibly be. It had assuredly ex-isted at any rate; for it seemed now to come over him that no gentleman of his age at Woollett could ever, to a lady of Mrs. Newsome's, which was not much less than his, have embarked on such a simile.

All sorts of things in fact now seemed to come over him, comparatively few of which his chronicler can hope for space to mention. It came over him for instance that Miss Gostrey looked perhaps like Mary Stuart: Lambert Strether had a candour of fancy which could rest for an instant gratified in such an antithesis. It came over him that never before — no, literally never — had a lady dined with him at a public place before going to the play. The publicity of the place was just, in the matter, for Strether, the rare strange thing; it affected him almost as the achievement of privacy might have affected a man of a different experience. He had married, in the far-away years, so young as to have missed the time natural in Boston for taking girls to the Museum; and it was absolutely true of him that — even after the close of the period of conscious detachment occupying the centre of his life, the grey middle desert of the two deaths, that of his wife and that, ten years later, of his boy — he had never taken any one anywhere. It came over him in especial — though the monition had, as happened, already sounded, fitfully gleamed, in other forms — that the business he had come out on had n't yet been so brought home to him as by the sight of the people about him. She gave him the impression, his friend, at first, more straight than he got it for himself — gave it simply by saying with off-hand illumination: "Oh yes, they're types!" — but after he had taken it he made to the full his own use of it; both while he kept silence for the four acts and while he talked in the intervals. It was an evening, it was a world of types, and this was a connexion above all in which the figures and faces in the stalls were interchangeable with those on the stage.

He felt as if the play itself penetrated him with the naked elbow of his neighbour, a great stripped handsome red-haired lady who conversed with a gentleman on her other side in stray dissyllables which had for his ear, in the oddest way in the world, so much sound that he wondered they had n't more sense; and he recognised by the same law, beyond the footlights, what he was pleased to take for the very flush of English life. He had distracted drops in which he could n't have said if it were actors or auditors who were most true, and the upshot of which, each time, was the consciousness of new contacts. However he viewed his job it was "types" he should have to tackle. Those before him and around him were not as the types of Woollett, where, for that matter, it had begun to seem to him that there must only have been the male and the female. These made two exactly, even with the individual varieties. Here, on the other hand, apart from the personal and the sexual range — which might be greater or less — a series of strong stamps had been applied, as it were, from without; stamps that his observation played with as, before a glass case on a table, it might have passed from medal to medal and from copper to gold. It befell that in the drama precisely there was a bad woman in a yellow frock who made a pleasant weak good-looking young man in perpetual evening dress do the most dreadful things.

53

Strether felt himself on the whole not afraid of the yellow frock, but he was vaguely anxious over a certain kindness into which he found himself drifting for its victim. He had n't come out, he reminded himself, to be too kind, or indeed to be kind at all, to Chadwick Newsome. Would Chad also be in perpetual evening dress? He somehow rather hoped it — it seemed so to add to *this* young man's general amenability; though he wondered too if, to fight him with his own weapons, he himself (a thought almost startling) would have likewise to be. This young man furthermore would have been much more easy to handle — at least for *him* — than appeared probable in respect to Chad.

It came up for him with Miss Gostrey that there were things of which she would really perhaps after all have heard; and she admitted when a little pressed that she was never quite sure of what she heard as distinguished from things such as, on occasions like the present, she only extravagantly guessed. "I seem with this freedom, you see, to have guessed Mr. Chad. He's a young man on whose head high hopes are placed at Woollett; a young man a wicked woman has got hold of and whom his family over there have sent you out to rescue. You've accepted the mission of separating him from the wicked woman. Are you quite sure she's very bad for him?"

Something in his manner showed it as quite pulling him up. "Of course we are. Would n't *you* be?"

"Oh I don't know. One never does — does one? — beforehand. One can only judge on the facts. Yours are quite new to me; I'm really not in the least, as you see, in possession of them: so it will be awfully interesting to have them from you. If you're satisfied, that's all that's required. I mean if you're sure you *are* sure: sure it won't do."

"That he should lead such a life? Rather!"

"Oh but I don't know, you see, about his life; you've not told me about his life. She may be charming — his life!"

"Charming?" — Strether stared before him. "She's base, venal — out of the streets."

"I see. And *he* — ?"

"Chad, wretched boy?"

"Of what type and temper is he?" she went on as Strether had lapsed.

"Well — the obstinate." It was as if for a moment he had been going to say more and had then controlled himself.

That was scarce what she wished. "Do you like him?"

This time he was prompt. "No. How *can* I?"

"Do you mean because of your being so saddled with him?"

"I'm thinking of his mother," said Strether after a moment. "He has darkened her admirable life." He spoke with austerity. "He has worried her half to death."

"Oh that's of course odious." She had a pause as if for renewed emphasis of this truth, but it ended on another note. "Is her life very admirable?"

"Extraordinarily."

There was so much in the tone that Miss Gostrey had to devote another pause to the appreciation of it.

"And has he only *her?* I don't mean the bad woman in Paris," she quickly added — "for I assure you I should n't even at the best be disposed to allow him more than one. But has he only his mother?"

"He has also a sister, older than himself and married; and they're both remarkably fine women."

"Very handsome, you mean?"

This promptitude — almost, as he might have thought, this precipitation, gave him a brief drop; but he came up again. "Mrs. Newsome, I think, is handsome, though she's not of course, with a son of twenty-eight and a daughter of thirty, in her very first youth. She married, however, extremely young."

"And is wonderful," Miss Gostrey asked, "for her age?"

Strether seemed to feel with a certain disquiet the pressure of it. "I don't say she's wonderful. Or rather," he went on the next moment, "I do say it. It's exactly what she *is* — wonderful. But I was n't thinking of her appearance," he explained — "striking as that doubtless is. I was thinking — well, of many other things." He seemed to look at these as if to mention some of them; then took, pulling himself up, another turn. "About Mrs. Pocock people may differ."

"Is that the daughter's name — 'Pocock'?"

"That's the daughter's name," Strether sturdily confessed.

"And people may differ, you mean, about *her* beauty?"

"About everything."

"But *you* admire her?"

He gave his friend a glance as to show how he could bear this. "I'm perhaps a little afraid of her."

"Oh," said Miss Gostrey, "I see her from here! You may say then I see very fast and very far, but I've already shown you I do. The young man and the two ladies," she went on, "are at any rate all the family?"

"Quite all. His father has been dead ten years, and there's no brother, nor any other sister. They'd do," said Strether, "anything in the world for him."

"And you'd do anything in the world for *them?*"

He shifted again; she had made it perhaps just a shade too affirmative for his nerves. "Oh I don't know!"

"You'd do at any rate this, and the 'anything' they'd do is represented by their *making* you do it."

"Ah they couldn't have come — either of them. They're very busy people and Mrs. Newsome in particular has a large full life. She's moreover highly nervous — and not at all strong."

"You mean she's an American invalid?"

He carefully distinguished. "There's nothing she likes less than to be called one, but she would consent to be one of those things, I think," he laughed, "if it were the only way to be the other."

"Consent to be an American in order to be an invalid?"

"No," said Strether, "the other way round. She's at any rate delicate sensitive high-strung. She puts so much of herself into everything —"

Ah Maria knew these things! "That she has nothing left for anything else? Of course she hasn't.

To whom do you say it? High-strung? Don't I spend my life, for them, jamming down the pedal? I see moreover how it has told on you."

Strether took this more lightly. "Oh I jam down the pedal too!"

"Well," she lucidly returned, "we must from this moment bear on it together with all our might." And she forged ahead. "Have they money?'

But it was as if, while her energetic image still held him, her enquiry fell short. "Mrs. Newsome," he wished further to explain, "has n't moreover your courage on the question of contact. If she had come it would have been to see the person herself."

"The woman? Ah but that's courage."

"No — it's exaltation, which is a very different thing. Courage," he, however, accommodatingly threw out, "is what *you* have."

She shook her head. "You say that only to patch me up — to cover the nudity of my want of exaltation. I've neither the one nor the other. I've mere battered indifference. I see that what you mean," Miss Gostrey pursued, "is that if your friend *had* come she would take great views, and the great views, to put it simply, would be too much for her."

Strether looked amused at her notion of the simple, but he adopted her formula. "Everything's too much for her."

"Ah then such a service as this of yours — "

"Is more for her than anything else? Yes — far more. But so long as it is n't too much for *me* —!"

"Her condition does n't matter? Surely not; we leave her condition out; we take it, that is, for granted.

I see it, her condition, as behind and beneath you; yet at the same time I see it as bearing you up."

"Oh it does bear me up!" Strether laughed.

"Well then as yours bears *me* nothing more's needed." With which she put again her question. "Has Mrs. Newsome money?"

This time he heeded. "Oh plenty. That's the root of the evil. There's money, to very large amounts, in the concern. Chad has had the free use of a great deal. But if he'll pull himself together and come home, all the same, he'll find his account in it."

She had listened with all her interest. "And I hope to goodness you'll find yours!"

"He'll take up his definite material reward," said Strether without acknowledgement of this. "He's at the parting of the ways. He can come into the business now — he can't come later."

"Is there a business?"

"Lord, yes — a big brave bouncing business. A roaring trade."

"A great shop?"

"Yes — a workshop; a great production, a great industry. The concern's a manufacture — and a manufacture that, if it's only properly looked after, may well be on the way to become a monopoly. It's a little thing they make — make better, it appears, than other people can, or than other people, at any rate, do. Mr. Newsome, being a man of ideas, at least in that particular line," Strether explained, "put them on it with great effect, and gave the place altogether, in his time, an immense lift."

"It's a place in itself?"

"Well, quite a number of buildings; almost a little industrial colony. But above all it's a thing. The article produced."

"And what *is* the article produced?"

Strether looked about him as in slight reluctance to say; then the curtain, which he saw about to rise, came to his aid. "I'll tell you next time." But when the next time came he only said he'd tell her later on — after they should have left the theatre; for she had immediately reverted to their topic, and even for himself the picture of the stage was now overlaid with another image. His postponements, however, made her wonder — wonder if the article referred to were anything bad. And she explained that she meant improper or ridiculous or wrong. But Strether, so far as that went, could satisfy her. "Unmentionable? Oh no, we constantly talk of it; we are quite familiar and brazen about it. Only, as a small, trivial, rather ridiculous object of the commonest domestic use, it's just wanting in — what shall I say? Well, dignity, or the least approach to distinction. Right here therefore, with everything about us so grand —!" In short he shrank.

"It's a false note?"

"Sadly. It's vulgar."

"But surely not vulgarer than this." Then on his wondering as she herself had done: "Than everything about us." She seemed a trifle irritated. "What do you take this for?"

"Why for — comparatively — divine!"

"This dreadful London theatre? It's impossible, if you really want to know."

BOOK SECOND

"Oh then," laughed Strether, "I *don't* really want to know!"

It made between them a pause, which she, however, still fascinated by the mystery of the production at Woollett, presently broke. "'Rather ridiculous'? Clothes-pins? Saleratus? Shoe-polish?"

It brought him round. "No — you don't even 'burn.' I don't think, you know, you'll guess it."

"How then can I judge how vulgar it is?"

"You'll judge when I do tell you" — and he persuaded her to patience. But it may even now frankly be mentioned that he in the sequel never *was* to tell her. He actually never did so, and it moreover oddly occurred that by the law, within her, of the incalculable, her desire for the information dropped and her attitude to the question converted itself into a positive cultivation of ignorance. In ignorance she could humour her fancy, and that proved a useful freedom. She could treat the little nameless object as indeed unnameable — she could make their abstention enormously definite. There might indeed have been for Strether the portent of this in what she next said.

"Is it perhaps then because it's so bad — because your industry, as you call it, *is* so vulgar — that Mr. Chad won't come back? Does he feel the taint? Is he staying away not to be mixed up in it?"

"Oh," Strether laughed, "it would n't appear — would it? — that he feels 'taints'! He's glad enough of the money from it, and the money's his whole basis. There's appreciation in that — I mean as to the allowance his mother has hitherto made him. She has of course the resource of cutting this allowance off; but

61

even then he has unfortunately, and on no small scale, his independent supply — money left him by his grandfather, her own father."

"Would n't the fact you mention then," Miss Gostrey asked, "make it just more easy for him to be particular? Is n't he conceivable as fastidious about the source — the apparent and public source — of his income?"

Strether was able quite good-humouredly to entertain the proposition. "The source of his grandfather's wealth — and thereby of his own share in it — was not particularly noble."

"And what source was it?"

Strether cast about. "Well — practices."

"In business? Infamies? He was an old swindler?"

"Oh," he said with more emphasis than spirit, "I shan't describe *him* nor narrate his exploits."

"Lord, what abysses! And the late Mr. Newsome then?"

"Well, what about him?"

"Was he like the grandfather?"

"No — he was on the other side of the house. And he was different."

Miss Gostrey kept it up. "Better?"

Her friend for a moment hung fire. "No."

Her comment on his hesitation was scarce the less marked for being mute. "Thank you. *Now* don't you see," she went on, "why the boy does n't come home? He's drowning his shame."

"His shame? What shame?"

"What shame? Comment donc? *The* shame."

BOOK SECOND

"But where and when," Strether asked, "is '*the shame*' — where is any shame — to-day? The men I speak of — they did as every one does; and (besides being ancient history) it was all a matter of appreciation."

She showed how she understood. "Mrs. Newsome has appreciated?"

"Ah I can't speak for *her!*"

"In the midst of such doings — and, as I understand you, profiting by them, she at least has remained exquisite?"

"Oh I can't talk of her!" Strether said.

"I thought she was just what you *could* talk of. You *don't* trust me," Miss Gostrey after a moment declared.

It had its effect. "Well, her money is spent, her life conceived and carried on with a large beneficence—"

"That's a kind of expiation of wrongs? Gracious," she added before he could speak, "how intensely you make me see her!"

"If you see her," Strether dropped, "it's all that's necessary."

She really seemed to have her. "I feel that. She *is*, in spite of everything, handsome."

This at least enlivened him. "What do you mean by everything?"

"Well, I mean *you.*" With which she had one of her swift changes of ground. "You say the concern needs looking after; but does n't Mrs. Newsome look after it?"

"So far as possible. She's wonderfully able, but

63

it's not her affair, and her life's a good deal over-charged. She has many, many things."

"And you also?"

"Oh yes — I've many too, if you will."

"I see. But what I mean is," Miss Gostrey amended, "do you also look after the business?"

"Oh no, I don't touch the business."

"Only everything else?"

"Well, yes — some things."

"As for instance — ?"

Strether obligingly thought. "Well, the Review."

"The Review? — you have a Review?"

"Certainly. Woollett has a Review — which Mrs. Newsome, for the most part, magnificently pays for and which I, not at all magnificently, edit. My name's on the cover," Strether pursued, "and I'm really rather disappointed and hurt that you seem never to have heard of it."

She neglected for a moment this grievance. "And what kind of a Review is it?"

His serenity was now completely restored. "Well, it's green."

"Do you mean in political colour as they say here — in thought?"

"No; I mean the cover's green — of the most lovely shade."

"And with Mrs. Newsome's name on it too?"

He waited a little. "Oh as for that you must judge if she peeps out. She's behind the whole thing; but she's of a delicacy and a discretion —!"

Miss Gostrey took it all. "I'm sure. She *would* be. I don't underrate her. She must be rather a swell."

"Oh yes, she's rather a swell!"

"A Woollett swell — *bon!* I like the idea of a Woollett swell. And you must be rather one too, to be so mixed up with her."

"Ah no," said Strether, "that's not the way it works."

But she had already taken him up. "The way it works — you need n't tell me! — is of course that you efface yourself."

"With my name on the cover?" he lucidly objected.

"Ah but you don't put it on for yourself."

"I beg your pardon — that's exactly what I do put it on for. It's exactly the thing that I'm reduced to doing for myself. It seems to rescue a little, you see, from the wreck of hopes and ambitions, the refuse-heap of disappointments and failures, my one presentable little scrap of an identity."

On this she looked at him as to say many things, but what she at last simply said was: "She likes to see it there. You're the bigger swell of the two," she immediately continued, "because you think you're not one. She thinks she *is* one. However," Miss Gostrey added, "she thinks you're one too. You're at all events the biggest she can get hold of." She embroidered, she abounded. "I don't say it to interfere between you, but on the day she gets hold of a bigger one —!" Strether had thrown back his head as in silent mirth over something that struck him in her audacity or felicity, and her flight meanwhile was already higher. "Therefore close with her —!"

"Close with her?" he asked as she seemed to hang poised.

65

"Before you lose your chance."

Their eyes met over it. "What do you mean by closing?"

"And what do I mean by your chance? I'll tell you when you tell me all the things *you* don't. Is it her *greatest* fad?" she briskly pursued.

"The Review?" He seemed to wonder how he could best describe it. This resulted however but in a sketch. "It's her tribute to the ideal."

"I see. You go in for tremendous things."

"We go in for the unpopular side — that is so far as we dare."

"And how far *do* you dare?"

"Well, she very far. I much less. I don't begin to have her faith. She provides," said Strether, "three fourths of that. And she provides, as I've confided to you, *all* the money."

It evoked somehow a vision of gold that held for a little Miss Gostrey's eyes, and she looked as if she heard the bright dollars shovelled in. "I hope then you make a good thing —"

"I *never* made a good thing!" he at once returned.

She just waited. "Don't you call it a good thing to be loved?"

"Oh we're not loved. We're not even hated. We're only just sweetly ignored."

She had another pause. "You don't trust me!" she once more repeated.

"Don't I when I lift the last veil? — tell you the very secret of the prison-house?"

Again she met his eyes, but to the result that after an instant her own turned away with impatience.

"You don't sell? Oh I'm glad of *that!*" After which however, and before he could protest, she was off again. "She's just a *moral* swell."

He accepted gaily enough the definition. "Yes — I really think that describes her."

But it had for his friend the oddest connexion. "How does she do her hair?"

He laughed out. "Beautifully!"

"Ah that does n't tell me. However, it does n't matter — I know. It's tremendously neat — a real reproach; quite remarkably thick and without, as yet, a single strand of white. There!"

He blushed for her realism, but gaped at her truth. "You're the very deuce."

"What else *should* I be? It was as the very deuce I pounced on you. But don't let it trouble you, for everything but the very deuce — at our age — is a bore and a delusion, and even he himself, after all, but half a joy." With which, on a single sweep of her wing, she resumed. "You assist her to expiate — which is rather hard when you've yourself not sinned."

"It's she who has n't sinned," Strether replied. "I've sinned the most."

"Ah," Miss Gostrey cynically laughed, "what a picture of *her!* Have you robbed the widow and the orphan?"

"I've sinned enough," said Strether.

"Enough for whom? Enough for what?"

"Well, to be where I am."

"Thank you!" They were disturbed at this moment by the passage between their knees and the back of the seats before them of a gentleman who had been absent during a part of the performance and who now returned for the close; but the interruption left Miss Gostrey time, before the subsequent hush, to express as a sharp finality her sense of the moral of all their talk. "I knew you had something up your sleeve!" This finality, however, left them in its turn, at the end of the play, as disposed to hang back as if they had still much to say; so that they easily agreed to let every one go before them — they found an interest in waiting. They made out from the lobby that the night had turned to rain; yet Miss Gostrey let her friend know that he was n't to see her home. He was simply to put her, by herself, into a four-wheeler; she liked so in London, of wet nights after wild pleasures, thinking things over, on the return, in lonely four-wheelers. This was her great time, she intimated, for pulling herself together. The delays caused by the weather, the struggle for vehicles at the door, gave them occasion to subside on a divan at the back of the vestibule and just beyond the reach of the fresh damp gusts from the street. Here Strether's comrade resumed that free handling of the subject to which his own imagination of it already owed so much. "Does your young friend in Paris like you?"

It had almost, after the interval, startled him. "Oh I hope not! Why *should* he?"

"Why should n't he?" Miss Gostrey asked. "That you're coming down on him need have nothing to do with it."

"You see more in it," he presently returned, "than I."

"Of course I see *you* in it."

"Well then you see more in 'me'!"

"Than you see in yourself? Very likely. That's always one's right. What I was thinking of," she explained, "is the possible particular effect on him of his *milieu.*"

"Oh his *milieu*—!" Strether really felt he could imagine it better now than three hours before.

"Do you mean it can only have been so lowering?"

"Why that's my very starting-point."

"Yes, but you start so far back. What do his letters say?"

"Nothing. He practically ignores us — or spares us. He does n't write."

"I see. But there are all the same," she went on, "two quite distinct things that — given the wonderful place he's in — may have happened to him. One is that he may have got brutalised. The other is that he may have got refined."

Strether stared — this *was* a novelty. "Refined?"

"Oh," she said quietly, "there *are* refinements."

The way of it made him, after looking at her, break into a laugh. "*You* have them!"

"As one of the signs," she continued in the same tone, "they constitute perhaps the worst."

He thought it over and his gravity returned. "Is it a refinement not to answer his mother's letters?"

She appeared to have a scruple, but she brought it out. "Oh I should say the greatest of all."

"Well," said Strether, "*I*'m quite content to let it, as one of the signs, pass for the worst that I know he believes he can do what he likes with me."

69

This appeared to strike her. "How do you know it?"

"Oh I'm sure of it. I feel it in my bones."

"Feel he *can* do it?"

"Feel that he believes he can. It may come to the same thing!" Strether laughed.

She would n't, however, have this. "Nothing for you will ever come to the same thing as anything else." And she understood what she meant, it seemed, sufficiently to go straight on. "You say that if he does break he'll come in for things at home?"

"Quite positively. He'll come in for a particular chance — a chance that any properly constituted young man would jump at. The business has so developed that an opening scarcely apparent three years ago, but which his father's will took account of as in certain conditions possible and which, under that will, attaches to Chad's availing himself of it a large contingent advantage — this opening, the conditions having come about, now simply awaits him. His mother has kept it for him, holding out against strong pressure, till the last possible moment. It requires, naturally, as it carries with it a handsome 'part,' a large share in profits, his being on the spot and making a big effort for a big result. That's what I mean by his chance. If he misses it he comes in, as you say, for nothing. And to see that he does n't miss it is, in a word, what I've come out for."

She let it all sink in. "What you've come out for then is simply to render him an immense service."

Well, poor Strether was willing to take it so. "Ah if you like."

"He stands, as they say, if you succeed with him, to gain —"

"Oh a lot of advantages." Strether had them clearly at his fingers' ends.

"By which you mean of course a lot of money."

"Well, not only. I'm acting with a sense for him of other things too. Consideration and comfort and security — the general safety of being anchored by a strong chain. He wants, as I see him, to be protected. Protected I mean from life."

"Ah voilà!" — her thought fitted with a click. "From life. What you *really* want to get him home for is to marry him."

"Well, that's about the size of it."

"Of course," she said, "it's rudimentary. But to any one in particular?"

He smiled at this, looking a little more conscious. "You get everything out."

For a moment again their eyes met. "You put everything in!"

He acknowledged the tribute by telling her. "To Mamie Pocock."

She wondered; then gravely, even exquisitely, as if to make the oddity also fit: "His own niece?"

"Oh you must yourself find a name for the relation. His brother-in-law's sister. Mrs. Jim's sister-in-law."

It seemed to have on Miss Gostrey a certain hardening effect. "And who in the world's Mrs. Jim?"

"Chad's sister — who was Sarah Newsome. She's married — did n't I mention it? — to Jim Pocock."

"Ah yes," she tacitly replied; but he had mentioned things —! Then, however, with all the sound it could have, "Who in the world's Jim Pocock?" she asked.

"Why Sally's husband. That's the only way we distinguish people at Woollett," he good-humoredly explained.

"And is it a great distinction — being Sally's husband?"

He considered. "I think there can be scarcely a greater — unless it may become one, in the future, to be Chad's wife."

"Then how do they distinguish *you?*"

"They *don't* — except, as I've told you, by the green cover."

Once more their eyes met on it, and she held him an instant. "The green cover won't — nor will *any* cover — avail you with *me*. You're of a depth of duplicity!" Still, she could in her own large grasp of the real condone it. "Is Mamie a great *parti?*"

"Oh the greatest we have — our prettiest brightest girl."

Miss Gostrey seemed to fix the poor child. "I know what they *can* be. And with money?"

"Not perhaps with a great deal of that — but with so much of everything else that we don't miss it. We *don't* miss money much, you know," Strether added, "in general, in America, in pretty girls."

"No," she conceded; "but I know also what you do sometimes miss. And do you," she asked, "yourself admire her?"

It was a question, he indicated, that there might be

several ways of taking; but he decided after an instant for the humorous. "Have n't I sufficiently showed you how I admire *any* pretty girl?"

Her interest in his problem was by this time such that it scarce left her freedom, and she kept close to the facts. "I supposed that at Woollett you wanted them — what shall I call it? — blameless. I mean your young men for your pretty girls."

"So did I!" Strether confessed. "But you strike there a curious fact — the fact that Woollett too accommodates itself to the spirit of the age and the increasing mildness of manners. Everything changes, and I hold that our situation precisely marks a date. We *should* prefer them blameless, but we have to make the best of them as we find them. Since the spirit of the age and the increasing mildness send them so much more to Paris —"

"You've to take them back as they come. When they *do* come. *Bon!*" Once more she embraced it all, but she had a moment of thought. "Poor Chad!"

"Ah," said Strether cheerfully, "Mamie will save him!"

She was looking away, still in her vision, and she spoke with impatience and almost as if he had n't understood her. "*You'll* save him. That's who'll save him."

"Oh but with Mamie's aid. Unless indeed you mean," he added, "that I shall effect so much more with yours!"

It made her at last again look at him. "You'll do more — as you're so much better — than all of us put together."

73

"I think I'm only better since I've known *you!*"
Strether bravely returned.

The depletion of the place, the shrinkage of the
crowd and now comparatively quiet withdrawal of its
last elements had already brought them nearer the
door and put them in relation with a messenger of
whom he bespoke Miss Gostrey's cab. But this left
them a few minutes more, which she was clearly in no
mood not to use. "You've spoken to me of what —
by your success — Mr. Chad stands to gain. But
you've not spoken to me of what you do."

"Oh I've nothing more to gain," said Strether very
simply.

She took it as even quite too simple. "You mean
you've got it all 'down'? You've been paid in
advance?"

"Ah don't talk about payment!" he groaned.

Something in the tone of it pulled her up, but as
their messenger still delayed she had another chance
and she put it in another way. "What — by failure —
do you stand to lose?"

He still, however, wouldn't have it. "Nothing!"
he exclaimed, and on the messenger's at this instant
reappearing he was able to sink the subject in their
responsive advance. When, a few steps up the street,
under a lamp, he had put her into her four-wheeler
and she had asked him if the man had called for him
no second conveyance, he replied before the door was
closed. "You won't take me with you?"

"Not for the world."

"Then I shall walk."

"In the rain?"

BOOK SECOND

"I like the rain," said Strether. "Good-night!"

She kept him a moment, while his hand was on the door, by not answering; after which she answered by repeating her question. "What do you stand to lose?"

Why the question now affected him as other he could n't have said; he could only this time meet it otherwise. "Everything."

"So I thought. Then you shall succeed. And to that end I'm yours —"

"Ah, dear lady!" he kindly breathed.

"Till death!" said Maria Gostrey. "Good-night."

II

STRETHER called, his second morning in Paris, on the bankers of the Rue Scribe to whom his letter of credit was addressed, and he made this visit attended by Waymarsh, in whose company he had crossed from London two days before. They had hastened to the Rue Scribe on the morrow of their arrival, but Strether had not then found the letters the hope of which prompted this errand. He had had as yet none at all; had n't expected them in London, but had counted on several in Paris, and, disconcerted now, had presently strolled back to the Boulevard with a sense of injury that he felt himself taking for as good a start as any other. It would serve, this spur to his spirit, he reflected, as, pausing at the top of the street, he looked up and down the great foreign avenue, it would serve to begin business with. His idea was to begin business immediately, and it did much for him the rest of his day that the beginning of business awaited him. He did little else till night but ask himself what he should do if he had n't fortunately had so much to do; but he put himself the question in many different situations and connexions. What carried him hither and yon was an admirable theory that nothing he could do would n't be in some manner related to what he fundamentally had on hand, or *would* be — should he happen to have a scruple — wasted for it. He did happen to have a scruple — a

76

scruple about taking no definite step till he should get letters; but this reasoning carried it off. A single day to feel his feet — he had felt them as yet only at Chester and in London — was, he could consider, none too much; and having, as he had often privately expressed it, Paris to reckon with, he threw these hours of freshness consciously into the reckoning. They made it continually greater, but that was what it had best be if it was to be anything at all, and he gave himself up till far into the evening, at the theatre and on the return, after the theatre, along the bright congested Boulevard, to feeling it grow. Waymarsh had accompanied him this time to the play, and the two men had walked together, as a first stage, from the Gymnase to the Café Riche, into the crowded "terrace" of which establishment — the night, or rather the morning, for midnight had struck, being bland and populous — they had wedged themselves for refreshment. Waymarsh, as a result of some discussion with his friend, had made a marked virtue of his having now let himself go; and there had been elements of impression in their half-hour over their watered beer-glasses that gave him his occasion for conveying that he held this compromise with his stiffer self to have become extreme. He conveyed it — for it was still, after all, his stiffer self who gloomed out of the glare of the terrace — in solemn silence; and there was indeed a great deal of critical silence, every way, between the companions, even till they gained the Place de l'Opéra, as to the character of their nocturnal progress.

This morning there *were* letters — letters which

had reached London, apparently all together, the day
of Strether's journey, and had taken their time to follow him; so that, after a controlled impulse to go into
them in the reception-room of the bank, which, reminding him of the post-office at Woollett, affected
him as the abutment of some transatlantic bridge, he
slipped them into the pocket of his loose grey overcoat with a sense of the felicity of carrying them off.
Waymarsh, who had had letters yesterday, had had
them again to-day, and Waymarsh suggested in this
particular no controlled impulses. The last one he was
at all events likely to be observed to struggle with was
clearly that of bringing to a premature close any visit
to the Rue Scribe. Strether had left him there yesterday; he wanted to see the papers, and he had spent, by
what his friend could make out, a succession of hours
with the papers. He spoke of the establishment, with
emphasis, as a post of superior observation; just as he
spoke generally of his actual damnable doom as a
device for hiding from him what was going on. Europe was best described, to his mind, as an elaborate
engine for dissociating the confined American from
that indispensable knowledge, and was accordingly
only rendered bearable by these occasional stations of
relief, traps for the arrest of wandering western airs.
Strether, on his side, set himself to walk again — he
had his relief in his pocket; and indeed, much as
he had desired his budget, the growth of restlessness
might have been marked in him from the moment he
had assured himself of the superscription of most of
the missives it contained. This restlessness became
therefore his temporary law; he knew he should recog-

nise as soon as see it the best place of all for settling down with his chief correspondent. He had for the next hour an accidental air of looking for it in the windows of shops; he came down the Rue de la Paix in the sun and, passing across the Tuileries and the river, indulged more than once — as if on finding himself determined — in a sudden pause before the book-stalls of the opposite quay. In the garden of the Tuileries he had lingered, on two or three spots, to look; it was as if the wonderful Paris spring had stayed him as he roamed. The prompt Paris morning struck its cheerful notes — in a soft breeze and a sprinkled smell, in the light flit, over the garden-floor, of bareheaded girls with the buckled strap of oblong boxes, in the type of ancient thrifty persons basking betimes where terrace-walls were warm, in the blue-frocked brass-labelled officialism of humble rakers and scrapers, in the deep references of a straight-pacing priest or the sharp ones of a white-gaitered red-legged soldier. He watched little brisk figures, figures whose movement was as the tick of the great Paris clock, take their smooth diagonal from point to point; the air had a taste as of something mixed with art, something that presented nature as a white-capped master-chef. The palace was gone, Strether remembered the palace; and when he gazed into the irremediable void of its site the historic sense in him might have been freely at play — the play under which in Paris indeed it so often winces like a touched nerve. He filled out spaces with dim symbols of scenes; he caught the gleam of white statues at the base of which, with his letters out, he could tilt back a straw-bottomed chair. But his drift was, for reasons, to the other side, and it floated him unspent up the Rue de Seine and as far as the Luxembourg.

In the Luxembourg Gardens he pulled up; here at last he found his nook, and here, on a penny chair from which terraces, alleys, vistas, fountains, little trees in green tubs, little women in white caps and shrill little girls at play all sunnily "composed" together, he passed an hour in which the cup of his impressions seemed truly to overflow. But a week had elapsed since he quitted the ship, and there were more things in his mind than so few days could account for. More than once, during the time, he had regarded himself as admonished; but the admonition this morning was formidably sharp. It took as it had n't done yet the form of a question — the question of what he was doing with such an extraordinary sense of escape. This sense was sharpest after he had read his letters, but that was also precisely why the question pressed. Four of the letters were from Mrs. Newsome and none of them short; she had lost no time, had followed on his heels while he moved, so expressing herself that he now could measure the probable frequency with which he should hear. They would arrive, it would seem, her communications, at the rate of several a week; he should be able to count, it might even prove, on more than one by each mail. If he had begun yesterday with a small grievance he had therefore an opportunity to begin to-day with its opposite. He read the letters successively and slowly, putting others back into his pocket but keeping these for a long time afterwards gathered in his lap. He held them there, lost in thought, as if to prolong the presence of what they gave him; or as if at the least to assure them their part in the constitution of some lucidity. His friend wrote admirably, and her tone was even more in her style than in her voice — he might almost, for the hour, have had to come this distance to get its full carrying quality; yet the plentitude of his consciousness of difference consorted perfectly with the deepened intensity of the connexion. It was the difference, the difference of being just where he was and *as* he was, that formed the escape — this difference was so much greater than he had dreamed it would be; and what he finally sat there turning over was the strange logic of his finding himself so free. He felt it in a manner his duty to think out his state, to approve the process, and when he came in fact to trace the steps and add up the items they sufficiently accounted for the sum. He had never expected — that was the truth of it — again to find himself young, and all the years and other things it had taken to make him so were exactly his present arithmetic. He had to make sure of them to put his scruple to rest.

It all sprang at bottom from the beauty of Mrs. Newsome's desire that he should be worried with nothing that was not of the essence of his task; by insisting that he should thoroughly intermit and break she had so provided for his freedom that she would, as it were, have only herself to thank. Strether could not at this point indeed have completed his thought by the image of what she might have to thank herself *for*: the image, at best, of his own likeness — poor Lambert Strether washed up on the sunny strand by the waves of a single day, poor Lambert Strether thankful for breathing-time and stiffening himself while he gasped. There he was, and with nothing in his aspect or his posture to scandalise: it was only true that if he had seen Mrs. Newsome coming he would instinctively have jumped up to walk away a little. He would have come round and back to her bravely, but he would have had first to pull himself together. She abounded in news of the situation at home, proved to him how perfectly she was arranging for his absence, told him who would take up this and who take up that exactly where he had left it, gave him in fact chapter and verse for the moral that nothing would suffer. It filled for him, this tone of hers, all the air; yet it struck him at the same time as the hum of vain things. This latter effect was what he tried to justify — and with the success that, grave though the appearance, he at last lighted on a form that was happy. He arrived at it by the inevitable recognition of his having been a fortnight before one of the weariest of men. If ever a man had come off tired Lambert Strether was that man; and had n't it been distinctly on the ground of his fatigue that his wonderful friend at home had so felt for him and so contrived? It seemed to him somehow at these instants that, could he only maintain with sufficient firmness his grasp of that truth, it might become in a manner his compass and his helm. What he wanted most was some idea that would simplify, and nothing would do this so much as the fact that he was done for and finished. If it had been in such a light that he had just detected in his cup the dregs of youth, that was a mere flaw of the surface of his scheme. He was so distinctly fagged-out that it must serve precisely as his convenience, and if he could but consistently be good for little enough he might do everything he wanted.

Everything he wanted was comprised moreover in a single boon — the common unattainable art of taking things as they came. He appeared to himself to have given his best years to an active appreciation of the way they did n't come; but 'perhaps — as they would seemingly here be things quite other — this long ache might at last drop to rest. He could easily see that from the moment he should accept the notion of his foredoomed collapse the last thing he would lack would be reasons and memories. Oh if he *should* do the sum no slate would hold the figures! The fact that he had failed, as he considered, in everything, in each relation and in half a dozen trades, as he liked luxuriously to put it, might have made, might still make, for an empty present; but it stood solidly for a crowded past. It had not been, so much achievement missed, a light yoke nor a short load. It was at present as if the backward picture had hung there, the long crooked course, grey in the shadow of his solitude. It had been a dreadful cheerful sociable solitude, a solitude of life or choice, of community; but though there had been people enough all round it there had been but three or four persons *in* it. Waymarsh was one of these, and the fact struck him just now as marking the record. Mrs. Newsome was another, and Miss Gostrey had of a sudden shown signs of becoming a third. Beyond, behind them was the pale figure of his

real youth, which held against its breast the two pre-
sences paler than itself — the young wife he had early
lost and the young son he had stupidly sacrificed. He
had again and again made out for himself that he
might have kept his little boy, his little dull boy who
had died at school of rapid diphtheria, if he had not
in those years so insanely given himself to merely
missing the mother. It was the soreness of his remorse that the child had in all likelihood not really
been dull — had been dull, as he had been banished
and neglected, mainly because the father had been
unwittingly selfish. This was doubtless but the secret
habit of sorrow, which had slowly given way to time;
yet there remained an ache sharp enough to make the
spirit, at the sight now and again of some fair young
man just growing up, wince with the thought of an
opportunity lost. Had ever a man, he had finally
fallen into the way of asking himself, lost so much
and even done so much for so little? There had been
particular reasons why all yesterday, beyond other
days, he should have had in one ear this cold enquiry.
His name on the green cover, where he had put it for
Mrs. Newsome, expressed him doubtless just enough
to make the world — the world as distinguished, both
for more and for less, from Woollett — ask who he
was. He had incurred the ridicule of having to have
his explanation explained. He was Lambert Strether
because he was on the cover, whereas it should have
been, for anything like glory, that he was on the cover
because he was Lambert Strether. He would have
done anything for Mrs. Newsome, have been still
more ridiculous — as he might, for that matter, have

occasion to be yet; which came to saying that this acceptance of fate was all he had to show at fifty-five.

He judged the quantity as small because it *was* small, and all the more egregiously since it could n't, as he saw the case, so much as thinkably have been larger. He had n't had the gift of making the most of what he tried, and if he had tried and tried again — no one but himself knew how often — it appeared to have been that he might demonstrate what else, in default of that, *could* be made. Old ghosts of experiments came back to him, old drudgeries and delusions, and disgusts, old recoveries with their relapses, old fevers with their chills, broken moments of good faith, others of still better doubt; adventures, for the most part, of the sort qualified as lessons. The special spring that had constantly played for him the day before was the recognition — frequent enough to surprise him — of the promises to himself that he had after his other visit never kept. The reminiscence to-day most quickened for him was that of the vow taken in the course of the pilgrimage that, newly-married, with the War just over, and helplessly young in spite of it, he had recklessly made with the creature who was so much younger still. It had been a bold dash, for which they had taken money set apart for necessities, but kept sacred at the moment in a hundred ways, and in none more so than by this private pledge of his own to treat the occasion as a relation formed with the higher culture and see that, as they said at Woollett, it should bear a good harvest. He had believed, sailing home again, that he had gained something great, and his theory — with an elaborate innocent plan of reading, digesting, coming back even, every few years — had then been to preserve, cherish and extend it. As such plans as these had come to nothing, however, in respect to acquisitions still more precious, it was doubtless little enough of a marvel that he should have lost account of that handful of seed. Buried for long years in dark corners at any rate these few germs had sprouted again under forty-eight hours of Paris. The process of yesterday had really been the process of feeling the general stirred life of connexions long since individually dropped. Strether had become acquainted even on this ground with short gusts of speculation — sudden flights of fancy in Louvre galleries, hungry gazes through clear plates behind which lemon-coloured volumes were as fresh as fruit on the tree.

There were instants at which he could ask whether, since there had been fundamentally so little question of his keeping anything, the fate after all decreed for him had n't been only to *be* kept. Kept for something, in that event, that he did n't pretend, did n't possibly dare as yet to divine; something that made him hover and wonder and laugh and sigh, made him advance and retreat, feeling half ashamed of his impulse to plunge and more than half afraid of his impulse to wait. He remembered for instance how he had gone back in the sixties with lemon-coloured volumes in general on the brain as well as with a dozen — selected for his wife too — in his trunk; and nothing had at the moment shown more confidence than this invocation of the finer taste. They were still somewhere at home, the dozen — stale and soiled and

never sent to the binder; but what had become of the
sharp initiation they represented ? They represented
now the mere sallow paint on the door of the temple
of taste that he had dreamed of raising up — a struct-
ure he had practically never carried further. Strether's present highest flights were perhaps those in
which this particular lapse figured to him as a symbol,
a symbol of his long grind and his want of odd moments, his want moreover of money, of opportunity,
of positive dignity. That the memory of the vow of his
youth should, in order to throb again, have had to wait
for this last, as he felt it, of all his accidents — that
was surely proof enough of how his conscience had
been encumbered. If any further proof were needed it
would have been to be found in the fact that, as he
perfectly now saw, he had ceased even to measure his
meagreness, a meagreness that sprawled, in this retro-
spect, vague and comprehensive, stretching back like
some unmapped Hinterland from a rough coast-set-
tlement. His conscience had been amusing itself for the
forty-eight hours by forbidding him the purchase of a
book; he held off from that, held off from everything;
from the moment he did n't yet call on Chad he would
n't for the world have taken any other step. On this
evidence, however, of the way they actually affected
him he glared at the lemon-coloured covers in confession of the subconsciousness that, all the same, in the
great desert of the years, he must have had of them.
The green covers at home comprised, by the law of
their purpose, no tribute to letters; it was of a mere
rich kernel of economics, politics, ethics that, glazed
and, as Mrs. Newsome maintained rather against *his*

view, pre-eminently pleasant to touch, they formed the specious shell. Without therefore any needed instinctive knowledge of what was coming out, in Paris, on the bright highway, he struck himself at present as having more than once flushed with a suspicion: he could n't otherwise at present be feeling so many fears confirmed. There were "movements" he was too late for: were n't they, with the fun of them, already spent? There were sequences he had missed and great gaps in the procession: he might have been watching it all recede in a golden cloud of dust. If the playhouse was n't closed his seat had at least fallen to somebody else. He had had an uneasy feeling the night before that if he was at the theatre at all — though he indeed justified the theatre, in the specific sense, and with a grotesqueness to which his imagination did all honour, as something he owed poor Waymarsh — he should have been there with, and as might have been said, *for* Chad.

This suggested the question of whether he could properly have taken him to such a play, and what effect — it was a point that suddenly rose — his peculiar responsibility might be held in general to have on his choice of entertainment. It had literally been present to him at the Gymnase — where one was held moreover comparatively safe — that having his young friend at his side would have been an odd feature of the work of redemption; and this quite in spite of the fact that the picture presented might well, confronted with Chad's own private stage, have seemed the pattern of propriety. He clearly had n't come out in the name of propriety but to visit unattended equivocal

performances; yet still less had he done so to under-
mine his authority by sharing them with the graceless
youth. Was he to renounce all amusement for the
sweet sake of that authority? and *would* such renouncement give him for Chad a moral glamour?
The little problem bristled the more by reason of poor
Strether's fairly open sense of the irony of things.
Were there then sides on which his predicament
threatened to look rather droll to him? Should he
have to pretend to believe — either to himself or the
wretched boy — that there was anything that could
make the latter worse? Was n't some such pretence
on the other hand involved in the assumption of possible processes that would make him better? His
greatest uneasiness seemed to peep at him out of the
imminent impression that almost any acceptance of
Paris might give one's authority away. It hung before
him this morning, the vast bright Babylon, like some
huge iridescent object, a jewel brilliant and hard,
in which parts were not to be discriminated nor differences comfortably marked. It twinkled and trembled
and melted together, and what seemed all surface one
moment seemed all depth the next. It was a place of
which, unmistakeably, Chad was fond; wherefore
if he, Strether, should like it too much, what on earth,
with such a bond, would become of either of them?
It all depended of course — which was a gleam of
light — on how the "too much" was measured;
though indeed our friend fairly felt, while he prolonged
the meditation I describe, that for himself even already a certain measure had been reached. It will
have been sufficiently seen that he was not a man to

neglect any good chance for reflexion. Was it at all possible for instance to like Paris enough without liking it too much? He luckily however had n't promised Mrs. Newsome not to like it at all. He was ready to recognise at this stage that such an engagement *would* have tied his hands. The Luxembourg Gardens were incontestably just so adorable at this hour by reason — in addition to their intrinsic charm — of his not having taken it. The only engagement he had taken, when he looked the thing in the face, was to do what he reasonably could.

It upset him a little none the less and after a while to find himself at last remembering on what current of association he had been floated so far. Old imaginations of the Latin Quarter had played their part for him, and he had duly recalled its having been with this scene of rather ominous legend that, like so many young men in fiction as well as in fact, Chad had begun. He was now quite out of it, with his "home," as Strether figured the place, in the Boulevard Malesherbes; which was perhaps why, repairing, not to fail of justice either, to the elder neighbourhood, our friend had felt he could allow for the element of the usual, the immemorial, without courting perturbation. He was not at least in danger of seeing the youth and the particular Person flaunt by together; and yet he was in the very air of which — just to feel what the early natural note must have been — he wished most to take counsel. It became at once vivid to him that he had originally had, for a few days, an almost envious vision of the boy's romantic privilege. Melancholy Mürger, with Francine and Musette and Rodolphe,

at home, in the company of the tattered, one — if he
not in his single self two or three — of the unbound,
the paper-covered dozen on the shelf; and when Chad
had written, five years ago, after a sojourn then already prolonged to six months, that he had decided to
go in for economy and the real thing, Strether's fancy
had quite fondly accompanied him in this migration,
which was to convey him, as they somewhat confus-
edly learned at Woollett, across the bridges and up the
Montagne Sainte-Geneviève. This was the region —
Chad had been quite distinct about it — in which the
best French, and many other things, were to be learned
at least cost, and in which all sorts of clever fellows,
compatriots there for a purpose, formed an awfully
pleasant set. The clever fellows, the friendly country-
men were mainly young painters, sculptors, architects,
medical students; but they were, Chad sagely opined,
a much more profitable lot to be with — even on the
footing of not being quite one of them — than the
"terrible toughs" (Strether remembered the edifying
discrimination) of the American bars and banks
roundabout the Opéra. Chad had thrown out, in the
communications following this one — for at that time
he did once in a while communicate — that several
members of a band of earnest workers under one of
the great artists had taken him right in, making him
dine every night, almost for nothing, at their place, and
even pressing him not to neglect the hypothesis of there
being as much "in him" as in any of them. There
had been literally a moment at which it appeared
there might be something in him; there had been
at any rate a moment at which he had written that

he did n't know but what a month or two more might see him enrolled in some atelier. The season had been one at which Mrs. Newsome was moved to gratitude for small mercies; it had broken on them all as a blessing that their absentee *had* perhaps a conscience — that he was sated in fine with idleness, was ambitious of variety. The exhibition was doubtless as yet not brilliant, but Strether himself, even by that time much enlisted and immersed, had determined, on the part of the two ladies, a temperate approval and in fact, as he now recollected, a certain austere enthusiasm.

But the very next thing that happened had been a dark drop of the curtain. The son and brother had not browsed long on the Montagne Sainte-Geneviève — his effective little use of the name of which, like his allusion to the best French, appeared to have been but one of the notes of his rough cunning. The light refreshment of these vain appearances had not accordingly carried any of them very far. On the other hand it had gained Chad time; it had given him a chance, unchecked, to strike his roots, had paved the way for initiations more direct and more deep. It was Strether's belief that he had been comparatively innocent before this first migration, and even that the first effects of the migration would not have been, without some particular bad accident, to have been deplored. There had been three months — he had sufficiently figured it out — in which Chad had wanted to try. He *had* tried, though not very hard — he had had his little hour of good faith. The weakness of this principle in him was that almost any accident attestedly bad enough was stronger. Such had at any rate markedly been the case for the precipitation of a special series of impressions. They had proved, successively, these impressions — all of Musette and Francine, but Musette and Francine vulgarised by the larger evolution of the type — irresistibly sharp: he had "taken up," by what was at the time to be shrinkingly gathered, as it was scantly mentioned, with one ferociously "interested" little person after another. Strether had read somewhere of a Latin motto, a description of the hours, observed on a clock by a traveller in Spain; and he had been led to apply it in thought to Chad's number one, number two, number three. *Omnes vulnerant, ultima necat* — they had all morally wounded, the last had morally killed. The last had been longest in possession — in possession, that is, of whatever was left of the poor boy's finer mortality. And it had n't been she, it had been one of her early predecessors, who had determined the second migration, the expensive return and relapse, the exchange again, as was fairly to be presumed, of the vaunted best French for some special variety of the worst.

He pulled himself then at last together for his own progress back; not with the feeling that he had taken his walk in vain. He prolonged it a little, in the immediate neighbourhood, after he had quitted his chair; and the upshot of the whole morning for him was that his campaign had begun. He had wanted to put himself in relation, and he would be hanged if he were *not* in relation. He was that at no moment so much as while, under the old arches of the Odéon, he lingered before the charming open-air array of literature classic and casual. He found the effect of tone and tint, in the long charged tables and shelves, delicate and appetising; the impression — substituting one kind of low-priced *consommation* for another — might have been that of one of the pleasant cafés that over-lapped, under an awning, to the pavement; but he edged along, grazing the tables, with his hands firmly behind him. He was n't there to dip, to consume — he was there to reconstruct. He was n't there for his own profit — not, that is, the direct; he was there on some chance of feeling the brush of the wing of the stray spirit of youth. He felt it in fact, he had it be-side him; the old arcade indeed, as his inner sense listened, gave out the faint sound, as from far off, of the wild waving of wings. They were folded now over the breasts of buried generations; but a flutter or two lived again in the turned page of shock-headed slouch-hatted loiterers whose young intensity of type, in the direction of pale acuteness, deepened his vi-sion, and even his appreciation, of racial differences, and whose manipulation of the uncut volume was too often, however, but a listening at closed doors. He reconstructed a possible groping Chad of three or four years before, a Chad who had, after all, simply — for that was the only way to see it — been too vulgar for his privilege. Surely it *was* a privilege to have been young and happy just there. Well, the best thing Strether knew of him was that he had had such a dream.

But his own actual business half an hour later was with a third floor on the Boulevard Malesherbes — so much as that was definite; and the fact of the enjoy-

ment by the third-floor windows of a continuous balcony, to which he was helped by this knowledge, had
perhaps something to do with his lingering for five
minutes on the opposite side of the street. There were
points as to which he had quite made up his mind,
and one of these bore precisely on the wisdom of the
abruptness to which events had finally committed
him, a policy that he was pleased to find not at all
shaken as he now looked at his watch and wondered.
He *had* announced himself — six months before; had
written out at least that Chad was n't to be surprised
should he see him some day turn up. Chad had thereupon, in a few words of rather carefully colourless
answer, offered him a general welcome; and Strether,
ruefully reflecting that he might have understood the
warning as a hint to hospitality, a bid for an invitation, had fallen back upon silence as the corrective
most to his own taste. He had asked Mrs. Newsome
moreover not to announce him again; he had so distinct an opinion on his attacking his job, should he
attack it at all, in his own way. Not the least of this
lady's high merits for him was that he could absolutely
rest on her word. She was the only woman he had
known, even at Woollett, as to whom his conviction
was positive that to lie was beyond her art. Sarah
Pocock, for instance, her own daughter, though with
social ideals, as they said, in some respects different
— Sarah who *was*, in her way, æsthetic, had never
refused to human commerce that mitigation of rigour; there were occasions when he had distinctly
seen her apply it. Since, accordingly, at all events, he
had had it from Mrs. Newsome that she had, at what-

ever cost to her more strenuous view, conformed, in the matter of preparing Chad, wholly to his restrictions, he now looked up at the fine continuous balcony with a safe sense that if the case had been bungled the mistake was at least his property. Was there perhaps just a suspicion of that in his present pause on the edge of the Boulevard and well in the pleasant light?

Many things came over him here, and one of them was that he should doubtless presently know whether he had been shallow or sharp. Another was that the balcony in question did n't somehow show as a convenience easy to surrender. Poor Strether had at this very moment to recognise the truth that wherever one paused in Paris the imagination reacted before one could stop it. This perpetual reaction put a price, if one would, on pauses; but it piled up consequences till there was scarce room to pick one's steps among them. What call had he, at such a juncture, for example, to like Chad's very house? High broad clear — he was expert enough to make out in a moment that it was admirably built — it fairly embarrassed our friend by the quality that, as he would have said, it "sprang" on him. He had struck off the fancy that it might, as a preliminary, be of service to him to be seen, by a happy accident, from the third-story windows, which took all the March sun, but of what service was it to find himself making out after a moment that the quality "sprung," the quality produced by measure and balance, the fine relation of part to part and space to space, was probably — aided by the presence of ornament as positive as it was discreet, and by the complexion of the stone, a cold fair grey, warmed and polished a little by life — neither more nor less than a case of distinction, such a case as he could only feel unexpectedly as a sort of delivered challenge ? Meanwhile, however, the chance he had allowed for — the chance of being seen in time from the balcony — had become a fact. Two or three of the windows stood open to the violet air; and, before Strether had cut the knot by crossing, a young man had come out and looked about him, had lighted a cigarette and tossed the match over, and then, resting on the rail, had given himself up to watching the life below while he smoked. His arrival contributed, in its order, to keeping Strether in position; the result of which in turn was that Strether soon felt himself noticed. The young man began to look at him as in acknowledgement of his being himself in observation.

This was interesting so far as it went, but the interest was affected by the young man's not being Chad. Strether wondered at first if he were perhaps Chad altered, and then saw that this was asking too much of alteration. The young man was light bright and alert — with an air too pleasant to have been arrived at by patching. Strether had conceived Chad as patched, but not beyond recognition. He was in presence, he felt, of amendments enough as they stood; it was a sufficient amendment that the gentleman up there should be Chad's friend. He was young too then, the gentleman up there — he was very young; young enough apparently to be amused at an elderly watcher, to be curious even to see what the elderly watcher would do on finding himself watched. There was youth in that, there was youth in the surrender to the balcony, there was youth for Strether at this moment in everything but his own business; and Chad's thus pronounced association with youth had given the next instant an extraordinary quick lift to the issue. The balcony, the distinguished front, testified suddenly, for Strether's fancy, to something that was up and up; they placed the whole case materially, and as by an admirable image, on a level that he found himself at the end of another moment rejoicing to think he might reach. The young man looked at him still, he looked at the young man; and the issue, by a rapid process, was that this knowledge of a perched privacy appeared to him the last of luxuries. To him too the perched privacy was open, and he saw it now but in one light — that of the only domicile, the only fireside, in the great ironic city, on which he had the shadow of a claim. Miss Gostrey had a fireside; she had told him of it, and it was something that doubtless awaited him; but Miss Gostrey had n't yet arrived — she might n't arrive for days; and the sole attenuation of his excluded state was his vision of the small, the admittedly secondary hotel in the bye-street from the Rue de la Paix, in which her solicitude for his purse had placed him, which affected him somehow as all indoor chill, glass-roofed court and slippery staircase, and which, by the same token, expressed the presence of Waymarsh even at times when Waymarsh might have been certain to be round at the bank. It came to pass before he moved that Waymarsh, and Waymarsh alone, Waymarsh not only undiluted but positively strengthened, struck him as the present alternative to the young man in the balcony. When he did move it was fairly to escape that alternative. Taking his way over the street at last and passing through the *porte-cochère* of the house was like consciously leaving Waymarsh out. However, he would tell him all about it.

BOOK THIRD

I

STRETHER told Waymarsh all about it that very evening, on their dining together at the hotel; which need n't have happened, he was all the while aware, had n't he chosen to sacrifice to this occasion a rarer opportunity. The mention to his companion of the sacrifice was moreover exactly what introduced his recital — or, as he would have called it with more confidence in his interlocutor, his confession. His confession was that he had been captured and that one of the features of the affair had just failed to be his engaging himself on the spot to dinner. As by such a freedom Waymarsh would have lost him he had obeyed his scruple; and he had likewise obeyed another scruple — which bore on the question of his himself bringing a guest.

Waymarsh looked gravely ardent, over the finished soup, at this array of scruples; Strether had n't yet got quite used to being so unprepared for the consequences of the impression he produced. It was comparatively easy to explain, however, that he had n't felt sure his guest would please. The person was a young man whose acquaintance he had made but that afternoon in the course of rather a hindered enquiry for another person — an enquiry his new friend had just prevented in fact from being vain. "Oh," said Strether, "I 've all sorts of things to tell you!" — and he put it in a way that was a virtual hint to Waymarsh to help him to enjoy the telling. He waited for his fish, he drank of his wine, he wiped his long moustache, he leaned back in his chair, he took in the two English ladies who had just creaked past them and whom he would even have articulately greeted if they had n't rather chilled the impulse; so that all he could do was — by way of doing something — to say "Merci, François!" out quite loud when his fish was brought. Everything was there that he wanted, everything that could make the moment an occasion, that would do beautifully — everything but what Waymarsh might give. The little waxed salle-à-manger was sallow and sociable; François, dancing over it, all smiles, was a man and a brother; the high-shouldered patronne, with her high-held, much-rubbed hands, seemed always assenting exuberantly to something unsaid; the Paris evening in short was, for Strether, in the very taste of the soup, in the goodness, as he was innocently pleased to think it, of the wine, in the pleasant coarse texture of the napkin and the crunch of the thick-crusted bread. These all were things congruous with his confession, and his confession was that he *had* — it would come out properly just there if Waymarsh would only take it properly — agreed to breakfast out, at twelve literally, the next day. He did n't quite know where; the delicacy of the case came straight up in the remembrance of his new friend's "We'll see; I'll take you somewhere!" — for it had required little more than that, after all, to let him right in. He was affected after a minute, face to face with his actual comrade, by the impulse to overcolour. There had already been things in respect to which he knew himself tempted by this perversity. If Waymarsh thought them bad he should at least have his reason for his discomfort; so Strether showed them as worse. Still, he was now, in his way, sincerely perplexed.

Chad had been absent from the Boulevard Malesherbes — was absent from Paris altogether; he had learned that from the concierge, but had nevertheless gone up, and gone up — there were no two ways about it — from an uncontrollable, a really, if one would, depraved curiosity. The concierge had mentioned to him that a friend of the tenant of the troisième was for the time in possession; and this had been Strether's pretext for a further enquiry, an experiment carried on, under Chad's roof, without his knowledge. "I found his friend in fact there keeping the place warm, as he called it, for him; Chad himself being, as appears, in the south. He went a month ago to Cannes and though his return begins to be looked for it can't be for some days. I might, you see, perfectly have waited a week; might have beaten a retreat as soon as I got this essential knowledge. But I beat no retreat; I did the opposite; I stayed, I dawdled, I trifled; above all I looked round. I saw, in fine; and — I don't know what to call it — I sniffed. It's a detail, but it's as if there were something — something very good — *to* sniff."

Waymarsh's face had shown his friend an attention apparently so remote that the latter was slightly surprised to find it at this point abreast with him. "Do you mean a smell? What of?"

"A charming scent. But I don't know."

Waymarsh gave an inferential grunt. "Does he live there with a woman?"

"I don't know."

Waymarsh waited an instant for more, then resumed. "Has he taken her off with him?"

"And will he bring her back?" — Strether fell into the enquiry. But he wound it up as before. "I don't know."

The way he wound it up, accompanied as this was with another drop back, another degustation of the Léoville, another wipe of his moustache and another good word for François, seemed to produce in his companion a slight irritation. "Then what the devil *do* you know?"

"Well," said Strether almost gaily, "I guess I don't know anything!" His gaiety might have been a tribute to the fact that the state he had been reduced to did for him again what had been done by his talk of the matter with Miss Gostrey at the London theatre. It was somehow enlarging; and the air of that amplitude was now doubtless more or less — and all for Waymarsh to feel — in his further response. "That's what I found out from the young man."

"But I thought you said you found out nothing."

"Nothing but that — that I don't know anything."

"And what good does that do you?"

"It's just," said Strether, "what I've come to you to help me to discover. I mean anything about anything over here. I *felt* that, up there. It regularly rose before me in its might. The young man moreover — Chad's friend — as good as told me so."

"As good as told you you know nothing about anything?" Waymarsh appeared to look at some one who might have as good as told *him*. "How old is he?"

"Well, I guess not thirty."

"Yet you had to take that from him?"

"Oh I took a good deal more — since, as I tell you, I took an invitation to déjeuner."

"And are you *going* to that unholy meal?"

"If you'll come with me. He wants you too, you know. I told him about you. He gave me his card," Strether pursued, "and his name's rather funny. It's John Little Bilham, and he says his two surnames are, on account of his being small, inevitably used together."

"Well," Waymarsh asked with due detachment from these details, "what's he doing up there?"

"His account of himself is that he's 'only a little artist-man.' That seemed to me perfectly to describe him. But he's yet in the phase of study; this, you know, is the great art-school — to pass a certain number of years in which he came over. And he's a great friend of Chad's, and occupying Chad's rooms just now because they're so pleasant. *He's* very pleasant and curious too," Strether added — "though he's not from Boston."

Waymarsh looked already rather sick of him. "Where *is* he from?"

Strether thought. "I don't know that, either. But he's 'notoriously,' as he put it himself, not from Boston."

"Well," Waymarsh moralised from dry depths, "every one can't notoriously *be* from Boston. Why," he continued, "is he curious?"

"Perhaps just for *that* — for one thing! But really," Strether added, "for everything. When you meet him you'll see."

"Oh I don't want to meet him," Waymarsh impatiently growled. "Why don't he go home?"

Strether hesitated. "Well, because he likes it over here."

This appeared in particular more than Waymarsh could bear. "He ought then to be ashamed of himself, and, as you admit that you think so too, why drag him in?"

Strether's reply again took time. "Perhaps I do think so myself — though I don't quite yet admit it. I'm not a bit sure — it's again one of the things I want to find out. I liked him, and *can* you like people —? But no matter." He pulled himself up. "There's no doubt I want you to come down on me and squash me."

Waymarsh helped himself to the next course, which, however, proving not the dish he had just noted as supplied to the English ladies, had the effect of causing his imagination temporarily to wander. But it presently broke out at a softer spot. "Have they got a handsome place up there?"

"Oh a charming place; full of beautiful and valuable things. I never saw such a place" — and Strether's thought went back to it. "For a little artist-man —!" He could in fact scarce express it.

But his companion, who appeared now to have a view, insisted. "Well?"

"Well, life can hold nothing better. Besides, they're things of which he's in charge."

BOOK THIRD

"So that he does doorkeeper for your precious pair ?
Can life," Waymarsh enquired, "hold nothing better
than *that?*" Then as Strether, silent, seemed even
yet to wonder, "Does n't he know what *she* is ?" he
went on.

"*I* don't know. I did n't ask him. I could n't. It
was impossible. You would n't either. Besides I
did n't want to. No more would you." Strether in
short explained it at a stroke. "You can't make out
over here what people do know."

"Then what did you come over for ?"

"Well, I suppose exactly to see for myself — without their aid."

"Then what do you want mine for ?"

"Oh," Strether laughed, "you 're not one of *them!*
I do know what *you* know."

As, however, this last assertion caused Waymarsh
again to look at him hard — such being the latter's
doubt of its implications — he felt his justification
lame. Which was still more the case when Waymarsh
presently said : "Look here, Strether. Quit this."

Our friend smiled with a doubt of his own. "Do
you mean my tone ?"

"No — damn your tone. I mean your nosing
round. Quit the whole job. Let them stew in their
juice. You 're being used for a thing you ain't fit for.
People don't take a fine-tooth comb to groom a horse."

"Am I a fine-tooth comb ?" Strether laughed. "It 's
something I never called myself !"

"It 's what you are, all the same. You ain't so
young as you were, but you 've kept your teeth."

He acknowledged his friend's humour. "Take care

I don't get them into *you!* You'd like them, my friends at home, Waymarsh," he declared; "you'd really particularly like them. And I know " — it was slightly irrelevant, but he gave it sudden and singular force — "I know they'd like you!"

"Oh don't work them off on *me!*" Waymarsh groaned.

Yet Strether still lingered with his hands in his pockets. "It's really quite as indispensable as I say that Chad should be got back."

"Indispensable to whom? To you?"

"Yes," Strether presently said.

"Because if you get him you also get Mrs. Newsome?"

Strether faced it. "Yes."

"And if you don't get him you don't get her?"

It might be merciless, but he continued not to flinch. "I think it might have some effect on our personal understanding. Chad's of real importance — or can easily become so if he will — to the business."

"And the business is of real importance to his mother's husband?"

"Well, I naturally want what my future wife wants. And the thing will be much better if we have our own man in it."

"If you have your own man in it, in other words," Waymarsh said, "you'll marry — you personally — more money. She's already rich, as I understand you, but she'll be richer still if the business can be made to boom on certain lines that you've laid down."

"*I* haven't laid them down," Strether promptly returned. "Mr. Newsome — who knew extraordinarily well what he was about — laid them down ten years ago."

Oh well, Waymarsh seemed to indicate with a shake of his mane, *that* did n't matter! "You're fierce for the boom anyway."

His friend weighed a moment in silence the justice of the charge. "I can scarcely be called fierce, I think, when I so freely take my chance of the possibility, the danger, of being influenced in a sense counter to Mrs. Newsome's own feelings."

Waymarsh gave this proposition a long hard look. "I see. You're afraid yourself of being squared. But you're a humbug," he added, "all the same."

"Oh!" Strether quickly protested.

"Yes, you ask me for protection — which makes you very interesting; and then you won't take it. You say you want to be squashed —"

"Ah but not so easily! Don't you see," Strether demanded, "where my interest, as already shown you, lies? It lies in my not being squared. If I'm squared where's my marriage? If I miss my errand I miss that; and if I miss that I miss everything — I'm nowhere."

Waymarsh — but all relentlessly — took this in. "What do I care where you are if you're spoiled?"

Their eyes met on it an instant. "Thank you awfully," Strether at last said. "But don't you think *her* judgement of that —?"

"Ought to content me? No."

It kept them again face to face, and the end of this was that Strether again laughed. "You do her injustice. You really *must* know her. Good-night."

He breakfasted with Mr. Bilham on the morrow, and, as inconsequently befell, with Waymarsh massively of the party. The latter announced, at the eleventh hour and much to his friend's surprise, that, damn it, he would as soon join him as do anything else; on which they proceeded together, strolling in a state of detachment practically luxurious for them to the Boulevard Malesherbes, a couple engaged that day with the sharp spell of Paris as confessedly, it might have been seen, as any couple among the daily thousands so compromised. They walked, wandered, wondered and, a little, lost themselves; Strether had n't had for years so rich a consciousness of time — a bag of gold into which he constantly dipped for a handful. It was present to him that when the little business with Mr. Bilham should be over he would still have shining hours to use absolutely as he liked. There was no great pulse of haste yet in this process of saving Chad; nor was that effect a bit more marked as he sat, half an hour later, with his legs under Chad's mahogany, with Mr. Bilham on one side, with a friend of Mr. Bilham's on the other, with Waymarsh stupendously opposite, and with the great hum of Paris coming up in softness, vagueness — for Strether himself indeed already positive sweetness — through the sunny windows toward which, the day before, his curiosity had raised its wings from below. The feeling strongest with him at that moment had borne fruit almost faster than he could taste it, and Strether literally felt at the present hour that there was a precipitation in his fate. He had known nothing and nobody as he stood in the street; but had n't his view

now taken a bound in the direction of every one and
of every thing?

"What's he up to, what's he up to?" — something
like that was at the back of his head all the while in
respect to little Bilham; but meanwhile, till he should
make out, every one and every thing were as good as
represented for him by the combination of his host and
the lady on his left. The lady on his left, the lady thus
promptly and ingeniously invited to "meet" Mr.
Strether and Mr. Waymarsh — it was the way she
herself expressed her case — was a very marked person, a person who had much to do with our friend's
asking himself if the occasion were n't in its essence
the most baited, the most gilded of traps. Baited it
could properly be called when the repast was of so
wise a savour, and gilded surrounding objects seemed
inevitably to need to be when Miss Barrace — which
was the lady's name — looked at them with convex
Parisian eyes and through a glass with a remarkably
long tortoise-shell handle. Why Miss Barrace, mature meagre erect and eminently gay, highly adorned,
perfectly familiar, freely contradictious and reminding
him of some last-century portrait of a clever head
without powder — why Miss Barrace should have
been in particular the note of a "trap" Strether
could n't on the spot have explained; he blinked in the
light of a conviction that he should know later on, and
know well — as it came over him, for that matter,
with force, that he should need to. He wondered what
he was to think exactly of either of his new friends;
since the young man, Chad's intimate and deputy,
had, in thus constituting the scene, practised so much

more subtly than he had been prepared for, and since in especial Miss Barrace, surrounded clearly by every consideration, had n't scrupled to figure as a familiar object. It was interesting to him to feel that he was in the presence of new measures, other standards, a different scale of relations, and that evidently here were a happy pair who did n't think of things at all as he and Waymarsh thought. Nothing was less to have been calculated in the business than that it should now be for him as if he and Waymarsh were comparatively quite at one.

The latter was magnificent — this at least was an assurance privately given him by Miss Barrace. "Oh your friend's a type, the grand old American — what shall one call it? The Hebrew prophet, Ezekiel, Jeremiah, who used when I was a little girl in the Rue Montaigne to come to see my father and who was usually the American Minister to the Tuileries or some other court. I have n't seen one these ever so many years; the sight of it warms my poor old chilled heart; this specimen is wonderful; in the right quarter, you know, he'll have a *succès fou*." Strether had n't failed to ask what the right quarter might be, much as he required his presence of mind to meet such a change in their scheme. "Oh the artist-quarter and that kind of thing; *here* already, for instance, as you see." He had been on the point of echoing "'Here'? — is *this* the artist-quarter?" but she had already disposed of the question with a wave of all her tortoise-shell and an easy "Bring him to *me!*" He knew on the spot how little he should be able to bring him, for the very air was by this time, to his sense, thick and hot with

poor Waymarsh's judgement of it. He was in the trap
still more than his companion and, unlike his companion, not making the best of it; which was precisely
what doubtless gave him his admirable sombre glow.
Little did Miss Barrace know that what was behind
it was his grave estimate of her own laxity. The general assumption with which our two friends had arrived had been that of finding Mr. Bilham ready to
conduct them to one or other of those resorts of the
earnest, the æsthetic fraternity which were shown
among the sights of Paris. In this character it would
have justified them in a proper insistence on discharg-
ing their score. Waymarsh's only proviso at the last
had been that nobody should pay for him; but he
found himself, as the occasion developed, paid for on
a scale as to which Strether privately made out that
he already nursed retribution. Strether was conscious
across the table of what worked in him, conscious
when they passed back to the small salon to which,
the previous evening, he himself had made so rich a
reference; conscious most of all as they stepped out
to the balcony in which one would have had to be an
ogre not to recognise the perfect place for easy after-
tastes. These things were enhanced for Miss Barrace
by a succession of excellent cigarettes — acknowledged, acclaimed, as a part of the wonderful supply
left behind him by Chad — in an almost equal absorption of which Strether found himself blindly,
almost wildly pushing forward. He might perish by
the sword as well as by famine, and he knew that his
having abetted the lady by an excess that was rare
with him would count for little in the sum — as Way-

marsh might so easily add it up — of her licence. Waymarsh had smoked of old, smoked hugely; but Waymarsh did nothing now, and that gave him his advantage over people who took things up lightly just when others had laid them heavily down. Strether had never smoked, and he felt as if he flaunted at his friend that this had been only because of a reason. The reason, it now began to appear even to himself, was that he had never had a lady to smoke with.

It was this lady's being there at all, however, that was the strange free thing; perhaps, since she *was* there, her smoking was the least of her freedoms. If Strether had been sure at each juncture of what — with Bilham in especial — she talked about, he might have traced others and winced at them and felt Waymarsh wince; but he was in fact so often at sea that his sense of the range of reference was merely general and that he on several different occasions guessed and interpreted only to doubt. He wondered what they meant, but there were things he scarce thought they could be supposed to mean, and "Oh no — not *that!*" was at the end of most of his ventures. This was the very beginning with him of a condition as to which, later on, it will be seen, he found cause to pull himself up; and he was to remember the moment duly as the first step in a process. The central fact of the place was neither more nor less, when analysed — and a pressure superficial sufficed — than the fundamental impropriety of Chad's situation, round about which they thus seemed cynically clustered. Accordingly, since they took it for granted, they took for granted all that was in connexion with it taken for granted at Woollett —

matters as to which, verily, he had been reduced with Mrs. Newsome to the last intensity of silence. That was the consequence of their being too bad to be talked about, and was the accompaniment, by the same token, of a deep conception of their badness. It befell therefore that when poor Strether put it to himself that their badness was ultimately, or perhaps even insolently, what such a scene as the one before him was, so to speak, built upon, he could scarce shirk the dilemma of reading a roundabout echo of them into almost anything that came up. This, he was well aware, was a dreadful necessity; but such was the stern logic, he could only gather, of a relation to the irregular life.

It was the way the irregular life sat upon Bilham and Miss Barrace that was the insidious, the delicate marvel. He was eager to concede that their relation to it was all indirect, for anything else in him would have shown the grossness of bad manners; but the indirectness was none the less consonant — *that* was striking — with a grateful enjoyment of everything that was Chad's. They spoke of him repeatedly, invoking his good name and good nature, and the worst confusion of mind for Strether was that all their mention of him was of a kind to do him honour. They commended his munificence and approved his taste, and in doing so sat down, as it seemed to Strether, in the very soil out of which these things flowered. Our friend's final predicament was that he himself was sitting down, for the time, *with* them, and there was a supreme moment at which, compared with his collapse, Waymarsh's erectness affected him as really high. One thing was certain — he saw he must make up his mind. He must approach Chad, must wait for him, deal with him, master him, but he must n't dispossess himself of the faculty of seeing things as they were. He must bring him to *him* — not go himself, as it were, so much of the way. He must at any rate be clearer as to what — should he continue to do that for convenience — he was still condoning. It was on the detail of this quantity — and what could the fact be but mystifying?—that Bilham and Miss Barrace threw so little light. So there they were.

II

WHEN Miss Gostrey arrived, at the end of a week, she
made him a sign; he went immediately to see her,
and it was n't till then that he could again close his
grasp on the idea of a corrective. This idea however
was luckily all before him again from the moment he
crossed the threshold of the little entresol of the Quar-
tier Marbœuf into which she had gathered, as she said,
picking them up in a thousand flights and funny little
passionate pounces, the makings of a final nest. He
recognised in an instant that there really, there only,
he should find the boon with the vision of which he
had first mounted Chad's stairs. He might have been
a little scared at the picture of how much more, in this
place, he should know himself "in" had n't his friend
been on the spot to measure the amount to his appetite. Her compact and crowded little chambers,
almost dusky, as they at first struck him, with accumulations, represented a supreme general adjustment
to opportunities and conditions. Wherever he looked
he saw an old ivory or an old brocade, and he scarce
knew where to sit for fear of a misappliance. The
life of the occupant struck him of a sudden as more
charged with possession even than Chad's or than
Miss Barrace's; wide as his glimpse had lately become of the empire of "things," what was before him
still enlarged it; the lust of the eyes and the pride of
life had indeed thus their temple. It was the inner-

most nook of the shrine — as brown as a pirate's cave. In the brownness were glints of gold; patches of purple were in the gloom; objects all that caught, through the muslin, with their high rarity, the light of the low windows. Nothing was clear about them but that they were precious, and they brushed his ignorance with their contempt as a flower, in a liberty taken with him, might have been whisked under his nose. But after a full look at his hostess he knew none the less what most concerned him. The circle in which they stood together was warm with life, and every question between them would live there as nowhere else. A question came up as soon as they had spoken, for his answer, with a laugh, was quickly: "Well, they've got hold of me!" Much of their talk on this first occasion was his development of that truth. He was extraordinarily glad to see her, expressing to her frankly what she most showed him, that one might live for years without a blessing unsuspected, but that to know it at last for no more than three days was to need it or miss it for ever. She was the blessing that had now become his need, and what could prove it better than that without her he had lost himself?

"What do you mean?" she asked with an absence of alarm that, correcting him as if he had mistaken the "period" of one of her pieces, gave him afresh a sense of her easy movement through the maze he had but begun to tread. "What in the name of all the Pococks have you managed to do?"

"Why exactly the wrong thing. I've made a frantic friend of little Bilham."

BOOK THIRD

"Ah that sort of thing was of the essence of your case and to have been allowed for from the first." And it was only after this that, quite as a minor matter, she asked who in the world little Bilham might be. When she learned that he was a friend of Chad's and living for the time in Chad's rooms in Chad's absence, quite as if acting in Chad's spirit and serving Chad's cause, she showed, however, more interest. "Should you mind my seeing him? Only once, you know," she added.

"Oh the oftener the better: he's amusing — he's original."

"He does n't shock you?" Miss Gostrey threw out.

"Never in the world! We escape that with a perfection —! I feel it to be largely, no doubt, because I don't half-understand him; but our *modus vivendi* is n't spoiled even by that. You must dine with me to meet him," Strether went on. "Then you'll see."

"Are you giving dinners?"

"Yes — there I am. That's what I mean."

All her kindness wondered. "That you're spending too much money?"

"Dear no — they seem to cost so little. But that I do it to *them*. I ought to hold off."

She thought again — she laughed. "The money you must be spending to think it cheap! But I must be out of it — to the naked eye."

He looked for a moment as if she were really failing him. "Then you won't meet them?" It was almost as if she had developed an unexpected personal prudence.

She hesitated. "Who are they — first?"

"Why little Bilham to begin with." He kept back for the moment Miss Barrace. "And Chad — when he comes — you must absolutely see."

"When then does he come?"

"When Bilham has had time to write him, and hear from him, about me. Bilham, however," he pursued, "will report favourably — favourably for Chad. That will make him not afraid to come. I want you the more therefore, you see, for my bluff."

"Oh you'll do yourself for your bluff." She was perfectly easy. "At the rate you've gone I'm quiet."

"Ah but I haven't," said Strether, "made one protest."

She turned it over. "Haven't you been seeing what there's to protest about?"

He let her, with this, however ruefully, have the whole truth. "I haven't yet found a single thing."

"Isn't there any one *with* him then?"

"Of the sort I came out about?" Strether took a moment. "How do I know? And what do I care?"

"Oh oh!" — and her laughter spread. He was struck in fact by the effect on her of his joke. He saw now how he meant it as a joke. *She* saw, however, still other things, though in an instant she had hidden them. "You've got at no facts at all?"

He tried to muster them. "Well, he has a lovely home."

"Ah that, in Paris," she quickly returned, "proves nothing. That is rather it *dis*proves nothing. They may very well, you see, the people your mission is concerned with, have done it *for* him."

BOOK THIRD

"Exactly. And it was on the scene of their doings then that Waymarsh and I sat guzzling."

"Oh if you forbore to guzzle here on scenes of doings," she replied, "you might easily die of starvation." With which she smiled at him. "You've worse before you."

"Ah I've *everything* before me. But on our hypothesis, you know, they must be wonderful."

"They *are!*" said Miss Gostrey. "You're not therefore, you see," she added, "wholly without facts. They've *been*, in effect, wonderful."

To have got at something comparatively definite appeared at last a little to help — a wave by which moreover, the next moment, recollection was washed. "My young man does admit furthermore that they're our friend's great interest."

"Is that the expression he uses?"

Strether more exactly recalled. "No — not quite."

"Something more vivid? Less?"

He had bent, with neared glasses, over a group of articles on a small stand; and at this he came up. "It was a mere allusion, but, on the lookout as I was, it struck me. 'Awful, you know, as Chad is' — those were Bilham's words."

"'Awful, you know' —? Oh!" — and Miss Gostrey turned them over. She seemed, however, satisfied. "Well, what more do you want?"

He glanced once more at a bibelot or two, and everything sent him back. "But it *is* all the same as if they wished to let me have it between the eyes."

She wondered. "Quoi donc?"

"Why what I speak of. The amenity. They

can stun you with that as well as with anything else."

"Oh," she answered, "you'll come round! I must see them each," she went on, "for myself. I mean Mr. Bilham and Mr. Newsome — Mr. Bilham naturally first. Once only — once for each; that will do. But face to face — for half an hour. What's Mr. Chad," she immediately pursued, "doing at Cannes? Decent men don't go to Cannes with the — well, with the kind of ladies you mean."

"Don't they?" Strether asked with an interest in decent men that amused her.

"No; elsewhere, but not to Cannes. Cannes is different. Cannes is better. Cannes is best. I mean it's all people you know — when you do know them. And if *he* does, why that's different too. He must have gone alone. She can't be with him."

"I have n't," Strether confessed in his weakness, "the least idea." There seemed much in what she said, but he was able after a little to help her to a nearer impression. The meeting with little Bilham took place, by easy arrangement, in the great gallery of the Louvre; and when, standing with his fellow visitor before one of the splendid Titians — the overwhelming portrait of the young man with the strangely-shaped glove and the blue-grey eyes — he turned to see the third member of their party advance from the end of the waxed and gilded vista, he had a sense of having at last taken hold. He had agreed with Miss Gostrey — it dated even from Chester — for a morning at the Louvre, and he had embraced independently the same idea as thrown out by little Bilham, whom he had already accompanied to the museum of the Luxembourg. The fusion of these schemes presented no difficulty, and it was to strike him again that in little Bilham's company contrarieties in general dropped.

"Oh he's all right — he's one of *us!*" Miss Gostrey, after the first exchange, soon found a chance to murmur to her companion; and Strether, as they proceeded and paused and while a quick unanimity between the two appeared to have phrased itself in half a dozen remarks — Strether knew that he knew almost immediately what she meant, and took it as still another sign that he had got his job in hand. This was the more grateful to him that he could think of the intelligence now serving him as an acquisition positively new. He would n't have known even the day before what she meant — that is if she meant, what he assumed, that they were intense Americans together. He had just worked round — and with a sharper turn of the screw than any yet — to the conception of an American intense as little Bilham was intense. The young man was his first specimen; the specimen had profoundly perplexed him; at present however there was light. It was by little Bilham's amazing serenity that he had at first been affected, but he had inevitably, in his circumspection, felt it as the trail of the serpent, the corruption, as he might conveniently have said, of Europe; whereas the promptness with which it came up for Miss Gostrey but as a special little form of the oldest thing they knew justified it at once to his own vision as well. He wanted to be able to like his specimen with a clear good conscience, and this fully permitted it. What had muddled him was precisely the small artist-man's way — it was so complete — of being more American than anybody. But it now for the time put Strether vastly at his ease to have this view of a new way.

The amiable youth then looked out, as it had first struck Strether, at a world in respect to which he had n't a prejudice. The one our friend most instantly missed was the usual one in favour of an occupation accepted. Little Bilham had an occupation, but it was only an occupation declined; and it was by his general exemption from alarm, anxiety or remorse on this score that the impression of his serenity was made. He had come out to Paris to paint — to fathom, that is, at large, that mystery; but study had been fatal to him so far as anything *could* be fatal, and his product-ive power faltered in proportion as his knowledge grew. Strether had gathered from him that at the mo-ment of his finding him in Chad's rooms he had n't saved from his shipwreck a scrap of anything but his beautiful intelligence and his confirmed habit of Paris. He referred to these things with an equal fond familiarity, and it was sufficiently clear that, as an outfit, they still served him. They were charming to Strether through the hour spent at the Louvre, where indeed they figured for him as an unseparated part of the charged iridescent air, the glamour of the name, the splendour of the space, the colour of the masters. Yet they were present too wherever the young man led, and the day after the visit to the Louvre they hung, in a different walk, about the steps of our party.

BOOK THIRD

He had invited his companions to cross the river with him, offering to show them his own poor place; and his own poor place, which was very poor, gave to his idiosyncrasies, for Strether — the small sublime indifferences and independences that had struck the latter as fresh — an odd and engaging dignity. He lived at the end of an alley that went out of an old short cobbled street, a street that went in turn out of a new long smooth avenue — street and avenue and alley having, however, in common a sort of social shabbiness; and he introduced them to the rather cold and blank little studio which he had lent to a comrade for the term of his elegant absence. The comrade was another ingenuous compatriot, to whom he had wired that tea was to await them "regardless," and this reckless repast, and the second ingenuous compatriot, and the faraway makeshift life, with its jokes and its gaps, its delicate daubs and its three or four chairs, its overflow of taste and conviction and its lack of nearly all else — these things wove round the occasion a spell to which our hero unreservedly surrendered.

He liked the ingenuous compatriots — for two or three others soon gathered; he liked the delicate daubs and the free discriminations — involving references indeed, involving enthusiasms and execrations that made him, as they said, sit up; he liked above all the legend of good-humoured poverty, of mutual accommodation fairly raised to the romantic, that he soon read into the scene. The ingenuous compatriots showed a candour, he thought, surpassing even the candour of Woollett; they were red-haired and long-legged, they were quaint and queer and dear and

droll; they made the place resound with the vernacu-
lar, which he had never known so marked as when
figuring for the chosen language, he must suppose, of
contemporary art. They twanged with a vengeance
the æsthetic lyre — they drew from it wonderful airs.
This aspect of their life had an admirable innocence;
and he looked on occasion at Maria Gostrey to see to
what extent that element reached her. She gave him
however for the hour, as she had given him the previous day, no further sign than to show how she dealt
with boys; meeting them with the air of old Parisian
practice that she had for every one, for everything, in
turn. Wonderful about the delicate daubs, masterful
about the way to make tea, trustful about the legs of
chairs and familiarly reminiscent of those, in the other
time, the named, the numbered or the caricatured,
who had flourished or failed, disappeared or arrived,
she had accepted with the best grace her second course
of little Bilham, and had said to Strether, the previous
afternoon, on his leaving them, that, since her impression was to be renewed, she would reserve judgement
till after the new evidence.

The new evidence was to come, as it proved, in a
day or two. He soon had from Maria a message to the
effect that an excellent box at the Français had been
lent her for the following night; it seeming on such
occasions not the least of her merits that she was subject to such approaches. The sense of how she was
always paying for something in advance was equalled
on Strether's part only by the sense of how she was
always being paid; all of which made for his consciousness, in the larger air, of a lively bustling traffic,

the exchange of such values as were not for him to handle. She hated, he knew, at the French play, anything but a box — just as she hated at the English anything but a stall; and a box was what he was already in this phase girding himself to press upon her. But she had for that matter her community with little Bilham: she too always, on the great issues, showed as having known in time. It made her constantly beforehand with him and gave him mainly the chance to ask himself how on the day of their settlement their account would stand. He endeavoured even now to keep it a little straight by arranging that if he accepted her invitation she should dine with him first; but the upshot of this scruple was that at eight o'clock on the morrow he awaited her with Waymarsh under the pillared portico. She had n't dined with him, and it was characteristic of their relation that she had made him embrace her refusal without in the least understanding it. She ever caused her rearrangements to affect him as her tenderest touches. It was on that principle for instance that, giving him the opportunity to be amiable again to little Bilham, she had suggested his offering the young man a seat in their box. Strether had dispatched for this purpose a small blue missive to the Boulevard Malesherbes, but up to the moment of their passing into the theatre he had received no response to his message. He held, however, even after they had been for some time conveniently seated, that their friend, who knew his way about, would come in at his own right moment. His temporary absence moreover seemed, as never yet, to make the right moment for Miss Gostrey. Strether had been waiting till to-night to get back from her in some mirrored form her impressions and conclusions. She had elected, as they said, to see little Bilham once; but now she had seen him twice and had nevertheless not said more than a word.

Waymarsh meanwhile sat opposite him with their hostess between; and Miss Gostrey spoke of herself as an instructor of youth introducing her little charges to a work that was one of the glories of literature. The glory was happily unobjectionable, and the little charges were candid; for herself she had travelled that road and she merely waited on their innocence. But she referred in due time to their absent friend, whom it was clear they should have to give up. "He either won't have got your note," she said, "or you won't have got his: he has had some kind of hindrance, and, of course, for that matter, you know, a man never writes about coming to a box." She spoke as if, with her look, it might have been Waymarsh who had written to the youth, and the latter's face showed a mixture of austerity and anguish. She went on however as if to meet this. "He's far and away, you know, the best of them."

"The best of whom, ma'am?"

"Why of all the long procession — the boys, the girls, or the old men and old women as they sometimes really are; the hope, as one may say, of our country. They've all passed, year after year; but there has been no one in particular I've ever wanted to stop. I feel — don't *you?* — that I want to stop little Bilham; he's so exactly right as he is." She continued to talk to Waymarsh. "He's too delightful. If he'll only not spoil it! But they always *will;* they always do; they always have."

"I don't think Waymarsh knows," Strether said after a moment, "quite what it's open to Bilham to spoil."

"It can't be a good American," Waymarsh lucidly enough replied; "for it did n't strike me the young man had developed much in *that* shape."

"Ah," Miss Gostrey sighed, "the name of the good American is as easily given as taken away! What *is* it, to begin with, to *be* one, and what's the extraordinary hurry? Surely nothing that's so pressing was ever so little defined. It's such an order, really, that before we cook you the dish we must at least have your receipt. Besides, the poor chicks have time! What I've seen so often spoiled," she pursued, "is the happy attitude itself, the state of faith and — what shall I call it? — the sense of beauty. You're right about him" — she now took in Strether; "little Bilham has them to a charm; we must keep little Bilham along." Then she was all again for Waymarsh. "The others have all wanted so dreadfully to do something, and they've gone and done it in too many cases indeed. It leaves them never the same afterwards; the charm's always somehow broken. Now *he*, I think, you know, really won't. He won't do the least dreadful little thing. We shall continue to enjoy him just as he is. No — he's quite beautiful. He sees everything. He is n't a bit ashamed. He has every scrap of the courage of it that one could ask. Only think what he *might* do. One wants really — for fear of some accident — to keep him in view. At this very moment perhaps

what may n't he be up to ? I 've had my disappointments — the poor things are never really safe; or only
at least when you have them under your eye. One
can never completely trust them. One's uneasy, and
I think that's why I most miss him now."

She had wound up with a laugh of enjoyment over her
embroidery of her idea — an enjoyment that her face
communicated to Strether, who almost wished none
the less at this moment that she would let poor Waymarsh alone. *He* knew more or less what she meant;
but the fact was n't a reason for her not pretending to
Waymarsh that he did n't. It was craven of him perhaps, but he would, for the high amenity of the occasion, have liked Waymarsh not to be so sure of his wit.
Her recognition of it gave him away and, before she
had done with him or with that article, would give him
worse. What was he, all the same, to do ? He looked
across the box at his friend; their eyes met; something
queer and stiff, something that bore on the situation
but that it was better not to touch, passed in silence
between them. Well, the effect of it for Strether was
an abrupt reaction, a final impatience of his own
tendency to temporise. Where was that taking him
anyway ? It was one of the quiet instants that sometimes settle more matters than the outbreaks dear to
the historic muse. The only qualification of the quiet-
ness was the synthetic "Oh hang it!" into which
Strether's share of the silence soundlessly flowered.
It represented, this mute ejaculation, a final impulse
to burn his ships. These ships, to the historic muse,
may seem of course mere cockles, but when he presently spoke to Miss Gostrey it was with the sense at

least of applying the torch. "Is it then a conspiracy?"

"Between the two young men? Well, I don't pretend to be a seer or a prophetess," she presently replied; "but if I'm simply a woman of sense he's working for you to-night. I don't quite know how — but it's in my bones." And she looked at him at last as if, little material as she yet gave him, he'd really understand. "For an opinion *that's* my opinion. He makes you out too well not to."

"Not to work for me to-night?" Strether wondered. "Then I hope he isn't doing anything very bad."

"They've got you," she portentously answered.

"Do you mean he *is* — ?"

"They've got you," she merely repeated. Though she disclaimed the prophetic vision she was at this instant the nearest approach he had ever met to the priestess of the oracle. The light was in her eyes. "You must face it now."

He faced it on the spot. "They *had* arranged — ?"

"Every move in the game. And they've been arranging ever since. He has had every day his little telegram from Cannes."

It made Strether open his eyes. "Do you *know* that?"

"I do better. I see it. This was, before I met him, what I wondered whether I *was* to see. But as soon as I met him I ceased to wonder, and our second meeting made me sure. I took him all in. He was acting — he is still — on his daily instructions."

"So that Chad has done the whole thing?"

"Oh no — not the whole. *We've* done some of it. You and I and 'Europe.'"

"Europe — yes," Strether mused.

"Dear old Paris," she seemed to explain. But there was more, and, with one of her turns, she risked it. "And dear old Waymarsh. You," she declared, "have been a good bit of it."

He sat massive. "A good bit of what, ma'am?"

"Why of the wonderful consciousness of our friend here. You've helped too in your way to float him to where he is."

"And where the devil *is* he?"

She passed it on with a laugh. "Where the devil, Strether, are you?"

He spoke as if he had just been thinking it out. "Well, quite already in Chad's hands, it would seem." And he had had with this another thought. "Will that be — just all through Bilham — the way he's going to work it? It would be, for him, you know, an idea. And Chad with an idea —!"

"Well?" she asked while the image held him.

"Well, is Chad — what shall I say? — monstrous?"

"Oh as much as you like! But the idea you speak of," she said, "won't have been his best. He'll have a better. It won't be all through little Bilham that he'll work it."

This already sounded almost like a hope destroyed. "Through whom else then?"

"That's what we shall see!" But quite as she spoke she turned, and Strether turned; for the door of the box had opened, with the click of the *ouvreuse*, from the lobby, and a gentleman, a stranger to them, had come in with a quick step. The door closed behind him, and, though their faces showed him his mistake, his air, which was striking, was all good confidence. The curtain had just again arisen, and, in the hush of the general attention, Strether's challenge was tacit, as was also the greeting, with a quickly-deprecating hand and smile, of the unannounced visitor. He discreetly signed that he would wait, would stand, and these things and his face, one look from which she had caught, had suddenly worked for Miss Gostrey. She fitted to them all an answer for Strether's last question. The solid stranger was simply the answer — as she now, turning to her friend, indicated. She brought it straight out for him — it presented the intruder. "Why, through this gentleman!" The gentleman indeed, at the same time, though sounding for Strether a very short name, did practically as much to explain. Strether gasped the name back — then only had he seen. Miss Gostrey had said more than she knew. They were in presence of Chad himself.

Our friend was to go over it afterwards again and again — he was going over it much of the time that they were together, and they were together constantly for three or four days: the note had been so strongly struck during that first half-hour that everything happening since was comparatively a minor development. The fact was that his perception of the young man's identity — so absolutely checked for a minute — had been quite one of the sensations that count in life; he certainly had never known one that had acted, as he

135

might have said, with more of a crowded rush. And the rush, though both vague and multitudinous, had lasted a long time, protected, as it were, yet at the same time aggravated, by the circumstance of its coinciding with a stretch of decorous silence. They could n't talk without disturbing the spectators in the part of the balcony just below them; and it, for that matter, came to Strether — being a thing of the sort that did come to him — that these were the accidents of a high civilisation; the imposed tribute to propriety, the frequent exposure to conditions, usually brilliant, in which relief has to await its time. Relief was never quite near at hand for kings, queens, comedians and other such people, and though you might be yourself not exactly one of those, you could yet, in leading the life of high pressure, guess a little how they sometimes felt. It was truly the life of high pressure that Strether had seemed to feel himself lead while he sat there, close to Chad, during the long tension of the act. He was in presence of a fact that occupied his whole mind, that occupied for the half-hour his senses themselves all together; but he could n't without inconvenience show anything — which moreover might count really as luck. What he might have shown, had he shown at all, was exactly the kind of emotion — the emotion of bewilderment — that he had proposed to himself from the first, whatever should occur, to show least. The phenomenon that had suddenly sat down there with him was a phenomenon of change so complete that his imagination, which had worked so beforehand, felt itself, in the connexion, without margin or allowance. It had faced every contingency but that Chad should not *be* Chad, and this was what it now had to face with a mere strained smile and an uncomfortable flush.

He asked himself if, by any chance, before he should have in some way to commit himself, he might feel his mind settled to the new vision, might habituate it, so to speak, to the remarkable truth. But oh it was too remarkable, the truth; for what could be more remarkable than this sharp rupture of an identity? You could deal with a man as himself — you could n't deal with him as somebody else. It was a small source of peace moreover to be reduced to wondering how little he might know in such an event what a sum he was setting you. He could n't absolutely not know, for you could n't absolutely not let him. It was a *case* then simply, a strong case, as people nowadays called such things, a case of transformation unsurpassed, and the hope was but in the general law that strong cases were liable to control from without. Perhaps he, Strether himself, was the only person after all aware of it. Even Miss Gostrey, with all her science, would n't be, would she? — and he had never seen any one less aware of anything than Waymarsh as he glowered at Chad. The social sightlessness of his old friend's survey marked for him afresh, and almost in an humiliating way, the inevitable limits of direct aid from this source. He was not certain, however, of not drawing a shade of compensation from the privilege, as yet untasted, of knowing more about something in particular than Miss Gostrey did. His situation too was a case, for that matter, and he was now so interested, quite so privately agog, about it, that he had already an eye to the fun it would be to open up to her afterwards. He derived during his half-hour no assistance from her, and just this fact of her not meeting his eyes played a little, it must be confessed, into his predicament.

He had introduced Chad, in the first minutes, under his breath, and there was never the primness in her of the person unacquainted; but she had none the less betrayed at first no vision but of the stage, where she occasionally found a pretext for an appreciative moment that she invited Waymarsh to share. The latter's faculty of participation had never had, all round, such an assault to meet; the pressure on him being the sharper for this chosen attitude in her, as Strether judged it, of isolating, for their natural intercourse, Chad and himself. This intercourse was meanwhile restricted to a frank friendly look from the young man, something markedly like a smile, but falling far short of a grin, and to the vivacity of Strether's private speculation as to whether *he* carried himself like a fool. He did n't quite see how he could so feel as one without somehow showing as one. The worst of that question moreover was that he knew it as a symptom the sense of which annoyed him. "If I'm going to be odiously conscious of how I may strike the fellow," he reflected, "it was so little what I came out for that I may as well stop before I begin." This sage consideration too, distinctly, seemed to leave untouched the fact that he *was* going to be conscious. He was conscious of everything but of what would have served him.

He was to know afterwards, in the watches of the night, that nothing would have been more open to him than after a minute or two to propose to Chad to seek with him the refuge of the lobby. He had n't only not proposed it, but had lacked even the presence of mind to see it as possible. He had stuck there like a school-boy wishing not to miss a minute of the show; though for that portion of the show then presented he had n't had an instant's real attention. He could n't when the curtain fell have given the slightest account of what had happened. He had therefore, further, not at that moment acknowledged the amenity added by this acceptance of his awkwardness to Chad's general pa-tience. Had n't he none the less known at the very time — known it stupidly and without reaction — that the boy was accepting something? He was mod-estly benevolent, the boy — that was at least what he had been capable of the superiority of making out his chance to be; and one had one's self literally not had the gumption to get in ahead of him. If we should go into all that occupied our friend in the watches of the night we should have to mend our pen; but an instance or two may mark for us the vividness with which he could remember. He remembered the two absurdities that, if his presence of mind *had* failed, were the things that had had most to do with it. He had never in his life seen a young man come into a box at ten o'clock at night, and would, if challenged on the ques-tion in advance, have scarce been ready to pronounce as to different ways of doing so. But it was in spite of this definite to him that Chad had had a way that was wonderful: a fact carrying with it an implication that, as one might imagine it, he knew, he had learned, how.

Here already then were abounding results; he had
on the spot and without the least trouble of intention
taught Strether that even in so small a thing as that
there were different ways. He had done in the same
line still more than this; had by a mere shake or two
of the head made his old friend observe that the
change in him was perhaps more than anything else,
for the eye, a matter of the marked streaks of grey,
extraordinary at his age, in his thick black hair; as
well as that this new feature was curiously becoming
to him, did something for him, as characterisation,
also even — of all things in the world — as refinement, that had been a good deal wanted. Strether
felt, however, he would have had to confess, that it
would n't have been easy just now, on this and other
counts, in the presence of what had been supplied, to
be quite clear as to what had been missed. A reflexion a candid critic might have made of old, for instance, was that it would have been happier for the
son to look more like the mother; but this was a reflexion that at present would never occur. The ground
had quite fallen away from it, yet no resemblance
whatever to the mother had supervened. It would
have been hard for a young man's face and air to dis-
connect themselves more completely than Chad's at
this juncture from any discerned, from any imagin-
able aspect of a New England female parent. That of
course was no more than had been on the cards; but it
produced in Strether none the less one of those frequent phenomena of mental reference with which all
judgement in him was actually beset.

Again and again as the days passed he had had a

sense of the pertinence of communicating quickly with Woollett — communicating with a quickness with which telegraphy alone would rhyme; the fruit really of a fine fancy in him for keeping things straight, for the happy forestalment of error. No one could explain better when needful, nor put more conscience into an account or a report; which burden of conscience is perhaps exactly the reason why his heart always sank when the clouds of explanation gathered. His highest ingenuity was in keeping the sky of life clear of them. Whether or no he had a grand idea of the lucid, he held that nothing ever was in fact — for any one else — explained. One went through the vain motions, but it was mostly a waste of life. A personal relation was a relation only so long as people either perfectly understood or, better still, did n't care if they did n't. From the moment they cared if they did n't it was living by the sweat of one's brow; and the sweat of one's brow was just what one might buy one's self off from by keeping the ground free of the wild weed of delusion. It easily grew too fast, and the Atlantic cable now alone could race with it. That agency would each day have testified for him to something that was not what Woollett had argued. He was not at this moment absolutely sure that the effect of the morrow's — or rather of the night's — appreciation of the crisis would n't be to determine some brief missive. "Have at last seen him, but oh dear!" — some temporary relief of that sort seemed to hover before him. It hovered somehow as preparing them all — yet preparing them for what? If he might do so more luminously and cheaply he would tick out in four words: "Awfully old — grey hair." To this particular item in Chad's appearance he constantly, during their mute half-hour, reverted; as if so very much more than he could have said had been involved in it. The most he could have said would have been: "If he's going to make me feel young —!" which indeed, however, carried with it quite enough. If Strether was to feel young, that is, it would be because Chad was to feel old; and an aged and hoary sinner had been no part of the scheme.

The question of Chadwick's true time of life was, doubtless, what came up quickest after the adjournment of the two, when the play was over, to a café in the Avenue de l'Opéra. Miss Gostrey had in due course been perfect for such a step; she had known exactly what they wanted — to go straight somewhere and talk; and Strether had even felt she had known what he wished to say and that he was arranging immediately to begin. She had n't pretended this, as she *had* pretended on the other hand, to have divined Waymarsh's wish to extend to her an independent protection homeward; but Strether nevertheless found how, after he had Chad opposite to him at a small table in the brilliant halls that his companion straightway selected, sharply and easily discriminated from others, it was quite, to his mind, as if she heard him speak; as if, sitting up, a mile away, in the little apartment he knew, she would listen hard enough to catch. He found too that he liked that idea, and he wished that, by the same token, Mrs. Newsome might have caught as well. For what had above all been determined in him as a necessity of the first order was

BOOK THIRD

not to lose another hour, nor a fraction of one; was to
advance, to overwhelm, with a rush. This was how
he would anticipate — by a night-attack, as might be
— any forced maturity that a crammed consciousness
of Paris was likely to take upon itself to assert on behalf of the boy. He knew to the full, on what he had
just extracted from Miss Gostrey, Chad's marks of
alertness; but they were a reason the more for not
dawdling. If he was himself moreover to be treated as
young he would n't at all events be so treated before
he should have struck out at least once. His arms
might be pinioned afterwards, but it would have been
left on record that he was fifty. The importance of
this he had indeed begun to feel before they left the
theatre; it had become a wild unrest, urging him to
seize his chance. He could scarcely wait for it as they
went; he was on the verge of the indecency of bringing
up the question in the street; he fairly caught himself
going on — so he afterwards invidiously named it —
as if there would be for him no second chance should
the present be lost. Not till, on the purple divan before the perfunctory *bock*, he had brought out the
words themselves, was he sure, for that matter, that
the present would be saved.

BOOK FOURTH

I

"I've come, you know, to make you break with everything, neither more nor less, and take you straight home; so you'll be so good as immediately and favourably to consider it!" — Strether, face to face with Chad after the play, had sounded these words almost breathlessly, and with an effect at first positively disconcerting to himself alone. For Chad's receptive attitude was that of a person who had been gracefully quiet while the messenger at last reaching him has run a mile through the dust. During some seconds after he had spoken Strether felt as if *he* had made some such exertion; he was not even certain that the perspiration was n't on his brow. It was the kind of consciousness for which he had to thank the look that, while the strain lasted, the young man's eyes gave him. They reflected — and the deuce of the thing was that they reflected really with a sort of shyness of kindness — his momentarily disordered state; which fact brought on in its turn for our friend the dawn of a fear that Chad might simply "take it out" — take everything out — in being sorry for him. Such a fear, any fear, was unpleasant. But everything was unpleasant; it was odd how everything had suddenly turned so. This however was no reason for letting the least thing go. Strether had the next minute proceeded as roundly as if with an advantage to follow up. "Of course I'm a busybody, if you want to fight the case to the death; but after all mainly in the sense of having known you and having given you such attention as you kindly permitted when you were in jackets and knickerbockers. Yes — it was knickerbockers, I'm busybody enough to remember that; and that you had, for your age — I speak of the first far-away time — tremendously stout legs. Well, we want you to break. Your mother's heart's passionately set upon it, but she has above and beyond that excellent arguments and reasons. I've not put them into her head — I need n't remind you how little she's a person who needs that. But they exist — you must take it from me as a friend both of hers and yours — for myself as well. I did n't invent them, I did n't originally work them out; but I understand them, I think I can explain them — by which I mean make you actively do them justice; and that's why you see me here. You had better know the worst at once. It's a question of an immediate rupture and an immediate return. I've been conceited enough to dream I can sugar that pill. I take at any rate the greatest interest in the question. I took it already before I left home; and I don't mind telling you that, altered as you are, I take it still more now that I've seen you. You're older and — I don't know what to call it! — more of a handful; but you're by so much the more, I seem to make out, to our purpose."

"Do I strike you as improved?" Strether was to recall that Chad had at this point enquired.

He was likewise to recall — and it had to count for some time as his greatest comfort — that it had been "given" him, as they said at Woollett, to reply with

some presence of mind: "I have n't the least idea."
He was really for a while to like thinking he had been
positively hard. On the point of conceding that Chad
had improved in appearance, but that to the question
of appearance the remark must be confined, he
checked even that compromise and left his reserva-
tion bare. Not only his moral, but also, as it were, his
æsthetic sense had a little to pay for this, Chad being
unmistakeably — and was n't it a matter of the con-
founded grey hair again ? — handsomer than he had
ever promised. That however fell in perfectly with
what Strether had said. They had no desire to keep
down his proper expansion, and he would n't be less
to their purpose for not looking, as he had too often
done of old, only bold and wild. There was indeed a
signal particular in which he would distinctly be more
so. Strether did n't, as he talked, absolutely follow
himself; he only knew he was clutching his thread and
that he held it from moment to moment a little tighter;
his mere uninterruptedness during the few minutes
helped him to do that. He had frequently, for a
month, turned over what he should say on this very
occasion, and he seemed at last to have said nothing
he had thought of — everything was so totally different.

But in spite of all he had put the flag at the window.
This was what he had done, and there was a minute
during which he affected himself as having shaken it
hard, flapped it with a mighty flutter, straight in front
of his companion's nose. It gave him really almost the
sense of having already acted his part. The momentary relief — as if from the knowledge that nothing of

that at least could be undone — sprang from a particular cause, the cause that had flashed into operation, in Miss Gostrey's box, with direct apprehension, with amazed recognition, and that had been concerned since then in every throb of his consciousness. What it came to was that with an absolutely *new* quantity to deal with one simply could n't know. The new quantity was represented by the fact that Chad had been made over. That was all; whatever it was it was everything. Strether had never seen the thing so done before — it was perhaps a speciality of Paris. If one had been present at the process one might little by little have mastered the result; but he was face to face, as matters stood, with the finished business. It had freely been noted for him that he might be received as a dog among skittles, but that was on the basis of the old quantity. He had originally thought of lines and tones as things to be taken, but these possibilities had now quite melted away. There was no computing at all what the young man before him would think or feel or say on any subject whatever. This intelligence Strether had afterwards, to account for his nervousness, reconstituted as he might, just as he had also reconstituted the promptness with which Chad had corrected his uncertainty. An extraordinarily short time had been required for the correction, and there had ceased to be anything negative in his companion's face and air as soon as it was made. "Your engagement to my mother has become then what they call here a *fait accompli?*" — it had consisted, the determinant touch, in nothing more than that.

Well, that was enough, Strether had felt while his

answer hung fire. He had felt at the same time, however, that nothing could less become him than that it
should hang fire too long. "Yes," he said brightly,
"it was on the happy settlement of the question that
I started. You see therefore to what tune I'm in your
family. Moreover," he added, "I've been supposing
you'd suppose it."

"Oh I've been supposing it for a long time, and
what you tell me helps me to understand that you
should want to do something. To do something, I
mean," said Chad, "to commemorate an event so —
what do they call it? — so auspicious. I see you make
out, and not unnaturally," he continued, "that bringing me home in triumph as a sort of wedding-present
to Mother would commemorate it better than anything else. You want to make a bonfire in fact," he
laughed, "and you pitch me on. Thank you, thank
you!" he laughed again.

He was altogether easy about it, and this made
Strether now see how at bottom, and in spite of the
shade of shyness that really cost him nothing, he had
from the first moment been easy about everything.
The shade of shyness was mere good taste. People
with manners formed could apparently have, as one
of their best cards, the shade of shyness too. He had
leaned a little forward to speak; his elbows were on
the table; and the inscrutable new face that he had
got somewhere and somehow was brought by the
movement nearer to his critic's. There was a fascina-
tion for that critic in its not being, this ripe physi-
ognomy, the face that, under observation at least, he
had originally carried away from Woollett. Strether

found a certain freedom on his own side in defining it as that of a man of the world — a formula that indeed seemed to come now in some degree to his relief; that of a man to whom things had happened and were variously known. In gleams, in glances, the past did perhaps peep out of it; but such lights were faint and instantly merged. Chad was brown and thick and strong, and of old Chad had been rough. Was all the difference therefore that he was actually smooth? Possibly; for that he *was* smooth was as marked as in the taste of a sauce or in the rub of a hand. The effect of it was general — it had retouched his features, drawn them with a cleaner line. It had cleared his eyes and settled his colour and polished his fine square teeth — the main ornament of his face; and at the same time that it had given him a form and a surface, almost a design, it had toned his voice, established his accent, encouraged his smile to more play and his other motions to less. He had formerly, with a great deal of action, expressed very little; and he now expressed whatever was necessary with almost none at all. It was as if in short he had really, copious perhaps but shapeless, been put into a firm mould and turned successfully out. The phenomenon — Strether kept eyeing it as a phenomenon, an eminent case — was marked enough to be touched by the finger. He finally put his hand across the table and laid it on Chad's arm. "If you'll promise me — here on the spot and giving me your word of honour — to break straight off, you'll make the future the real right thing for all of us alike. You'll ease off the strain of this decent but none the less acute suspense in which

BOOK FOURTH

I've for so many days been waiting for you, and let
me turn in to rest. I shall leave you with my blessing
and go to bed in peace."

Chad again fell back at this and, his hands pocketed,
settled himself a little; in which posture he looked,
though he rather anxiously smiled, only the more
earnest. Then Strether seemed to see that he was
really nervous, and he took that as what he would have
called a wholesome sign. The only mark of it hitherto
had been his more than once taking off and putting on
his wide-brimmed crush hat. He had at this moment
made the motion again to remove it, then had only
pushed it back, so that it hung informally on his
strong young grizzled crop. It was a touch that gave
the note of the familiar — the intimate and the belated — to their quiet colloquy; and it was indeed by
some such trivial aid that Strether became aware at
the same moment of something else. The observation
was at any rate determined in him by some light too
fine to distinguish from so many others, but it was
none the less sharply determined. Chad looked unmistakeably during these instants — well, as Strether
put it to himself, all he was worth. Our friend had a
sudden apprehension of what that would on certain
sides be. He saw him in a flash as the young man
marked out by women; and for a concentrated minute
the dignity, the comparative austerity, as he funnily
fancied it, of this character affected him almost with
awe. There was an experience on his interlocutor's
part that looked out at him from under the displaced
hat, and that looked out moreover by a force of its
own, the deep fact of its quantity and quality, and not

through Chad's intending bravado or swagger. That was then the way men marked out by women *were* — and also the men by whom the women were doubtless in turn sufficiently distinguished. It affected Strether for thirty seconds as a relevant truth; a truth which, however, the next minute, had fallen into its relation. "Can't you imagine there being some questions," Chad asked, "that a fellow — however much impressed by your charming way of stating things — would like to put to you first?"

"Oh yes — easily. I'm here to answer everything. I think I can even tell you things, of the greatest interest to you, that you won't know enough to ask me. We'll take as many days to it as you like. But I want," Strether wound up, "to go to bed now."

"Really?"

Chad had spoken in such surprise that he was amused. "Can't you believe it? — with what you put me through?"

The young man seemed to consider. "Oh I have n't put you through much — yet."

"Do you mean there's so much more to come?" Strether laughed. "All the more reason then that I should gird myself." And as if to mark what he felt he could by this time count on he was already on his feet.

Chad, still seated, stayed him, with a hand against him, as he passed between their table and the next. "Oh we shall get on!"

The tone was, as who should say, everything Strether could have desired; and quite as good the expression of face with which the speaker had looked up at him and kindly held him. All these things lacked was their not showing quite so much as the fruit of experience. Yes, experience was what Chad did play on him, if he did n't play any grossness of defiance. Of course experience was in a manner defiance; but it was n't, at any rate — rather indeed quite the contrary! — grossness; which was so much gained. He fairly grew older, Strether thought, while he himself so reasoned. Then with his mature pat of his visitor's arm he also got up; and there had been enough of it all by this time to make the visitor feel that something *was* settled. Was n't it settled that he had at least the testimony of Chad's own belief in a settlement? Strether found himself treating Chad's profession that they would get on as a sufficient basis for going to bed. He had n't nevertheless after this gone to bed directly; for when they had again passed out together into the mild bright night a check had virtually sprung from nothing more than a small circumstance which might have acted only as confirming quiescence. There were people, expressive sound, projected light, still abroad, and after they had taken in for a moment, through everything, the great clear architectural street, they turned off in tacit union to the quarter of Strether's hotel. "Of course," Chad here abruptly began, "of course Mother's making things out with you about me has been natural — and of course also you 've had a good deal to go upon. Still, you must have filled out."

He had stopped, leaving his friend to wonder a little what point he wished to make; and this it was that enabled Strether meanwhile to make one. "Oh we 've never pretended to go into detail. We were n't in the least bound to *that*. It was 'filling out' enough to miss you as we did."

But Chad rather oddly insisted, though under the high lamp at their corner, where they paused, he had at first looked as if touched by Strether's allusion to the long sense, at home, of his absence. "What I mean is you must have imagined."

"Imagined what?"

"Well — horrors."

It affected Strether: horrors were so little — superficially at least — in this robust and reasoning image. But he was none the less there to be veracious. "Yes, I dare say we *have* imagined horrors. But where's the harm if we have n't been wrong?"

Chad raised his face to the lamp, and it was one of the moments at which he had, in his extraordinary way, most his air of designedly showing himself. It was as if at these instants he just presented himself, his identity so rounded off, his palpable presence and his massive young manhood, as such a link in the chain as might practically amount to a kind of demonstration. It was as if — and how but anomalously? — he could n't after all help thinking sufficiently well of these things to let them go for what they were worth. What could there be in this for Strether but the hint of some self-respect, some sense of power, oddly perverted; something latent and beyond access, ominous and perhaps enviable? The intimation had the next thing, in a flash, taken on a name — a name on which our friend seized as he asked himself if he were n't perhaps really dealing with an irreducible young Pa-

gan. This description — he quite jumped at it — had
a sound that gratified his mental ear, so that of a sudden he had already adopted it. Pagan — yes, that
was, was n't it? what Chad *would* logically be. It was
what he must be. It was what he was. The idea was
a clue and, instead of darkening the prospect, projected a certain clearness. Strether made out in this
quick ray that a Pagan was perhaps, at the pass they
had come to, the thing most wanted at Woollett.
They'd be able to do with one — a good one; he'd
find an opening — yes; and Strether's imagination
even now prefigured and accompanied the first appearance there of the rousing personage. He had only
the slight discomfort of feeling, as the young man
turned away from the lamp, that his thought had in
the momentary silence possibly been guessed. "Well,
I've no doubt," said Chad, "you've come near
enough. The details, as you say, don't matter. It *has*
been generally the case that I've let myself go. But
I'm coming round — I'm not so bad now." With
which they walked on again to Strether's hotel.

"Do you mean," the latter asked as they approached the door, "that there is n't any woman with
you now?"

"But pray what has that to do with it?"

"Why it's the whole question."

"Of my going home?" Chad was clearly surprised.
"Oh not much! Do you think that when I want to go
any one will have any power —"

"To keep you" — Strether took him straight up —
"from carrying out your wish? Well, our idea has
been that somebody has hitherto — or a good many

persons perhaps — kept you pretty well from 'wanting.' That's what — if you're in anybody's hands — may again happen. You don't answer my question " — he kept it up; "but if you are n't in anybody's hands so much the better. There's nothing then but what makes for your going."

Chad turned this over. "I don't answer your question?" He spoke quite without resenting it. "Well, such questions have always a rather exaggerated side. One does n't know quite what you mean by being in women's 'hands.' It's all so vague. One is when one is n't. One is n't when one is. And then one can't quite give people away." He seemed kindly to explain. "I've *never* got stuck — so very hard; and, as against anything at any time really better, I don't think I've ever been afraid." There was something in it that held Strether to wonder, and this gave him time to go on. He broke out as with a more helpful thought. "Don't you know how I like Paris itself?"

The upshot was indeed to make our friend marvel. "Oh if *that's* all that's the matter with you —!" It was *he* who almost showed resentment.

Chad's smile of a truth more than met it. "But is n't that enough?"

Strether hesitated, but it came out. "Not enough for your mother!" Spoken, however, it sounded a trifle odd — the effect of which was that Chad broke into a laugh. Strether, at this, succumbed as well, though with extreme brevity. "Permit us to have still our theory. But if you *are* so free and so strong you're inexcusable. I'll write in the morning," he added with decision. "I'll say I've got you."

BOOK FOURTH

This appeared to open for Chad a new interest. "How often do you write?"

"Oh perpetually."

"And at great length?"

Strether had become a little impatient. "I hope it's not found too great."

"Oh I'm sure not. And you hear as often?"

Again Strether paused. "As often as I deserve."

"Mother writes," said Chad, "a lovely letter."

Strether, before the closed porte-cochère, fixed him a moment. "It's more, my boy, than *you* do! But our suppositions don't matter," he added, "if you're actually not entangled."

Chad's pride seemed none the less a little touched. "I never *was* that — let me insist. I always had my own way." With which he pursued: "And I have it at present."

"Then what are you here for? What has kept you," Strether asked, "if you *have* been able to leave?"

It made Chad, after a stare, throw himself back. "Do you think one's kept only by women?" His surprise and his verbal emphasis rang out so clear in the still street that Strether winced till he remembered the safety of their English speech. "Is that," the young man demanded, "what they think at Woollett?" At the good faith in the question Strether had changed colour, feeling that, as he would have said, he had put his foot in it. He had appeared stupidly to misrepresent what they thought at Woollett; but before he had time to rectify Chad again was upon him. "I must say then you show a low mind!"

It so fell in, unhappily for Strether, with that reflexion of his own prompted in him by the pleasant air of the Boulevard Malesherbes, that its disconcerting force was rather unfairly great. It was a dig that, administered by himself — and administered even to poor Mrs. Newsome — was no more than salutary; but administered by Chad — and quite logically — it came nearer drawing blood. They *had n't* a low mind — nor any approach to one; yet incontestably they had worked, and with a certain smugness, on a basis that might be turned against them. Chad had at any rate pulled his visitor up; he had even pulled up his admirable mother; he had absolutely, by a turn of the wrist and a jerk of the far-flung noose, pulled up, in a bunch, Woollett browsing in its pride. There was no doubt Woollett *had* insisted on his coarseness; and what he at present stood there for in the sleeping street was, by his manner of striking the other note, to make of such insistence a preoccupation compromising to the insisters. It was exactly as if they had imputed to him a vulgarity that he had by a mere gesture caused to fall from him. The devil of the case was that Strether felt it, by the same stroke, as falling straight upon himself. He had been wondering a minute ago if the boy were n't a Pagan, and he found himself wondering now if he were n't by chance a gentleman. It did n't in the least, on the spot, spring up helpfully for him that a person could n't at the same time be both. There was nothing at this moment in the air to challenge the combination; there was everything to give it on the contrary something of a flourish. It struck Strether into the bargain as doing something to meet the most difficult of the questions; though perhaps indeed only by substituting another. Would n't it be precisely by having learned to be a gentleman that he had mastered the consequent trick of looking so well that one could scarce speak to him straight? But what in the world was the clue to such a prime producing cause? There were too many clues then that Strether still lacked, and these clues to clues were among them. What it accordingly amounted to for him was that he had to take full in the face a fresh attribution of ignorance. He had grown used by this time to reminders, especially from his own lips, of what he did n't know; but he had borne them because in the first place they were private and because in the second they practically conveyed a tribute. He did n't know what was bad, and — as others did n't know how little he knew it — he could put up with his state. But if he did n't know, in so important a particular, what was good, Chad at least was now aware he did n't; and that, for some reason, affected our friend as curiously public. It was in fact an exposed condition that the young man left him in long enough for him to feel its chill — till he saw fit, in a word, generously again to cover him. This last was in truth what Chad quite gracefully did. But he did it as with a simple thought that met the whole of the case. "Oh I'm all right!" It was what Strether had rather bewilderedly to go to bed on.

II

IT really looked true moreover from the way Chad was to behave after this. He was full of attentions to his mother's ambassador; in spite of which, all the while, the latter's other relations rather remarkably contrived to assert themselves. Strether's sittings pen in hand with Mrs. Newsome up in his own room were broken, yet they were richer; and they were more than ever interspersed with the hours in which he reported himself, in a different fashion, but with scarce less earnestness and fulness, to Maria Gostrey. Now that, as he would have expressed it, he had really something to talk about he found himself, in respect to any oddity that might reside for him in the double connexion, at once more aware and more indifferent. He had been fine to Mrs. Newsome about his useful friend, but it had begun to haunt his imagination that Chad, taking up again for her benefit a pen too long disused, might possibly be finer. It would n't at all do, he saw, that anything should come up for him at Chad's hand but what specifically *was* to have come; the greatest divergence from which would be precisely the element of any lubrication of their intercourse by levity. It was accordingly to forestall such an accident that he frankly put before the young man the several facts, just as they had occurred, of his funny alliance. He spoke of these facts, pleasantly and obligingly, as "the whole story," and felt that he might qualify the alliance as funny if he remained sufficiently grave about it. He flattered himself that he even exaggerated the wild freedom of his original encounter with the wonderful lady; he was scrupulously definite about the absurd conditions in which they had made acquaintance — their having picked each other up almost in the street; and he had (finest inspiration of all!) a conception of carrying the war into the enemy's country by showing surprise at the enemy's ignorance.

He had always had a notion that this last was the grand style of fighting; the greater therefore the reason for it, as he could n't remember that he had ever before fought in the grand style. Every one, according to this, knew Miss Gostrey: how came it Chad did n't know her? The difficulty, the impossibility, was really to escape it; Strether put on him, by what he took for granted, the burden of proof of the contrary. This tone was so far successful as that Chad quite appeared to recognise her as a person whose fame had reached him, but against his acquaintance with whom much mischance had worked. He made the point at the same time that his social relations, such as they could be called, were perhaps not to the extent Strether supposed with the rising flood of their compatriots. He hinted at his having more and more given way to a different principle of selection; the moral of which seemed to be that he went about little in the "colony." For the moment certainly he had quite another interest. It was deep, what he understood; and Strether, for himself, could only so observe it. He could n't see as yet how deep. Might he not all too soon! For there was really too much of their question that Chad had already committed himself to liking. He liked, to begin with, his prospective stepfather; which was distinctly what had not been on the cards. His hating him was the untowardness for which Strether had been best prepared; he had n't expected the boy's actual form to give him more to do than his imputed. It gave him more through suggesting that he must somehow make up to himself for not being sure he was sufficiently disagreeable. That had really been present to him as his only way to be sure he was sufficiently thorough. The point was that if Chad's tolerance of his thoroughness were insincere, were but the best of devices for gaining time, it none the less did treat everything as tacitly concluded.

That seemed at the end of ten days the upshot of the abundant, the recurrent talk through which Strether poured into him all it concerned him to know, put him in full possession of facts and figures. Never cutting these colloquies short by a minute, Chad behaved, looked and spoke as if he were rather heavily, perhaps even a trifle gloomily, but none the less fundamentally and comfortably free. He made no crude profession of eagerness to yield, but he asked the most intelligent questions, probed, at moments, abruptly, even deeper than his friend's layer of information, justified by these touches the native estimate of his latent stuff, and had in every way the air of trying to live, reflectively, into the square bright picture. He walked up and down in front of this production, sociably took Strether's arm at the points at which he stopped, surveyed it repeatedly from the right and from the left, inclined a critical head to either quarter, and, while he puffed a still more critical cigarette, animadverted to his companion on this passage and that. Strether sought relief — there were hours when he required it — in repeating himself; it was in truth not to be blinked that Chad had a way. The main question as yet was of what it was a way *to*. It made vulgar questions no more easy; but that was unimportant when all questions save those of his own asking had dropped. That he was free was answer enough, and it wasn't quite ridiculous that this freedom should end by presenting itself as what was difficult to move. His changed state, his lovely home, his beautiful things, his easy talk, his very appetite for Strether, insatiable and, when all was said, flattering — what were such marked matters all but the notes of his freedom? He had the effect of making a sacrifice of it just in these handsome forms to his visitor; which was mainly the reason the visitor was privately, for the time, a little out of countenance. Strether was at this period again and again thrown back on a felt need to remodel somehow his plan. He fairly caught himself shooting rueful glances, shy looks of pursuit, toward the embodied influence, the definite adversary, who had by a stroke of her own failed him and on a fond theory of whose palpable presence he had, under Mrs. Newsome's inspiration, altogether proceeded. He had once or twice, in secret, literally expressed the irritated wish that *she* would come out and find her.

He couldn't quite yet force it upon Woollett that such a career, such a perverted young life, showed after all a certain plausible side, *did* in the case before them flaunt something like an impunity for the social man; but he could at least treat himself to the statement that would prepare him for the sharpest echo. This echo — as distinct over there in the dry thin air as some shrill "heading" above a column of print — seemed to reach him even as he wrote. "He says there's no woman," he could hear Mrs. Newsome report, in capitals almost of newspaper size, to Mrs. Pocock; and he could focus in Mrs. Pocock the response of the reader of the journal. He could see in the younger lady's face the earnestness of her attention and catch the full scepticism of her but slightly delayed "What is there then?" Just so he could again as little miss the mother's clear decision: "There's plenty of disposition, no doubt, to pretend there is n't." Strether had, after posting his letter, the whole scene out; and it was a scene during which, coming and going, as befell, he kept his eye not least upon the daughter. He had his fine sense of the conviction Mrs. Pocock would take occasion to reaffirm — a conviction bearing, as he had from the first deeply divined it to bear, on Mr. Strether's essential inaptitude. She had looked him in his conscious eyes even before he sailed, and that she did n't believe *he* would find the woman had been written in her book. Had n't she at the best but a scant faith in his ability to find women? It was n't even as if he had found her mother — so much more, to her discrimination, had her mother performed the finding. Her mother had, in a case her private judgement of which remained educative of Mrs. Pocock's critical sense, found the man. The man owed his unchallenged state, in general, to the fact that Mrs. Newsome's discoveries were accepted at Woollett; but he knew in his bones, our friend did, how almost irresistibly Mrs. Pocock would now be moved to show what she thought of his own. Give *her* a free hand, would be the moral, and the woman would soon be found.

His impression of Miss Gostrey after her introduction to Chad was meanwhile an impression of a person almost unnaturally on her guard. He struck himself as at first unable to extract from her what he wished; though indeed *of* what he wished at this special juncture he would doubtless have contrived to make but a crude statement. It sifted and settled nothing to put to her, *tout bêtement*, as she often said, "Do you like him, eh?" — thanks to his feeling it actually the least of his needs to heap up the evidence in the young man's favour. He repeatedly knocked at her door to let her have it afresh that Chad's case — whatever else of minor interest it might yield — was first and foremost a miracle almost monstrous. It was the alteration of the entire man, and was so signal an instance that nothing else, for the intelligent observer, could — *could* it? — signify. "It's a plot," he declared — "there's more in it than meets the eye." He gave the rein to his fancy. "It's a plant!"

His fancy seemed to please her. "Whose then?"

"Well, the party responsible is, I suppose, the fate that waits for one, the dark doom that rides. What I mean is that with such elements one can't count. I've but my poor individual, my modest human means. It isn't playing the game to turn on the uncanny. All one's energy goes to facing it, to tracking it. One wants, confound it, don't you see?" he confessed with a queer face — "one wants to enjoy anything so rare. Call it then life" — he puzzled it out — "call it poor dear old life simply that springs the surprise. Nothing alters the fact that the surprise is paralysing, or at any rate engrossing — all, practically, hang it, that one sees, that one *can* see."

Her silences were never barren, nor even dull. "Is that what you've written home?"

He tossed it off. "Oh dear, yes!"

She had another pause while, across her carpets, he had another walk. "If you don't look out you'll have them straight over."

"Oh but I've said he'll go back."

"And *will* he?" Miss Gostrey asked.

The special tone of it made him, pulling up, look at her long. "What's that but just the question I've spent treasures of patience and ingenuity in giving *you*, by the sight of him — after everything had led up — every facility to answer? What is it but just the thing I came here to-day to get out of you? Will h ?"

"No — he won't," she said at last. "He's not free."

The air of it held him. "Then you've all the while known — ?"

"I've known nothing but what I've seen; and I wonder," she declared with some impatience, "that you did n't see as much. It was enough to be with him there —"

"In the box? Yes," he rather blankly urged.

"Well — to feel sure."

"Sure of what?"

BOOK FOURTH

She got up from her chair, at this, with a nearer approach than she had ever yet shown to dismay at his dimness. She even, fairly pausing for it, spoke with a shade of pity. "Guess!"

It was a shade, fairly, that brought a flush into his face; so that for a moment, as they waited together, their difference was between them. "You mean that just your hour with him told you so much of his story? Very good; I'm not such a fool, on my side, as that I don't understand you, or as that I did n't in some degree understand *him*. That he has done what he liked most is n't, among any of us, a matter the least in dispute. There's equally little question at this time of day of what it is he does like most. But I'm not talking," he reasonably explained, "of any mere wretch he may still pick up. I'm talking of some person who in his present situation may have held her own, may really have counted."

"That's exactly what *I* am!" said Miss Gostrey. But she as quickly made her point. "I thought you thought — or that they think at Woollett — that that's what mere wretches necessarily do. Mere wretches necessarily *don't!*" she declared with spirit. "There must, behind every appearance to the contrary, still be somebody — somebody who's not a mere wretch, since we accept the miracle. What else but such a somebody can such a miracle be?"

He took it in. "Because the fact itself *is* the woman?"

"*A* woman. Some woman or other. It's one of the things that *have* to be."

"But you mean then at least a good one."

"A good woman?" She threw up her arms with a laugh. "I should call her excellent!"

"Then why does he deny her?"

Miss Gostrey thought a moment. "Because she's too good to admit! Don't you see," she went on, "how she accounts for him?"

Strether clearly, more and more, did see; yet it made him also see other things. "But is n't what we want that he shall account for *her?*"

"Well, he does. What you have before you is his way. You must forgive him if it is n't quite outspoken. In Paris such debts are tacit."

Strether could imagine; but still —! "Even when the woman's good?"

Again she laughed out. "Yes, and even when the man is! There's always a caution in such cases," she more seriously explained — "for what it may seem to show. There's nothing that's taken as showing so much here as sudden unnatural goodness."

"Ah then you 're speaking now," Strether said, "of people who are *not* nice."

"I delight," she replied, "in your classifications. But do you want me," she asked, "to give you in the matter, on this ground, the wisest advice I'm capable of? Don't consider her, don't judge her at all in herself. Consider her and judge her only in Chad."

He had the courage at least of his companion's logic. "Because then I shall like her?" He almost looked, with his quick imagination, as if he already did, though seeing at once also the full extent of how little it would suit his book. "But is that what I came out for?"

BOOK FOURTH

She had to confess indeed that it was n't. But there was something else. "Don't make up your mind. There are all sorts of things. You have n't seen him all."

This on his side Strether recognised; but his acuteness none the less showed him the danger. "Yes, but if the more I see the better he seems?"

Well, she found something. "That may be — but his disavowal of her is n't, all the same, pure consideration. There's a hitch." She made it out. "It's the effort to sink her."

Strether winced at the image. "To 'sink' — ?"

"Well, I mean there's a struggle, and a part of it is just what he hides. Take time — that's the only way not to make some mistake that you'll regret. Then you'll see. He does really want to shake her off."

Our friend had by this time so got into the vision that he almost gasped. "After all she has done for him?"

Miss Gostrey gave him a look which broke the next moment into a wonderful smile. "He's not so good as you think!"

They remained with him, these words, promising him, in their character of warning, considerable help; but the support he tried to draw from them found itself on each renewal of contact with Chad defeated by something else. What could it be, this disconcerting force, he asked himself, but the sense, constantly renewed, that Chad *was* — quite in fact insisted on being — as good as he thought? It seemed somehow as if he could n't *but* be as good from the moment he was n't as bad. There was a succession of days at all events when contact with him — and in its immediate effect, as if it could produce no other — elbowed out of Strether's consciousness everything but itself. Little Bilham once more pervaded the scene, but little Bilham became even in a higher degree than he had originally been one of the numerous forms of the inclusive relation; a consequence promoted, to our friend's sense, by two or three incidents with which we have yet to make acquaintance. Waymarsh himself, for the occasion, was drawn into the eddy; it absolutely, though but temporarily, swallowed him down, and there were days when Strether seemed to bump against him as a sinking swimmer might brush a submarine object. The fathomless medium held them — Chad's manner was the fathomless medium; and our friend felt as if they passed each other, in their deep immersion, with the round impersonal eye of silent fish. It was practically produced between them that Waymarsh was giving him then his chance; and the shade of discomfort that Strether drew from the allowance resembled not a little the embarrassment he had known at school, as a boy, when members of his family had been present at exhibitions. He could perform before strangers, but relatives were fatal, and it was now as if, comparatively, Waymarsh were a relative. He seemed to hear him say "Strike up then!" and to enjoy a foretaste of conscientious domestic criticism. He *had* struck up, so far as he actually could; Chad knew by this time in profusion what he wanted; and what vulgar violence did his fellow pilgrim expect of him when he had really emptied his mind ? It went somehow to and fro that what poor

BOOK FOURTH

Waymarsh meant was "I told you so — that you'd lose your immortal soul!" but it was also fairly explicit that Strether had his own challenge and that, since they must go to the bottom of things, he wasted no more virtue in watching Chad than Chad wasted in watching him. His dip for duty's sake — where was it worse than Waymarsh's own? For *he* need n't have stopped resisting and refusing, need n't have parleyed, at that rate, with the foe.

The strolls over Paris to see something or call somewhere were accordingly inevitable and natural, and the late sessions in the wondrous troisième, the lovely home, when men dropped in and the picture composed more suggestively through the haze of tobacco, of music more or less good and of talk more or less polyglot, were on a principle not to be distinguished from that of the mornings and the afternoons. Nothing, Strether had to recognise as he leaned back and smoked, could well less resemble a scene of violence than even the liveliest of these occasions. They were occasions of discussion, none the less, and Strether had never in his life heard so many opinions on so many subjects. There were opinions at Woollett, but only on three or four. The differences were there to match; if they were doubtless deep, though few, they were quiet — they were, as might be said, almost as shy as if people had been ashamed of them. People showed little diffidence about such things, on the other hand, in the Boulevard Malesherbes, and were so far from being ashamed of them — or indeed of anything else — that they often seemed to have invented them to avert those agreements that destroy the taste of talk. No one had ever done that at Woollett, though Strether could remember times when he himself had been tempted to it without quite knowing why. He saw why at present — he had but wanted to promote intercourse.

These, however, were but parenthetic memories; and the turn taken by his affair on the whole was positively that if his nerves were on the stretch it was because he missed violence. When he asked himself if none would then, in connexion with it, ever come at all, he might almost have passed as wondering how to provoke it. It would be too absurd if such a vision as *that* should have to be invoked for relief; it was already marked enough as absurd that he should actually have begun with flutters and dignities on the score of a single accepted meal. What sort of a brute had he expected Chad to be, anyway ? — Strether had occasion to make the enquiry but was careful to make it in private. He could himself, comparatively recent as it was — it was truly but the fact of a few days since — focus his primal crudity; but he would on the approach of an observer, as if handling an illicit possession, have slipped the reminiscence out of sight. There were echoes of it still in Mrs. Newsome's letters, and there were moments when these echoes made him exclaim on her want of tact. He blushed of course, at once, still more for the explanation than for the ground of it : it came to him in time to save his manners that she could n't at the best become tactful as quickly as he. Her tact had to reckon with the Atlantic Ocean, the General Post-Office and the extravagant curve of the globe.

BOOK FOURTH

Chad had one day offered tea at the Boulevard Malesherbes to a chosen few, a group again including the unobscured Miss Barrace; and Strether had on coming out walked away with the acquaintance whom in his letters to Mrs. Newsome he always spoke of as the little artist-man. He had had full occasion to mention him as the other party, so oddly, to the only close personal alliance observation had as yet detected in Chad's existence. Little Bilham's way this afternoon was not Strether's, but he had none the less kindly come with him, and it was somehow a part of his kindness that as it had sadly begun to rain they suddenly found themselves seated for conversation at a café in which they had taken refuge. He had passed no more crowded hour in Chad's society than the one just ended; he had talked with Miss Barrace, who had reproached him with not having come to see her, and he had above all hit on a happy thought for causing Waymarsh's tension to relax. Something might possibly be extracted for the latter from the idea of his success with that lady, whose quick apprehension of what might amuse her had given Strether a free hand. What had she meant if not to ask whether she could n't help him with his splendid encumbrance, and might n't the sacred rage at any rate be kept a little in abeyance by thus creating for his comrade's mind even in a world of irrelevance the possibility of a relation? What was it but a relation to be regarded as so decorative and, in especial, on the strength of it, to be whirled away, amid flounces and feathers, in a coupé lined, by what Strether could make out, with dark blue brocade? He himself had never been whirled away — never at least in a coupé and behind a footman; he had driven with Miss Gostrey in cabs, with Mrs. Pocock, a few times, in an open buggy, with Mrs. Newsome in a four-seated cart and, occasionally up at the mountains, on a buckboard; but his friend's actual adventure transcended his personal experience. He now showed his companion soon enough indeed how inadequate, as a general monitor, this last queer quantity could once more feel itself.

"What game under the sun is he playing?" He signified the next moment that his allusion was not to the fat gentleman immersed in dominoes on whom his eyes had begun by resting, but to their host of the previous hour, as to whom, there on the velvet bench, with a final collapse of all consistency, he treated himself to the comfort of indiscretion. "Where do you see him come out?"

Little Bilham, in meditation, looked at him with a kindness almost paternal. "Don't you like it over here?"

Strether laughed out — for the tone was indeed droll; he let himself go. "What has that to do with it? The only thing I've any business to like is to feel that I'm moving him. That's why I ask you whether you believe I *am?* Is the creature" — and he did his best to show that he simply wished to ascertain — "honest?"

His companion looked responsible, but looked it through a small dim smile. "What creature do you mean?"

It was on this that they did have for a little a mute interchange. "Is it untrue that he's free? How then," Strether asked wondering, "does he arrange his life?"

"Is the creature you mean Chad himself?" little Bilham said.

Strether here, with a rising hope, just thought, "We must take one of them at a time." But his coherence lapsed. "*Is* there some woman? Of whom he's really afraid of course I mean — or who does with him what she likes."

"It's awfully charming of you," Bilham presently remarked, "not to have asked me that before."

"Oh I'm not fit for my job!"

The exclamation had escaped our friend, but it made little Bilham more deliberate. "Chad's a rare case!" he luminously observed. "He's awfully changed," he added.

"Then you see it too?"

"The way he has improved? Oh yes — I think every one must see it. But I'm not sure," said little Bilham, "that I did n't like him about as well in his other state."

"Then this *is* really a new state altogether?"

"Well," the young man after a moment returned, "I'm not sure he was really meant by nature to be quite so good. It's like the new edition of an old book that one has been fond of — revised and amended, brought up to date, but not quite the thing one knew and loved. However that may be at all events," he pursued, "I don't think, you know, that he's really playing, as you call it, any game. I believe he really wants to go back and take up a career. He's capable of one, you know, that will improve and enlarge him still more. He won't then," little Bilham continued to remark, "be my pleasant well-rubbed old-fashioned volume at all. But of course I 'm beastly immoral. I 'm afraid it would be a funny world altogether — a world with things the way I like them. I ought, I dare say, to go home and go into business myself. Only I 'd simply rather die — simply. And I 've not the least difficulty in making up my mind not to, and in knowing exactly why, and in defending my ground against all comers. All the same," he wound up, "I assure you I don't say a word against it — for himself, I mean — to Chad. I seem to see it as much the best thing for him. You see he 's not happy."

"*Do* I ?" — Strether stared. "I 've been supposing I see just the opposite — an extraordinary case of the equilibrium arrived at and assured."

"Oh there 's a lot behind it."

"Ah there you are!" Strether exclaimed. "That's just what I want to get at. You speak of your familiar volume altered out of recognition. Well, who's the editor ?"

Little Bilham looked before him a minute in silence. "He ought to get married. *That* would do it. And he wants to."

"Wants to marry her ?"

Again little Bilham waited, and, with a sense that he had information, Strether scarce knew what was coming. "He wants to be free. He is n't used, you see," the young man explained in his lucid way, "to being so good."

Strether hesitated. "Then I may take it from you that he *is* good ?"

BOOK FOURTH

His companion matched his pause, but making it up with a quiet fulness. "*Do* take it from me."

"Well then why is n't he free? He swears to me he is, but meanwhile does nothing — except of course that he's so kind to me — to prove it; and could n't really act much otherwise if he were n't. My question to you just now was exactly on this queer impression of his diplomacy: as if instead of really giving ground his line were to keep me on here and set me a bad example."

As the half-hour meanwhile had ebbed Strether paid his score, and the waiter was presently in the act of counting out change. Our friend pushed back to him a fraction of it, with which, after an emphatic recognition, the personage in question retreated. "You give too much," little Bilham permitted himself benevolently to observe.

"Oh I always give too much!" Strether helplessly sighed. "But you don't," he went on as if to get quickly away from the contemplation of that doom, "answer my question. Why is n't he free?"

Little Bilham had got up as if the transaction with the waiter had been a signal, and had already edged out between the table and the divan. The effect of this was that a minute later they had quitted the place, the gratified waiter alert again at the open door. Strether had found himself deferring to his companion's abruptness as to a hint that he should be answered as soon as they were more isolated. This happened when after a few steps in the outer air they had turned the next corner. There our friend had kept it up. "Why is n't he free if he's good?"

Little Bilham looked him full in the face. "Because it's a virtuous attachment."

This had settled the question so effectually for the time — that is for the next few days — that it had given Strether almost a new lease of life. It must be added however that, thanks to his constant habit of shaking the bottle in which life handed him the wine of experience, he presently found the taste of the lees rising as usual into his draught. His imagination had in other words already dealt with his young friend's assertion; of which it had made something that sufficiently came out on the very next occasion of his seeing Maria Gostrey. This occasion moreover had been determined promptly by a new circumstance — a circumstance he was the last man to leave her for a day in ignorance of. "When I said to him last night," he immediately began, "that without some definite word from him now that will enable me to speak to them over there of our sailing — or at least of mine, giving them some sort of date — my responsibility becomes uncomfortable and my situation awkward; when I said that to him what do you think was his reply?" And then as she this time gave it up: "Why that he has two particular friends, two ladies, mother and daughter, about to arrive in Paris — coming back from an absence; and that he wants me so furiously to meet them, know them and like them, that I shall oblige him by kindly not bringing our business to a crisis till he has had a chance to see them again himself. Is that," Strether enquired, "the way he's going to try to get off? These are the people," he explained, "that he must have gone down to see before I arrived.

BOOK FOURTH

They're the best friends he has in the world, and they
take more interest than any one else in what concerns
him. As I'm his next best he sees a thousand reasons
why we should comfortably meet. He has n't broached
the question sooner because their return was un-
certain — seemed in fact for the present impossible.
But he more than intimates that — if you can believe
it — their desire to make my acquaintance has had to
do with their surmounting difficulties."

"They're dying to see you?" Miss Gostrey asked.

"Dying. Of course," said Strether, "they're the
virtuous attachment." He had already told her about
that — had seen her the day after his talk with little
Bilham; and they had then threshed out together the
bearing of the revelation. She had helped him to put
into it the logic in which little Bilham had left it
slightly deficient. Strether had n't pressed him as to
the object of the preference so unexpectedly described;
feeling in the presence of it, with one of his irrepressible scruples, a delicacy from which he had in the quest
of the quite other article worked himself sufficiently
free. He had held off, as on a small principle of pride,
from permitting his young friend to mention a name;
wishing to make with this the great point that Chad's
virtuous attachments were none of his business. He
had wanted from the first not to think too much of his
dignity, but that was no reason for not allowing it any
little benefit that might turn up. He had often enough
wondered to what degree his interference might pass
for interested; so that there was no want of luxury in
letting it be seen whenever he could that he did n't
interfere. That had of course at the same time not

deprived him of the further luxury of much private astonishment; which however he had reduced to some order before communicating his knowledge. When he had done this at last it was with the remark that, surprised as Miss Gostrey might, like himself, at first be, she would probably agree with him on reflexion that such an account of the matter did after all fit the confirmed appearances. Nothing certainly, on all the indications, could have been a greater change for him than a virtuous attachment, and since they had been in search of the "word" as the French called it, of that change, little Bilham's announcement — though so long and so oddly delayed — would serve as well as another. She had assured Strether in fact after a pause that the more she thought of it the more it did serve; and yet her assurance had n't so weighed with him as that before they parted he had n't ventured to challenge her sincerity. Did n't she believe the attachment *was* virtuous ? — he had made sure of her again with the aid of that question. The tidings he brought her on this second occasion were moreover such as would help him to make surer still.

She showed at first none the less as only amused. "You say there are two ? An attachment to them both then would, I suppose, almost necessarily be innocent."

Our friend took the point, but he had his clue. "May n't he be still in the stage of not quite knowing which of them, mother or daughter, he likes best ?"

She gave it more thought. "Oh it must be the daughter — at his age."

BOOK FOURTH

"Possibly. Yet what do we know," Strether asked, "about hers? She may be old enough."

"Old enough for what?"

"Why to marry Chad. That may be, you know, what they want. And if Chad wants it too, and little Bilham wants it, and even *we*, at a pinch, could do with it — that is if she does n't prevent repatriation — why it may be plain sailing yet."

It was always the case for him in these counsels that each of his remarks, as it came, seemed to drop into a deeper well. He had at all events to wait a moment to hear the slight splash of this one. "I don't see why if Mr. Newsome wants to marry the young lady he has n't already done it or has n't been prepared with some statement to you about it. And if he both wants to marry her and is on good terms with them why is n't he 'free'?"

Strether, responsively, wondered indeed. "Perhaps the girl herself does n't like him."

"Then why does he speak of them to you as he does?"

Strether's mind echoed the question, but also again met it. "Perhaps it's with the mother he's on good terms."

"As against the daughter?"

"Well, if she's trying to persuade the daughter to consent to him, what could make him like the mother more? Only," Strether threw out, "why should n't the daughter consent to him?"

"Oh," said Miss Gostrey, "may n't it be that every one else is n't quite so struck with him as you?"

"Does n't regard him you mean as such an 'eligi-

183

ble' young man? *Is* that what I've come to?" he audibly and rather gravely sought to know. "However," he went on, "his marriage is what his mother most desires — that is if it will help. And ought n't *any* marriage to help? They must want him" — he had already worked it out — "to be better off. Almost any girl he may marry will have a direct interest in his taking up his chances. It won't suit *her* at least that he shall miss them."

Miss Gostrey cast about. "No — you reason well! But of course on the other hand there's always dear old Woollett itself."

"Oh yes," he mused — "there's always dear old Woollett itself."

She waited a moment. "The young lady may n't find herself able to swallow *that* quantity. She may think it's paying too much; she may weigh one thing against another."

Strether, ever restless in such debates, took a vague turn. "It will all depend on who she is. That of course — the proved ability to deal with dear old Woollett, since I'm sure she does deal with it — is what makes so strongly for Mamie."

"Mamie?"

He stopped short, at her tone, before her; then, though seeing that it represented not vagueness, but a momentary embarrassed fulness, let his exclamation come. "You surely have n't forgotten about Mamie!"

"No, I have n't forgotten about Mamie," she smiled. "There's no doubt whatever that there's ever so much to be said for her. Mamie's *my* girl!" she roundly declared.

BOOK FOURTH

Strether resumed for a minute his walk. "She's really perfectly lovely, you know. Far prettier than any girl I've seen over here yet."

"That's precisely on what I perhaps most build." And she mused a moment in her friend's way. "I should positively like to take her in hand!"

He humoured the fancy, though indeed finally to deprecate it. "Oh but don't, in your zeal, go over to her! I need you most and can't, you know, be left."

But she kept it up. "I wish they'd send her out to me!"

"If they knew you," he returned, "they would."

"Ah but don't they? — after all that, as I've understood you, you've told them about me?"

He had paused before her again, but he continued his course. "They *will* — before, as you say, I've done." Then he came out with the point he had wished after all most to make. "It seems to give away now his game. This is what he has been doing — keeping me along for. He has been waiting for them."

Miss Gostrey drew in her lips. "You see a good deal in it!"

"I doubt if I see as much as you. Do you pretend," he went on, "that you don't see — ?"

"Well, what?" — she pressed him as he paused.

"Why that there must be a lot between them — and that it has been going on from the first; even from before I came."

She took a minute to answer. "Who are they then — if it's so grave?"

"It may n't be grave — it may be gay. But at any rate it's marked. Only I don't know," Strether had to confess, "anything about them. Their name for instance was a thing that, after little Bilham's information, I found it a kind of refreshment not to feel obliged to follow up."

"Oh," she returned, "if you think you've got off —!"

Her laugh produced in him a momentary gloom. "I don't think I've got off. I only think I'm breathing for about five minutes. I dare say I *shall* have, at the best, still to get on." A look, over it all, passed between them, and the next minute he had come back to good humour. "I don't meanwhile take the smallest interest in their name."

"Nor in their nationality? — American, French, English, Polish?"

"I don't care the least little 'hang,'" he smiled, "for their nationality. It would be nice if they're Polish!" he almost immediately added.

"Very nice indeed." The transition kept up her spirits. "So you see you do care."

He did this contention a modified justice. "I think I should if they *were* Polish. Yes," he thought — "there might be joy in *that*."

"Let us then hope for it." But she came after this nearer to the question. "If the girl's of the right age of course the mother can't be. I mean for the virtuous attachment. If the girl's twenty — and she can't be less — the mother must be at least forty. So it puts the mother out. *She's* too old for him."

Strether, arrested again, considered and demurred.

186

BOOK FOURTH

"Do you think so? Do you think any one would be too old for him? *I'm* eighty, and I'm too young. But perhaps the girl," he continued, "*is n't* twenty. Perhaps she's only ten — but such a little dear that Chad finds himself counting her in as an attraction of the acquaintance. Perhaps she's only five. Perhaps the mother's but five-and-twenty — a charming young widow."

Miss Gostrey entertained the suggestion. "She *is* a widow then?"

"I have n't the least idea!" They once more, in spite of this vagueness, exchanged a look — a look that was perhaps the longest yet. It seemed in fact, the next thing, to require to explain itself; which it did as it could. "I only feel what I've told you — that he has some reason."

Miss Gostrey's imagination had taken its own flight. "Perhaps she's *not* a widow."

Strether seemed to accept the possibility with reserve. Still he accepted it. "Then that's why the attachment — if it's to her — is virtuous."

But she looked as if she scarce followed. "Why is it virtuous if — since she's free — there's nothing to impose on it any condition?"

He laughed at her question. "Oh I perhaps don't mean as virtuous as *that!* Your idea is that it can be virtuous — in any sense worthy of the name — only if she's *not* free? But what does it become then," he asked, "for *her?*"

"Ah that's another matter." He said nothing for a moment, and she soon went on. "I dare say you're right, at any rate, about Mr. Newsome's little plan.

He *has* been trying you — has been reporting on you to these friends."

Strether meanwhile had had time to think more. "Then where's his straightness?"

"Well, as we say, it's struggling up, breaking out, asserting itself as it can. We can be on the side, you see, of his straightness. We can help him. But he has made out," said Miss Gostrey, "that you'll do."

"Do for what?"

"Why, for *them* — for *ces dames*. He has watched you, studied you, liked you — and recognised that *they* must. It's a great compliment to you, my dear man; for I'm sure they're particular. You came out for a success, Well," she gaily declared, " you're having it!"

He took it from her with momentary patience and then turned abruptly away. It was always convenient to him that there were so many fine things in her room to look at. But the examination of two or three of them appeared soon to have determined a speech that had little to do with them. "You don't believe in it!"

"In what?"

"In the character of the attachment. In its innocence."

But she defended herself. "I don't pretend to know anything about it. Everything's possible. We must see."

"See?" he echoed with a groan. "Have n't we seen enough?"

"*I* have n't," she smiled.

"But do you suppose then little Bilham has lied?"

BOOK FOURTH

"You must find out."

It made him almost turn pale. "Find out any *more?*"

He had dropped on a sofa for dismay; but she seemed, as she stood over him, to have the last word. "Was n't what you came out for to find out *all?*"

BOOK FIFTH

I

THE Sunday of the next week was a wonderful day, and Chad Newsome had let his friend know in advance that he had provided for it. There had already been a question of his taking him to see the great Gloriani, who was at home on Sunday afternoons and at whose house, for the most part, fewer bores were to be met than elsewhere; but the project, through some accident, had not had instant effect, and now revived in happier conditions. Chad had made the point that the celebrated sculptor had a queer old garden, for which the weather — spring at last frank and fair — was propitious; and two or three of his other allusions had confirmed for Strether the expectation of something special. He had by this time, for all introductions and adventures, let himself recklessly go, cherishing the sense that whatever the young man showed him he was showing at least himself. He could have wished indeed, so far as this went, that Chad were less of a mere cicerone; for he was not without the impression — now that the vision of his game, his plan, his deep diplomacy, did recurrently assert itself — of his taking refuge from the realities of their intercourse in profusely dispensing, as our friend mentally phrased it, *panem et circenses*. Our friend continued to feel rather smothered in flowers, though he made in his other moments the almost angry inference that this was only because of his odious ascetic suspicion of any

form of beauty. He periodically assured himself —
for his reactions were sharp — that he should n't
reach the truth of anything till he had at least got
rid of that.

He had known beforehand that Madame de Vionnet and her daughter would probably be on view, an
intimation to that effect having constituted the only
reference again made by Chad to his good friends from
the south. The effect of Strether's talk about them
with Miss Gostrey had been quite to consecrate his
reluctance to pry; something in the very air of Chad's
silence — judged in the light of that talk — offered it
to him as a reserve he could markedly match. It
shrouded them about with he scarce knew what, a
consideration, a distinction; he was in presence at any
rate — so far as it placed him there — of ladies; and
the one thing that was definite for him was that they
themselves should be, to the extent of his responsibility, in presence of a gentleman. Was it because they
were very beautiful, very clever, or even very good —
was it for one of these reasons that Chad was, so to
speak, nursing his effect? Did he wish to spring them,
in the Woollett phrase, with a fuller force — to confound his critic, slight though as yet the criticism, with
some form of merit exquisitely incalculable? The
most the critic had at all events asked was whether
the persons in question were French; and that enquiry
had been but a proper comment on the sound of their
name. "Yes. That is no!" had been Chad's reply;
but he had immediately added that their English was
the most charming in the world, so that if Strether
were wanting an excuse for not getting on with them

he would n't in the least find one. Never in fact had Strether — in the mood into which the place had quickly launched him — felt, for himself, less the need of an excuse. Those he might have found would have been, at the worst, all for the others, the people before him, in whose liberty to be as they were he was aware that he positively rejoiced. His fellow guests were multiplying, and these things, their. liberty, their intensity, their variety, their conditions at large, were in fusion in the admirable medium of the scene.

The place itself was a great impression — a small pavilion, clear-faced and sequestered, an effect of polished parquet, of fine white panel and spare sallow gilt, of decoration delicate and rare, in the heart of the Faubourg Saint-Germain and on the edge of a cluster of gardens attached to old noble houses. Far back from streets and unsuspected by crowds, reached by a long passage and a quiet court, it was as striking to the unprepared mind, he immediately saw, as a treasure dug up; giving him too, more than anything yet, the note of the range of the immeasurable town and sweeping away, as by a last brave brush, his usual landmarks and terms. It was in the garden, a spacious cherished remnant, out of which a dozen persons had already passed, that Chad's host presently met them; while the tall bird-haunted trees, all of a twitter with the spring and the weather, and the high party-walls, on the other side of which grave *hôtels* stood off for privacy, spoke of survival, transmission, association, a strong indifferent persistent order. The day was so soft that the little party had practically adjourned to the open air, but the open air was in such conditions all a chamber of state. Strether had presently the sense of a great convent, a convent of missions, famous for he scarce knew what, a nursery of young priests, of scattered shade, of straight alleys and chapel-bells, that spread its mass in one quarter; he had the sense of names in the air, of ghosts at the windows, of signs and tokens, a whole range of expression, all about him, too thick for prompt discrimination.

This assault of images became for a moment, in the address of the distinguished sculptor, almost formidable: Gloriani showed him, in such perfect confidence, on Chad's introduction of him, a fine worn handsome face, a face that was like an open letter in a foreign tongue. With his genius in his eyes, his manners on his lips, his long career behind him and his honours and rewards all round, the great artist, in the course of a single sustained look and a few words of delight at receiving him, affected our friend as a dazzling prodigy of type. Strether had seen in museums — in the Luxembourg as well as, more reverently, later on, in the New York of the billionaires — the work of his hand; knowing too that after an earlier time in his native Rome he had migrated, in mid-career, to Paris, where, with a personal lustre almost violent, he shone in a constellation: all of which was more than enough to crown him, for his guest, with the light, with the romance, of glory. Strether, in contact with that element as he had never yet so intimately been, had the consciousness of opening to it, for the happy instant, all the windows of his mind, of letting this rather grey interior drink in for once the sun of a clime not marked in his old geography. He was to remember again repeatedly the medal-like Italian face, in which every line was an artist's own, in which time told only as tone and consecration; and he was to recall in especial, as the penetrating radiance, as the communication of the illustrious spirit itself, the manner in which, while they stood briefly, in welcome and response, face to face, he was held by the sculptor's eyes. He was n't soon to forget them, was to think of them, all unconscious, unintending, preoccupied though they were, as the source of the deepest intellectual sounding to which he had ever been exposed. He was in fact quite to cherish his vision of it, to play with it in idle hours; only speaking of it to no one and quite aware he could n't have spoken without appearing to talk nonsense. Was what it had told him or what it had asked him the greater of the mysteries? Was it the most special flare, unequalled, supreme, of the æsthetic torch, lighting that wondrous world for ever, or was it above all the long straight shaft sunk by a personal acuteness that life had seasoned to steel? Nothing on earth could have been stranger and no one doubtless more surprised than the artist himself, but it was for all the world to Strether just then as if in the matter of his accepted duty he had positively been on trial. The deep human expertness in Gloriani's charming smile — oh the terrible life behind it! — was flashed upon him as a test of his stuff.

Chad meanwhile, after having easily named his companion, had still more easily turned away and was already greeting other persons present. He was as easy, clever Chad, with the great artist as with his obscure compatriot, and as easy with every one else as with either: this fell into its place for Strether and made almost a new light, giving him, as a concatenation, something more he could enjoy. He liked Gloriani, but should never see him again; of that he was sufficiently sure. Chad accordingly, who was wonderful with both of them, was a kind of link for hopeless fancy, an implication of possibilities — oh if everything had been different! Strether noted at all events that he was thus on terms with illustrious spirits, and also that — yes, distinctly — he had n't in the least swaggered about it. Our friend had n't come there only for this figure of Abel Newsome's son, but that presence threatened to affect the observant mind as positively central. Gloriani indeed, remembering something and excusing himself, pursued Chad to speak to him, and Strether was left musing on many things. One of them was the question of whether, since he had been tested, he had passed. Did the artist drop him from having made out that he would n't do? He really felt just to-day that he might do better than usual. Had n't he done well enough, so far as that went, in being exactly so dazzled? and in not having too, as he almost believed, wholly hidden from his host that he felt the latter's plummet? Suddenly, across the garden, he saw little Bilham approach, and it was a part of the fit that was on him that as their eyes met he guessed also *his* knowledge. If he had said to him on the instant what was uppermost he would have said: "*Have* I passed? — for of course I know one has to pass here." Little Bilham would have reassured him, have told him that he exaggerated, and have adduced happily enough the argument of little Bilham's own very presence; which, in truth, he could see, was as easy a one as Gloriani's own or as Chad's. He himself would perhaps then after a while cease to be frightened, would get the point of view for some of the faces — types tremendously alien, alien to Woollett — that he had already begun to take in. Who were they all, the dispersed groups and couples, the ladies even more unlike those of Woollett than the gentlemen ? — this was the enquiry that, when his young friend had greeted him, he did find himself making.

"Oh they're every one — all sorts and sizes; of course I mean within limits, though limits down perhaps rather more than limits up. There are always artists — he's beautiful and inimitable to the *cher confrère;* and then *gros bonnets* of many kinds — ambassadors, cabinet ministers, bankers, generals, what do I know ? even Jews. Above all always some awfully nice women — and not too many; sometimes an actress, an artist, a great performer — but only when they're not monsters; and in particular the right *femmes du monde*. You can fancy his history on that side — I believe it's fabulous: they *never* give him up. Yet he keeps them down: no one knows how he manages; it's too beautiful and bland. Never too many — and a mighty good thing too; just a perfect choice. But there are not in any way many bores; it has always been so; he has some secret. It's extraordinary. And you don't find it out. He's the same to every one. He doesn't ask questions."

"Ah does n't he?" Strether laughed.

Bilham met it with all his candour. "How then should *I* be here?"

"Oh for what you tell me. You're part of the perfect choice."

Well, the young man took in the scene. "It seems rather good to-day."

Strether followed the direction of his eyes. "Are they all, this time, *femmes du monde?*"

Little Bilham showed his competence. "Pretty well."

This was a category our friend had a feeling for; a light, romantic and mysterious, on the feminine element, in which he enjoyed for a little watching it. "Are there any Poles?"

His companion considered. "I think I make out a ' Portuguee.' But I've seen Turks."

Strether wondered, desiring justice. "They seem — all the women — very harmonious."

"Oh in closer quarters they come out!" And then, while Strether was aware of fearing closer quarters, though giving himself again to the harmonies, "Well," little Bilham went on, "it *is* at the worst rather good, you know. If you like it, you feel it, this way, that shows you're not in the least out. But you always know things," he handsomely added, "immediately."

Strether liked it and felt it only too much; so "I say, don't lay traps for me!" he rather helplessly murmured.

"Well," his companion returned, "he's wonderfully kind to *us*."

"To us Americans you mean?"

BOOK FIFTH

"Oh no — he does n't know anything about *that*. That's half the battle here — that you can never hear politics. We don't talk them. I mean to poor young wretches of all sorts. And yet it's always as charming as this; it's as if, by something in the air, our squalor did n't show. It puts us all back — into the last century."

"I'm afraid," Strether said, amused, "that it puts me rather forward: oh ever so far!"

"Into the next? But is n't that only," little Bilham asked, "because you're really of the century before?"

"The century before the last? Thank you!" Strether laughed. "If I ask you about some of the ladies it can't be then that I may hope, as such a specimen of the rococo, to please them."

"On the contrary they adore — we all adore here — the rococo, and where is there a better setting for it than the whole thing, the pavilion and the garden, together? There are lots of people with collections," little Bilham smiled as he glanced round. "You'll be secured!"

It made Strether for a moment give himself again to contemplation. There were faces he scarce knew what to make of. Were they charming or were they only strange? He might n't talk politics, yet he suspected a Pole or two. The upshot was the question at the back of his head from the moment his friend had joined him. "Have Madame de Vionnet and her daughter arrived?"

"I have n't seen them yet, but Miss Gostrey has come. She's in the pavilion looking at objects. One can see *she's* a collector," little Bilham added without offence.

"Oh yes, she's a collector, and I knew she was to come. Is Madame de Vionnet a collector?" Strether went on.

"Rather, I believe; almost celebrated." The young man met, on it, a little, his friend's eyes. "I happen to know — from Chad, whom I saw last night — that they've come back; but only yesterday. He was n't sure — up to the last. This, accordingly," little Bilham went on, "will be — if they *are* here — their first appearance after their return."

Strether, very quickly, turned these things over. "Chad told you last night? To me, on our way here, he said nothing about it."

"But did you ask him?"

Strether did him the justice. "I dare say not."

"Well," said little Bilham, "you're not a person to whom it's easy to tell things you don't want to know. Though it *is* easy, I admit — it's quite beautiful," he benevolently added, "when you do want to."

Strether looked at him with an indulgence that matched his intelligence. "Is that the deep reasoning on which — about these ladies — you've been yourself so silent?"

Little Bilham considered the depth of his reasoning. "I have n't been silent. I spoke of them to you the other day, the day we sat together after Chad's tea-party."

Strether came round to it. "They then are the virtuous attachment?"

"I can only tell you that it's what they pass for.

But is n't that enough ? What more than a vain appearance does the wisest of us know ? I commend you," the young man declared with a pleasant emphasis, "the vain appearance."

Strether looked more widely round, and what he saw, from face to face, deepened the effect of his young friend's words. "Is it so good ?"

"Magnificent."

Strether had a pause. "The husband 's dead ?"

"Dear no. Alive."

"Oh!" said Strether. After which, as his companion laughed: "How then can it be so good ?"

"You 'll see for yourself. One does see."

"Chad 's in love with the daughter ?"

"That 's what I mean."

Strether wondered. "Then where 's the difficulty ?"

"Why, are n't you and I — with our grander bolder ideas ?"

"Oh mine — !" Strether said rather strangely. But then as if to attenuate: "You mean they won't hear of Woollett ?"

Little Bilham smiled. "Is n't that just what you must see about ?"

It had brought them, as she caught the last words, into relation with Miss Barrace, whom Strether had already observed — as he had never before seen a lady at a party — moving about alone. Coming within sound of them she had already spoken, and she took again, through her long-handled glass, all her amused and amusing possession. "How much, poor Mr. Strether, you seem to have to see about! But you can't say," she gaily declared, "that I don't do what

I can to help you. Mr. Waymarsh is placed. I've left him in the house with Miss Gostrey."

"The way," little Bilham exclaimed, "Mr. Strether gets the ladies to work for him! He's just preparing to draw in another; to pounce — don't you see him? — on Madame de Vionnet."

"Madame de Vionnet? Oh, oh, oh!" Miss Barrace cried in a wonderful crescendo. There was more in it, our friend made out, than met the ear. Was it after all a joke that he should be serious about anything? He envied Miss Barrace at any rate her power of not being. She seemed, with little cries and protests and quick recognitions, movements like the darts of some fine high-feathered free-pecking bird, to stand before life as before some full shop-window. You could fairly hear, as she selected and pointed, the tap of her tortoise-shell against the glass. "It's certain that we do need seeing about; only I'm glad it's not I who have to do it. One does, no doubt, begin that way; then suddenly one finds that one has given it up. It's too much, it's too difficult. You're wonderful, you people," she continued to Strether, "for not feeling those things — by which I mean impossibilities. You never feel them. You face them with a fortitude that makes it a lesson to watch you."

"Ah but" — little Bilham put it with discouragement — "what do we achieve after all? We see about you and report — when we even go so far as reporting. But nothing's done."

"Oh you, Mr. Bilham," she replied as with an impatient rap on the glass, "you're not worth sixpence! You come over to convert the savages — for I know you verily did, I remember you — and the savages simply convert *you*."

"Not even!" the young man woefully confessed: "they have n't gone through that form. They 've simply — the cannibals! — eaten me; converted me if you like, but converted me into food. I 'm but the bleached bones of a Christian."

"Well then there we are! Only" — and Miss Barrace appealed again to Strether — "don't let it discourage you. You 'll break down soon enough, but you 'll meanwhile have had your moments. *Il faut en avoir.* I always like to see you while you last. And I 'll tell you who *will* last."

"Waymarsh?" — he had already taken her up.

She laughed out as at the alarm of it. "He 'll resist even Miss Gostrey: so grand is it not to understand. He 's wonderful."

"He is indeed," Strether conceded. "He would n't tell me of this affair — only said he had an engagement; but with such a gloom, you must let me insist, as if it had been an engagement to be hanged. Then silently and secretly he turns up here with you. Do you call *that* 'lasting'?"

"Oh I hope it 's lasting!" Miss Barrace said. "But he only, at the best, bears with me. He does n't understand — not one little scrap. He 's delightful. He 's wonderful," she repeated.

"Michelangelesque!" — little Bilham completed her meaning. "He *is* a success. Moses, on the ceiling, brought down to the floor; overwhelming, colossal, but somehow portable."

"Certainly, if you mean by portable," she returned,

"looking so well in one's carriage. He's too funny beside me in his corner; he looks like somebody, somebody foreign and famous, *en exil;* so that people wonder — it's very amusing — whom I'm taking about. I show him Paris, show him everything, and he never turns a hair. He's like the Indian chief one reads about, who, when he comes up to Washington to see the Great Father, stands wrapt in his blanket and gives no sign. *I* might be the Great Father — from the way he takes everything." She was delighted at this hit of her identity with that personage — it fitted so her character; she declared it was the title she meant henceforth to adopt. "And the way he sits, too, in the corner of my room, only looking at my visitors very hard and as if he wanted to start something! They wonder what he does want to start. But he's wonderful," Miss Barrace once more insisted. "He has never started anything yet."

It presented him none the less, in truth, to her actual friends, who looked at each other in intelligence, with frank amusement on Bilham's part and a shade of sadness on Strether's. Strether's sadness sprang — for the image had its grandeur — from his thinking how little he himself was wrapt in his blanket, how little, in marble halls, all too oblivious of the Great Father, he resembled a really majestic aboriginal. But he had also another reflexion. "You've all of you here so much visual sense that you've somehow all 'run' to it. There are moments when it strikes one that you have n't any other."

"Any moral," little Bilham explained, watching

serenely, across the garden, the several *femmes du monde*. "But Miss Barrace has a moral distinction," he kindly continued; speaking as if for Strether's benefit not less than for her own.

"*Have* you?" Strether, scarce knowing what he was about, asked of her almost eagerly.

"Oh not a distinction" — she was mightily amused at his tone — "Mr. Bilham's too good. But I think I may say a sufficiency. Yes, a sufficiency. Have you supposed strange things of me?" — and she fixed him again, through all her tortoise-shell, with the droll interest of it. "You *are* all indeed wonderful. I should awfully disappoint you. I do take my stand on my sufficiency. But I know, I confess," she went on, "strange people. I don't know how it happens; I don't do it on purpose; it seems to be my doom — as if I were always one of their habits: it's wonderful! I dare say moreover," she pursued with an interested gravity, "that I do, that we all do here, run too much to mere eye. But how can it be helped? We're all looking at each other — and in the light of Paris one sees what things resemble. That's what the light of Paris seems always to show. It's the fault of the light of Paris — dear old light!"

"Dear old Paris!" little Bilham echoed.

"Everything, every one shows," Miss Barrace went on.

"But for what they really are?" Strether asked.

"Oh I like your Boston 'reallys'! But sometimes — yes."

"Dear old Paris then!" Strether resignedly sighed while for a moment they looked at each other. Then he broke out: "Does Madame de Vionnet do that? I mean really show for what she is?"

Her answer was prompt. "She's charming. She's perfect."

"Then why did you a minute ago say 'Oh, oh, oh!' at her name?"

She easily remembered. "Why just because —! She's wonderful."

"Ah she too?" — Strether had almost a groan.

But Miss Barrace had meanwhile perceived relief. "Why not put your question straight to the person who can answer it best?"

"No," said little Bilham; "don't put any question; wait, rather — it will be much more fun — to judge for yourself. He has come to take you to her."

II

On which Strether saw that Chad was again at hand, and he afterwards scarce knew, absurd as it may seem, what had then quickly occurred. The moment concerned him, he felt, more deeply than he could have explained, and he had a subsequent passage of speculation as to whether, on walking off with Chad, he had n't looked either pale or red. The only thing he was clear about was that, luckily, nothing indiscreet had in fact been said, and that Chad himself was more than ever, in Miss Barrace's great sense, wonderful. It was one of the connexions — though really why it should be, after all, was none so apparent — in which the whole change in him came out as most striking. Strether recalled as they approached the house that he had impressed him that first night as knowing how to enter a box. Well, he impressed him scarce less now as knowing how to make a presentation. It did something for Strether's own quality — marked it as estimated; so that our poor friend, conscious and passive, really seemed to feel himself quite handed over and delivered; absolutely, as he would have said, made a present of, given away. As they reached the house a young woman, about to come forth, appeared, unaccompanied, on the steps; at the exchange with whom of a word on Chad's part Strether immediately perceived that, obligingly, kindly, she was there to meet them. Chad had left her in the house, but she had afterwards come halfway and then the next moment had joined them in the garden. Her air of youth, for Strether, was at first almost disconcerting, while his second impression was, not less sharply, a degree of relief at there not having just been, with the others, any freedom used about her. It was upon him at a touch that she was no subject for that, and meanwhile, on Chad's introducing him, she had spoken to him, very simply and gently, in an English clearly of the easiest to her, yet unlike any other he had ever heard. It was n't as if she tried; nothing, he could see after they had been a few minutes together, was as if she tried; but her speech, charming correct and odd, was like a precaution against her passing for a Pole. There were precautions, he seemed indeed to see, only when there were really dangers.

Later on he was to feel many more of them, but by that time he was to feel other things besides. She was dressed in black, but in black that struck him as light and transparent; she was exceedingly fair, and, though she was as markedly slim, her face had a roundness, with eyes far apart and a little strange. Her smile was natural and dim; her hat not extravagant; he had only perhaps a sense of the clink, beneath her fine black sleeves, of more gold bracelets and bangles than he had ever seen a lady wear. Chad was excellently free and light about their encounter; it was one of the occasions on which Strether most wished he himself might have arrived at such ease and such humour: "Here you are then, face to face at last; you're made for each other — *vous allez voir;* and I bless your union." It was indeed, after he had gone off, as if he had been partly serious too. This latter motion had been determined by an enquiry from him about "Jeanne"; to which her mother had replied that she was probably still in the house with Miss Gostrey, to whom she had lately committed her. "Ah but you know," the young man had rejoined, "he must see her"; with which, while Strether pricked up his ears, he had started as if to bring her, leaving the other objects of his interest together. Strether wondered to find Miss Gostrey already involved, feeling that he missed a link; but feeling also, with small delay, how much he should like to talk with her of Madame de Vionnet on this basis of evidence.

The evidence as yet in truth was meagre; which, for that matter, was perhaps a little why his expectation had had a drop. There was somehow not quite a wealth in her; and a wealth was all that, in his simplicity, he had definitely prefigured. Still, it was too much to be sure already that there was but a poverty. They moved away from the house, and, with eyes on a bench at some distance, he proposed that they should sit down. "I've heard a great deal about you," she said as they went; but he had an answer to it that made her stop short. "Well, about *you*, Madame de Vionnet, I've heard, I'm bound to say, almost nothing"—those struck him as the only words he himself could utter with any lucidity; conscious as he was, and as with more reason, of the determination to be in respect to the rest of his business perfectly plain and go perfectly straight. It hadn't at any rate been in the least his idea to spy on Chad's proper freedom. It was possibly, however, at this very instant and under the impression of Madame de Vionnet's pause, that going straight began to announce itself as a matter for care. She had only after all to smile at him ever so gently in order to make him ask himself if he were n't already going crooked. It might be going crooked to find it of a sudden just only clear that she intended very definitely to be what he would have called nice to him. This was what passed between them while, for another instant, they stood still; he could n't at least remember afterwards what else it might have been. The thing indeed really unmistakeable was its rolling over him as a wave that he had been, in conditions incalculable and unimaginable, a subject of discussion. He had been, on some ground that concerned her, answered for; which gave her an advantage he should never be able to match.

"Has n't Miss Gostrey," she asked, "said a good word for me?"

What had struck him first was the way he was bracketed with that lady; and he wondered what account Chad would have given of their acquaintance. Something not as yet traceable, at all events, had obviously happened. "I did n't even know of her knowing you."

"Well, now she'll tell you all. I'm so glad you're in relation with her."

This was one of the things — the "all" Miss Gostrey would now tell him — that, with every deference to present preoccupation, was uppermost for Strether after they had taken their seat. One of the others was, at the end of five minutes, that she — oh incontestably, yes — *differed* less; differed, that is, scarcely at all — well, superficially speaking, from Mrs. Newsome or even from Mrs. Pocock. She was ever so much younger than the one and not so young as the other; but what *was* there in her, if anything, that would have made it impossible he should meet her at Woollett? And wherein was her talk during their moments on the bench together not the same as would have been found adequate for a Woollett garden-party? — unless perhaps truly in not being quite so bright. She observed to him that Mr. Newsome had, to her knowledge, taken extraordinary pleasure in his visit; but there was no good lady at Woollett who would n't have been at least up to that. Was there in Chad, by chance, after all, deep down, a principle of aboriginal loyalty that had made him, for sentimental ends, attach himself to elements, happily encountered, that would remind him most of the old air and the old soil? Why accordingly be in a flutter — Strether could even put it that way — about this unfamiliar phenomenon of the *femme du monde?* On these terms Mrs. Newsome herself was as much of one. Little Bilham verily had testified that they came out, the ladies of the type, in close quarters; but it was just in these quarters — now comparatively close — that he felt Madame de Vionnet's common humanity. She did come out, and certainly to his relief, but she came out as the usual thing. There might be motives behind, but so could there often be even at Woollett. The only thing was that if she showed him she wished to like him — as the motives behind might conceivably prompt — it would possibly have been more thrilling for him that she should have shown as more

vividly alien. Ah she was neither Turk nor Pole!—
which would be indeed flat once more for Mrs. Newsome and Mrs. Pocock. A lady and two gentlemen
had meanwhile, however, approached their bench,
and this accident stayed for the time further developments.

They presently addressed his companion, the brilliant strangers; she rose to speak to them, and Strether
noted how the escorted lady, though mature and by
no means beautiful, had more of the bold high look,
the range of expensive reference, that he had, as
might have been said, made his plans for. Madame
de Vionnet greeted her as "Duchesse" and was
greeted in turn, while talk started in French, as "Ma
toute-belle"; little facts that had their due, their vivid
interest for Strether. Madame de Vionnet did n't,
none the less, introduce him — a note he was conscious of as false to the Woollett scale and the Woollett humanity; though it did n't prevent the Duchess,
who struck him as confident and free, very much
what he had obscurely supposed duchesses, from looking at him as straight and as hard — for it *was* hard
— as if she would have liked, all the same, to know
him. "Oh yes, my dear, it's all right, it's *me;* and
who are *you*, with your interesting wrinkles and your
most effective (is it the handsomest, is it the ugliest?)
of noses?" — some such loose handful of bright
flowers she seemed, fragrantly enough, to fling at him.
Strether almost wondered — at such a pace was he
going — if some divination of the influence of either
party were what determined Madame de Vionnet's
abstention. One of the gentlemen, in any case, suc-

ceeded in placing himself in close relation with our
friend's companion; a gentleman rather stout and
importantly short, in a hat with a wonderful wide
curl to its brim and a frock coat buttoned with an
effect of superlative decision. His French had quickly
turned to equal English, and it occurred to Strether
that he might well be one of the ambassadors. His
design was evidently to assert a claim to Madame de
Vionnet's undivided countenance, and he made it
good in the course of a minute — led her away with a
trick of three words; a trick played with a social art of
which Strether, looking after them as the four, whose
backs were now all turned, moved off, felt himself no
master.

He sank again upon his bench and, while his eyes
followed the party, reflected, as he had done before, on
Chad's strange communities. He sat there alone for
five minutes, with plenty to think of; above all with
his sense of having suddenly been dropped by a
charming woman overlaid now by other impressions
and in fact quite cleared and indifferent. He had n't
yet had so quiet a surrender; he did n't in the least
care if nobody spoke to him more. He might have
been, by his attitude, in for something of a march so
broad that the want of ceremony with which he had
just been used could fall into its place as but a minor
incident of the procession. Besides, there would be
incidents enough, as he felt when this term of contemplation was closed by the reappearance of little Bilham, who stood before him a moment with a suggestive "Well?" in which he saw himself reflected as
disorganised, as possibly floored. He replied with a

"Well!" intended to show that he was n't floored in the least. No indeed; he gave it out, as the young man sat down beside him, that if, at the worst, he had been overturned at all, he had been overturned into the upper air, the sublimer element with which he had an affinity and in which he might be trusted a while to float. It was n't a descent to earth to say after an instant and in sustained response to the reference: "You're quite sure her husband's living?"

"Oh dear, yes."

"Ah then—!"

"Ah then what?"

Strether had after all to think. "Well, I'm sorry for them." But it did n't for the moment matter more than that. He assured his young friend he was quite content. They would n't stir; were all right as they were. He did n't want to be introduced; had been introduced already about as far as he could go. He had seen moreover an immensity; liked Gloriani, who, as Miss Barrace kept saying, was wonderful; had made out, he was sure, the half-dozen other men who were distinguished, the artists, the critics and oh the great dramatist—*him* it was easy to spot; but wanted—no, thanks, really—to talk with none of them; having nothing at all to say and finding it would do beautifully as it was; do beautifully because what it was—well, was just simply too late. And when after this little Bilham, submissive and responsive, but with an eye to the consolation nearest, easily threw off some "Better late than never!" all he got in return for it was a sharp "Better early than late!" This note indeed the next thing overflowed for Strether into a quiet

216

stream of demonstration that as soon as he had let himself go he felt as the real relief. It had consciously gathered to a head, but the reservoir had filled sooner than he knew, and his companion's touch was to make the waters spread. There were some things that had to come in time if they were to come at all. If they did n't come in time they were lost for ever. It was the general sense of them that had overwhelmed him with its long slow rush.

"It's not too late for *you*, on any side, and you don't strike me as in danger of missing the train; besides which people can be in general pretty well trusted, of course — with the clock of their freedom ticking as loud as it seems to do here — to keep an eye on the fleeting hour. All the same don't forget that you're young — blessedly young; be glad of it on the contrary and live up to it. Live all you can; it's a mistake not to. It does n't so much matter what you do in particular, so long as you have your life. If you have n't had that what *have* you had? This place and these impressions — mild as you may find them to wind a man up so; all my impressions of Chad and of people I've seen at *his* place — well, have had their abundant message for me, have just dropped *that* into my mind. I see it now. I have n't done so enough before — and now I'm old; too old at any rate for what I see. Oh I *do* see, at least; and more than you'd believe or I can express. It's too late. And it's as if the train had fairly waited at the station for me without my having had the gumption to know it was there. Now I hear its faint receding whistle miles and miles down the line. What one loses one loses; make no mistake about that. The affair— I mean the affair of life— could n't, no doubt, have been different for me; for it's at the best a tin mould, either fluted and embossed, with ornamental excrescences, or else smooth and dreadfully plain, into which, a helpless jelly, one's consciousness is poured— so that one 'takes' the form, as the great cook says, and is more or less compactly held by it: one lives in fine as one can. Still, one has the illusion of freedom; therefore don't be, like me, without the memory of that illusion. I was either, at the right time, too stupid or too intelligent to have it; I don't quite know which. Of course at present I'm a case of reaction against the mistake; and the voice of reaction should, no doubt, always be taken with an allowance. But that does n't affect the point that the right time is now yours. The right time is *any* time that one is still so lucky as to have. You've plenty; that's the great thing; you're, as I say, damn you, so happily and hatefully young. Don't at any rate miss things out of stupidity. Of course I don't take you for a fool, or I should n't be addressing you thus awfully. Do what you like so long as you don't make *my* mistake. For it was a mistake. Live!" . . . Slowly and sociably, with full pauses and straight dashes, Strether had so delivered himself; holding little Bilham from step to step deeply and gravely attentive. The end of all was that the young man had turned quite solemn, and that this was a contradiction of the innocent gaiety the speaker had wished to promote. He watched for a moment the consequence of his words, and then, laying a hand on his listener's knee and as if to end with the proper joke: "And now for the eye I shall keep on you!"

"Oh but I don't know that I want to be, at your age, too different from you!"

"Ah prepare while you're about it," said Strether, "to be more amusing."

Little Bilham continued to think, but at last had a smile. "Well, you *are* amusing — to *me*."

"*Impayable*, as you say, no doubt. But what am I to myself?" Strether had risen with this, giving his attention now to an encounter that, in the middle of the garden, was in the act of taking place between their host and the lady at whose side Madame de Vionnet had quitted him. This lady, who appeared within a few minutes to have left her friends, awaited Gloriani's eager approach with words on her lips that Strether could n't catch, but of which her interesting witty face seemed to give him the echo. He was sure she was prompt and fine, but also that she had met her match, and he liked — in the light of what he was quite sure was the Duchess's latent insolence — the good humour with which the great artist asserted equal resources. Were they, this pair, of the "great world"? — and was he himself, for the moment and thus related to them by his observation, *in* it? Then there was something in the great world covertly tiger-ish, which came to him across the lawn and in the charming air as a waft from the jungle. Yet it made him admire most of the two, made him envy, the glossy male tiger, magnificently marked. These absurdities of the stirred sense, fruits of suggestion ripening on the instant, were all reflected in his next words to little Bilham. "I know — if we talk of that — whom *I* should enjoy being like!"

Little Bilham followed his eyes; but then as with a shade of knowing surprise: "Gloriani?"

Our friend had in fact already hesitated, though not on the hint of his companion's doubt, in which there were depths of critical reserve. He had just made out, in the now full picture, something and somebody else; another impression had been superimposed. A young girl in a white dress and a softly plumed white hat had suddenly come into view, and what was presently clear was that her course was toward them. What was clearer still was that the handsome young man at her side was Chad Newsome, and what was clearest of all was that she was therefore Mademoiselle de Vionnet, that she was unmistakeably pretty — bright gentle shy happy wonderful — and that Chad now, with a consummate calculation of effect, was about to present her to his old friend's vision. What was clearest of all indeed was something much more than this, something at the single stroke of which — and was n't it simply juxtaposition? — all vagueness vanished. It was the click of a spring — he saw the truth. He had by this time also met Chad's look; there was more of it in that; and the truth, accordingly, so far as Bilham's enquiry was concerned, had thrust in the answer. "Oh Chad!" — it was that rare youth he should have enjoyed being "like." The virtuous attachment would be all there before him; the virtuous attachment would be in the very act of appeal for his blessing; Jeanne de Vionnet, this charming creature, would be — exquisitely, intensely

BOOK FIFTH

now — the object of it. Chad brought her straight up to him, and Chad was, oh yes, at this moment — for the glory of Woollett or whatever — better still even than Gloriani. He had plucked this blossom; he had kept it over-night in water; and at last as he held it up to wonder he did enjoy his effect. That was why Strether had felt at first the breath of calculation — and why moreover, as he now knew, his look at the girl would be, for the young man, a sign of the latter's success. What young man had ever paraded about that way, without a reason, a maiden in her flower? And there was nothing in his reason at present obscure. Her type sufficiently told of it — they would n't, they could n't, want her to go to Woollett. Poor Woollett, and what it might miss! — though brave Chad indeed too, and what it might gain! Brave Chad however had just excellently spoken. "This is a good little friend of mine who knows all about you and has moreover a message for you. And this, my dear" — he had turned to the child herself — "is the best man in the world, who has it in his power to do a great deal for us and whom I want you to like and revere as nearly as possible as much as I do."

She stood there quite pink, a little frightened, prettier and prettier and not a bit like her mother. There was in this last particular no resemblance but that of youth to youth; and here was in fact suddenly Strether's sharpest impression. It went wondering, dazed, embarrassed, back to the woman he had just been talking with; it was a revelation in the light of which he already saw she would become more interesting. So slim and fresh and fair, she had yet put forth this perfection; so that for really believing it of her, for seeing her to any such developed degree as a mother, comparison would be urgent. Well, what was it now but fairly thrust upon him? "Mamma wishes me to tell you before we go," the girl said, "that she hopes very much you'll come to see us very soon. She has something important to say to you."

"She quite reproaches herself," Chad helpfully explained: "you were interesting her so much when she accidentally suffered you to be interrupted."

"Ah don't mention it!" Strether murmured, looking kindly from one to the other and wondering at many things.

"And I'm to ask you for myself," Jeanne continued with her hands clasped together as if in some small learnt prayer — "I'm to ask you for myself if you won't positively come."

"Leave it to me, dear — I'll take care of it!" Chad genially declared in answer to this, while Strether himself almost held his breath. What was in the girl was indeed too soft, too unknown for direct dealing; so that one could only gaze at it as at a picture, quite staying one's own hand. But with Chad he was now on ground — Chad he could meet; so pleasant a confidence in that and in everything did the young man freely exhale. There was the whole of a story in his tone to his companion, and he spoke indeed as if already of the family. It made Strether guess the more quickly what it might be about which Madame de Vionnet was so urgent. Having seen him then she had found him easy; she wished to have it out with him that some way for the young people must be discovered, some way that would not impose as a condition the transplantation of her daughter. He already saw himself discussing with this lady the attractions of Woollett as a residence for Chad's companion. Was that youth going now to trust her with the affair — so that it would be after all with one of his "lady-friends" that his mother's missionary should be condemned to deal? It was quite as if for an instant the two men looked at each other on this question. But there was no mistaking at last Chad's pride in the display of such a connexion. This was what had made him so carry himself while, three minutes before, he was bringing it into view; what had caused his friend, first catching sight of him, to be so struck with his air. It was, in a word, just when he thus finally felt Chad putting things straight off on him that he envied him, as he had mentioned to little Bilham, most. The whole exhibition however was but a matter of three or four minutes, and the author of it had soon explained that, as Madame de Vionnet was immediately going "on," this could be for Jeanne but a snatch. They would all meet again soon, and Strether was meanwhile to stay and amuse himself — "I'll pick you up again in plenty of time." He took the girl off as he had brought her, and Strether, with the faint sweet foreignness of her "Au revoir, monsieur!" in his ears as a note almost unprecedented, watched them recede side by side and felt how, once more, her companion's relation to her got an accent from it. They disappeared among the others and apparently into the house; whereupon our friend turned round to give out to little Bilham the conviction of which he was full. But

there was no little Bilham any more; little Bilham had
within the few moments, for reasons of his own, proceeded further: a circumstance by which, in its order,
Strether was also sensibly affected

III

Chad was not in fact on this occasion to keep his promise of coming back; but Miss Gostrey had soon presented herself with an explanation of his failure. There had been reasons at the last for his going off with *ces dames;* and he had asked her with much instance to come out and take charge of their friend. She did so, Strether felt as she took her place beside him, in a manner that left nothing to desire. He had dropped back on his bench, alone again for a time, and the more conscious for little Bilham's defection of his unexpressed thought; in respect to which however this next converser was a still more capacious vessel. "It's the child!" he had exclaimed to her almost as soon as she appeared; and though her direct response was for some time delayed he could feel in her meanwhile the working of this truth. It might have been simply, as she waited, that they were now in presence altogether of truth spreading like a flood and not for the moment to be offered her in the mere cupful; inasmuch as who should *ces dames* prove to be but persons about whom — once thus face to face with them — she found she might from the first have told him almost everything? This would have freely come had he taken the simple precaution of giving her their name. There could be no better example — and she appeared to note it with high amusement — than the way, making things out already so much for himself, he was at last throwing precautions to the winds. They were neither more nor less, she and the child's mother, than old school-friends — friends who had scarcely met for years but whom this unlooked-for chance had brought together with a rush. It was a relief, Miss Gostrey hinted, to feel herself no longer groping; she was unaccustomed to grope and as a general thing, he might well have seen, made straight enough for her clue. With the one she had now picked up in her hands there need be at least no waste of wonder. "She's coming to see me — that's for *you*," Strether's counsellor continued; "but I don't require it to know where I am."

The waste of wonder might be proscribed; but Strether, characteristically, was even by this time in the immensity of space. "By which you mean that you know where *she* is?"

She just hesitated. "I mean that if she comes to see me I shall — now that I've pulled myself round a bit after the shock — not be at home."

Strether hung poised. "You call it — your recognition — a shock?"

She gave one of her rare flickers of impatience. "It was a surprise, an emotion. Don't be so literal. I wash my hands of her."

Poor Strether's face lengthened. "She's impossible — ?"

"She's even more charmng than I remembered her."

"Then what's the matter?"

She had to think how to put it. "Well, *I'm* impossible. It's impossible. Everything's impossible."

226

BOOK FIFTH

He looked at her an instant. "I see where you're coming out. Everything's possible." Their eyes had on it in fact an exchange of some duration; after which he pursued: "Isn't it that beautiful child?" Then as she still said nothing: "Why don't you mean to receive her?"

Her answer in an instant rang clear. "Because I wish to keep out of the business."

It provoked in him a weak wail. "You're going to abandon me *now?*"

"No, I'm only going to abandon *her*. She'll want me to help her with you. And I won't."

"You'll only help me with her? Well then —!" Most of the persons previously gathered had, in the interest of tea, passed into the house, and they had the gardens mainly to themselves. The shadows were long, the last call of the birds, who had made a home of their own in the noble interspaced quarter, sounded from the high trees in the other gardens as well, those of the old convent and of the old *hôtels;* it was as if our friends had waited for the full charm to come out. Strether's impressions were still present; it was as if something had happened that "nailed" them, made them more intense; but he was to ask himself soon afterwards, that evening, what really *had* happened — conscious as he could after all remain that for a gentleman taken, and taken the first time, into the "great world," the world of ambassadors and duchesses, the items made a meagre total. It was nothing new to him, however, as we know, that a man might have — at all events such a man as he — an amount of experience out of any proportion to his adventures;

so that, though it was doubtless no great adventure to sit on there with Miss Gostrey and hear about Madame de Vionnet, the hour, the picture, the immediate, the recent, the possible — as well as the communication itself, not a note of which failed to reverberate — only gave the moments more of the taste of history.

It was history, to begin with, that Jeanne's mother had been three-and-twenty years before, at Geneva, schoolmate and good girl-friend to Maria Gostrey, who had moreover enjoyed since then, though interruptedly and above all with a long recent drop, other glimpses of her. Twenty-three years put them both on, no doubt; and Madame de Vionnet — though she had married straight after school — could n't be to-day an hour less than thirty-eight. This made her ten years older than Chad — though ten years, also, if Strether liked, older than she looked; the least, at any rate, that a prospective mother-in-law could be expected to do with. She would be of all mothers-in-law the most charming; unless indeed, through some perversity as yet insupposeable, she should utterly belie herself in that relation. There was none surely in which, as Maria remembered her, she must n't be charming; and this frankly in spite of the stigma of failure in the tie where failure always most showed. It was no test there — when indeed *was* it a test there ? — for Monsieur de Vionnet had been a brute. She had lived for years apart from him — which was of course always a horrid position; but Miss Gostrey's impression of the matter had been that she could scarce have made a better thing of it had she done it on purpose to show she was amiable. She was so amiable that nobody had had a word to say; which was luckily not the case for her husband. He was so impossible that she had the advantage of all her merits.

It was still history for Strether that the Comte de Vionnet — it being also history that the lady in question was a Countess — should now, under Miss Gostrey's sharp touch, rise before him as a high distinguished polished impertinent reprobate, the product of a mysterious order; it was history, further, that the charming girl so freely sketched by his companion should have been married out of hand by a mother, another figure of striking outline, full of dark personal motive; it was perhaps history most of all that this company was, as a matter of course, governed by such considerations as put divorce out of the question. "*Ces gens-là* don't divorce, you know, any more than they emigrate or abjure — they think it impious and vulgar"; a fact in the light of which they seemed but the more richly special. It was all special; it was all, for Strether's imagination, more or less rich. The girl at the Genevese school, an isolated interesting attaching creature, then both sensitive and violent, audacious but always forgiven, was the daughter of a French father and an English mother who, early left a widow, had married again — tried afresh with a foreigner; in her career with whom she had apparently given her child no example of comfort. All these people — the people of the English mother's side — had been of condition more or less eminent; yet with oddities and disparities that had often since made

Maria, thinking them over, wonder what they really quite rhymed to. It was in any case her belief that the mother, interested and prone to adventure, had been without conscience, had only thought of ridding herself most quickly of a possible, an actual encumbrance. The father, by her impression, a Frenchman with a name one knew, had been a different matter, leaving his child, she clearly recalled, a memory all fondness, as well as an assured little fortune which was unluckily to make her more or less of a prey later on. She had been in particular, at school, dazzlingly, though quite booklessly, clever; as polgylot as a little Jewess (which she was n't, oh no!) and chattering French, English, German, Italian, anything one would, in a way that made a clean sweep, if not of prizes and parchments, at least of every "part," whether memorised or improvised, in the curtained costumed school repertory, and in especial of all mysteries of race and vagueness of reference, all swagger about "home," among their variegated mates.

It would doubtless be difficult to-day, as between French and English, to name her and place her; she would certainly show, on knowledge, Miss Gostrey felt, as one of those convenient types who don't keep you explaining — minds with doors as numerous as the many-tongued cluster of confessionals at Saint Peter's. You might confess to her with confidence in Roumelian, and even Roumelian sins. Therefore —! But Strether's narrator covered her implication with a laugh; a laugh by which his betrayal of a sense of the lurid in the picture was also perhaps sufficiently protected. He had a moment of wondering, while his

friend went on, what sins might be especially Roumelian. She went on at all events to the mention of
her having met the young thing — again by some
Swiss lake — in her first married state, which had appeared for the few intermediate years not at least
violently disturbed. She had been lovely at that moment, delightful to *her*, full of responsive emotion, of
amused recognitions and amusing reminders; and
then, once more, much later, after a long interval,
equally but differently charming — touching and
rather mystifying for the five minutes of an encounter
at a railway-station *en province*, during which it had
come out that her life was all changed. Miss Gostrey
had understood enough to see, essentially, what had
happened, and yet had beautifully dreamed that she
was herself faultless. There were doubtless depths in
her, but she was all right; Strether would see if she
was n't. She was another person however — that had
been promptly marked — from the small child of nature at the Geneva school; a little person quite made
over (as foreign women *were*, compared with American) by marriage. Her situation too had evidently
cleared itself up; there would have been — all that
was possible — a judicial separation. She had settled
in Paris, brought up her daughter, steered her boat.
It was no very pleasant boat — especially there — to
be in; but Marie de Vionnet would have headed
straight. She would have friends, certainly — and
very good ones. There she was at all events — and it
was very interesting. Her knowing Mr. Chad did n't
in the least prove she had n't friends; what it proved
was what good ones *he* had. "I saw that," said Miss

Gostrey, "that night at the Français; it came out for me in three minutes. I saw *her* — or somebody like her. And so," she immediately added, "did you."

"Oh no — not anybody like her!" Strether laughed. "But you mean," he as promptly went on, "that she has had such an influence on him?"

Miss Gostrey was on her feet; it was time for them to go. "She has brought him up for her daughter."

Their eyes, as so often, in candid conference, through their settled glasses, met over it long; after which Strether's again took in the whole place. They were quite alone there now. "Must n't she rather — in the time then — have rushed it?"

"Ah she won't of course have lost an hour. But that's just the good mother — the good French one. You must remember that of her — that as a mother she's French, and that for them there's a special providence. It precisely however — that she may n't have been able to begin as far back as she'd have liked — makes her grateful for aid."

Strether took this in as they slowly moved to the house on their way out. "She counts on me then to put the thing through?"

"Yes — she counts on you. Oh and first of all of course," Miss Gostrey added, "on her — well, convincing you."

"Ah," her friend returned, "she caught Chad young!"

"Yes, but there are women who are for all your 'times of life.' They're the most wonderful sort."

She had laughed the words out, but they brought

her companion, the next thing, to a stand. "Is what you mean that she'll try to make a fool of me?"

"Well, I'm wondering what she *will* — with an opportunity — make."

"What do you call," Strether asked, "an opportunity? My going to see her?"

"Ah you must go to see her" — Miss Gostrey was a trifle evasive. "You can't not do that. You'd have gone to see the other woman. I mean if there had been one — a different sort. It's what you came out for."

It might be; but Strether distinguished. "I did n't come out to see *this* sort."

She had a wonderful look at him now. "Are you disappointed she is n't worse?"

He for a moment entertained the question, then found for it the frankest of answers. "Yes. If she were worse she'd be better for our purpose. It would be simpler."

"Perhaps," she admitted. "But won't this be pleasanter?"

"Ah you know," he promptly replied, "I did n't come out — was n't that just what you originally reproached me with? — for the pleasant."

"Precisely. Therefore I say again what I said at first. You must take things as they come. Besides," Miss Gostrey added, "I'm not afraid for myself."

"For yourself — ?"

"Of your seeing her. I trust her. There's nothing she'll say about me. In fact there's nothing she *can*."

Strether wondered — little as he had thought of this. Then he broke out. "Oh you women!"

There was something in it at which she flushed.

"Yes — there we are. We're abysses." At last she smiled. "But I risk her!"

He gave himself a shake. "Well then so do I!" But he added as they passed into the house that he would see Chad the first thing in the morning.

This was the next day the more easily effected that the young man, as it happened, even before he was down, turned up at his hotel. Strether took his coffee, by habit, in the public room; but on his descending for this purpose Chad instantly proposed an adjournment to what he called greater privacy. He had himself as yet had nothing — they would sit down somewhere together; and when after a few steps and a turn into the Boulevard they had, for their greater privacy, sat down among twenty others, our friend saw in his companion's move a fear of the advent of Waymarsh. It was the first time Chad had to that extent given this personage "away"; and Strether found himself wondering of what it was symptomatic. He made out in a moment that the youth was in earnest as he had n't yet seen him; which in its turn threw a ray perhaps a trifle startling on what they had each up to that time been treating as earnestness. It was sufficiently flattering however that the real thing — if this *was* at last the real thing — should have been determined, as appeared, precisely by an accretion of Strether's importance. For this was what it quickly enough came to — that Chad, rising with the lark, had rushed down to let him know while his morning consciousness was yet young that he had literally made the afternoon before a tremendous impression. Madame de Vionnet would n't, could n't rest till she should have some assurance from him that he *would* consent again to see her. The announcement was made, across their marble-topped table, while the foam of the hot milk was in their cups and its plash still in the air, with the smile of Chad's easiest urbanity; and this expression of his face caused our friend's doubts to gather on the spot into a challenge of the lips. "See here" — that was all; he only for the moment said again "See here." Chad met it with all his air of straight intelligence, while Strether remembered again that fancy of the first impression of him, the happy young Pagan, handsome and hard but oddly indulgent, whose mysterious measure he had under the street-lamp tried mentally to take. The young Pagan, while a long look passed between them, sufficiently understood. Strether scarce needed at last to say the rest — "I want to know where I am." But he said it, adding before any answer something more. "Are you engaged to be married — is that your secret? — to the young lady?"

Chad shook his head with the slow amenity that was one of his ways of conveying that there was time for everything. "I have no secret — though I may have secrets! I have n't at any rate that one. We're not engaged. No."

"Then where's the hitch?"

"Do you mean why I have n't already started with you?" Chad, beginning his coffee and buttering his roll, was quite ready to explain. "Nothing would have induced me — nothing will still induce me — not to try to keep you here as long as you can be made to stay. It's too visibly good for you." Strether had him-self plenty to say about this, but it was amusing also to measure the march of Chad's tone. He had never been more a man of the world, and it was always in his company present to our friend that one was seeing how in successive connexions a man of the world acquitted himself. Chad kept it up beautifully. "My idea — *voyons!* — is simply that you should let Madame de Vionnet know you, simply that you should consent to know *her*. I don't in the least mind telling you that, clever and charming as she is, she's ever so much in my confidence. All I ask of you is to let her talk to you. You've asked me about what you call my hitch, and so far as it goes she'll explain it to you. She's herself my hitch, hang it — if you must really have it all out. But in a sense," he hastened in the most wonderful manner to add, "that you'll quite make out for yourself. She's too good a friend, confound her. Too good, I mean, for me to leave without — without —" It was his first hesitation.

"Without what?"

"Well, without my arranging somehow or other the damnable terms of my sacrifice."

"It *will* be a sacrifice then?"

"It will be the greatest loss I ever suffered. I owe her so much."

It was beautiful, the way Chad said these things, and his plea was now confessedly — oh quite flagrantly and publicly — interesting. The moment really took on for Strether an intensity. Chad owed Madame de Vionnet so much? What *did* that do then but clear up the whole mystery? He was indebted for alterations, and she was thereby in a position to have sent in her bill for expenses incurred in reconstruction.

BOOK FIFTH

What was this at bottom but what had been to be arrived at? Strether sat there arriving at it while he munched toast and stirred his second cup. To do this with the aid of Chad's pleasant earnest face was also to do more besides. No, never before had he been so ready to take him as he was. What was it that had suddenly so cleared up? It was just everybody's character; that is everybody's but — in a measure — his own. Strether felt *his* character receive for the instant a smutch from all the wrong things he had suspected or believed. The person to whom Chad owed it that he could positively turn out such a comfort to other persons — such a person was sufficiently raised above any "breath" by the nature of her work and the young man's steady light. All of which was vivid enough to come and go quickly; though indeed in the midst of it Strether could utter a question. "Have I your word of honour that if I surrender myself to Madame de Vionnet you'll surrender yourself to *me*?"

Chad laid his hand firmly on his friend's. "My dear man, you have it."

There was finally something in his felicity almost embarrassing and oppressive — Strether had begun to fidget under it for the open air and the erect posture. He had signed to the waiter that he wished to pay, and this transaction took some moments, during which he thoroughly felt, while he put down money and pretended — it was quite hollow — to estimate change, that Chad's higher spirit, his youth, his practice, his paganism, his felicity, his assurance, his impudence, whatever it might be, had consciously scored a success. Well, that was all right so far as it went; his sense of the thing in question covered our friend for a minute like a veil through which — as if he had been muffled—he heard his interlocutor ask him if he might n't take him over about five. "Over" was over the river, and over the river was where Madame de Vionnet lived, and five was that very afternoon. They got at last out of the place — got out before he answered. He lighted, in the street, a cigarette, which again gave him more time. But it was already sharp for him that there was no use in time. "What does she propose to do to me?" he had presently demanded.

Chad had no delays. "Are you afraid of her?"

"Oh immensely. Don't you see it?"

"Well," said Chad, "she won't do anything worse to you than make you like her."

"It's just of that I'm afraid."

"Then it's not fair to me."

Strether cast about. "It's fair to your mother."

"Oh," said Chad, "are you afraid of *her?*"

"Scarcely less. Or perhaps even more. But is this lady against your interests at home?" Strether went on.

"Not directly, no doubt; but she's greatly in favour of them here."

"And what — 'here' — does she consider them to be?"

"Well, good relations!"

"With herself?"

"With herself."

"And what is it that makes them so good?"

"What? Well, that's exactly what you'll make out if you'll only go, as I'm supplicating you, to see her."

BOOK FIFTH

Strether stared at him with a little of the wanness, no doubt, that the vision of more to "make out" could scarce help producing. "I mean *how* good are they?"

"Oh awfully good."

Again Strether had faltered, but it was brief. It was all very well, but there was nothing now he would n't risk. "Excuse me, but I must really — as I began by telling you — know where I am. Is she bad?"

"'Bad'?" — Chad echoed it, but without a shock. "Is that what's implied — ?"

"When relations are good?" Strether felt a little silly, and was even conscious of a foolish laugh, at having it imposed on him to have appeared to speak so. What indeed was he talking about? His stare had relaxed; he looked now all round him. But something in him brought him back, though he still did n't know quite how to turn it. The two or three ways he thought of, and one of them in particular, were, even with scruples dismissed, too ugly. He none the less at last found something. "Is her life without reproach?"

It struck him, directly he had found it, as pompous and priggish; so much so that he was thankful to Chad for taking it only in the right spirit. The young man spoke so immensely to the point that the effect was practically of positive blandness. "Absolutely without reproach. A beautiful life. *Allez donc voir!*"

These last words were, in the liberality of their confidence, so imperative that Strether went through no form of assent; but before they separated it had been confirmed that he should be picked up at a quarter to five.

BOOK SIXTH

I

IT was quite by half-past five — after the two men
had been together in Madame de Vionnet's drawing-
room not more than a dozen minutes — that Chad,
with a look at his watch and then another at their
hostess, said genially, gaily: "I've an engagement,
and I know you won't complain if I leave him with
you. He'll interest you immensely; and as for her,"
he declared to Strether, "I assure you, if you're at
all nervous, she's perfectly safe."

He had left them to be embarrassed or not by this
guarantee, as they could best manage, and embarrassment was a thing that Strether wasn't at first sure
Madame de Vionnet escaped. He escaped it himself,
to his surprise; but he had grown used by this time
to thinking of himself as brazen. She occupied, his
hostess, in the Rue de Bellechasse, the first floor of an
old house to which our visitors had had access from
an old clean court. The court was large and open, full
of revelations, for our friend, of the habit of privacy,
the peace of intervals, the dignity of distances and approaches; the house, to his restless sense, was in the
high homely style of an elder day, and the ancient
Paris that he was always looking for — sometimes
intensely felt, sometimes more acutely missed — was
in the immemorial polish of the wide waxed staircase
and in the fine *boiseries*, the medallions, mouldings,
mirrors, great clear spaces, of the greyish-white salon

243

into which he had been shown. He seemed at the very outset to see her in the midst of possessions not vulgarly numerous, but hereditary cherished charming. While his eyes turned after a little from those of his hostess and Chad freely talked — not in the least about *him*, but about other people, people he did n't know, and quite as if he did know them — he found himself making out, as a background of the occupant, some glory, some prosperity of the First Empire, some Napoleonic glamour, some dim lustre of the great legend; elements clinging still to all the consular chairs and mythological brasses and sphinxes' heads and faded surfaces of satin striped with alternate silk.

The place itself went further back — that he guessed, and how old Paris continued in a manner to echo there; but the post-revolutionary period, the world he vaguely thought of as the world of Châteaubriand, of Madame de Staël, even of the young Lamartine, had left its stamp of harps and urns and torches, a stamp impressed on sundry small objects, ornaments and relics. He had never before, to his knowledge, had present to him relics, of any special dignity, of a private order — little old miniatures, medallions, pictures, books; books in leather bindings, pinkish and greenish, with gilt garlands on the back, ranged, together with other promiscuous properties, under the glass of brass-mounted cabinets. His attention took them all tenderly into account. They were among the matters that marked Madame de Vionnet's apartment as something quite different from Miss Gostrey's little museum of bargains and from Chad's lovely home; he recognised it as founded much more

on old accumulations that had possibly from time to
time shrunken than on any contemporary method of
acquisition or form of curiosity. Chad and Miss Gostrey had rummaged and purchased and picked up
and exchanged, sifting, selecting, comparing; whereas
the mistress of the scene before him, beautifully passive under the spell of transmission — transmission
from her father's line, he quite made up his mind —
had only received, accepted and been quiet. When she
had n't been quiet she had been moved at the most
to some occult charity for some fallen fortune. There
had been objects she or her predecessors might even
conceivably have parted with under need, but Strether
could n't suspect them of having sold old pieces to get
"better" ones. They would have felt no difference as
to better or worse. He could but imagine their having
felt — perhaps in emigration, in proscription, for his
sketch was slight and confused — the pressure of want
or the obligation of sacrifice.

The pressure of want — whatever might be the
case with the other force — was, however, presumably not active now, for the tokens of a chastened
ease still abounded after all, many marks of a taste
whose discriminations might perhaps have been called
eccentric. He guessed at intense little preferences and
sharp little exclusions, a deep suspicion of the vulgar
and a personal view of the right. The general result
of this was something for which he had no name on
the spot quite ready, but something he would have
come nearest to naming in speaking of it as the air of
supreme respectability, the consciousness, small, still,
reserved, but none the less distinct and diffused, of

private honour. The air of supreme respectability —
that was a strange blank wall for his adventure to
have brought him to break his nose against. It had in
fact, as was now aware, filled all the approaches,
hovered in the court as he passed, hung on the staircase as he mounted, sounded in the grave rumble of
the old bell, as little electric as possible, of which
Chad, at the door, had pulled the ancient but neatly-
kept tassel; it formed in short the clearest medium of
its particular kind that he had ever breathed. He
would have answered for it at the end of a quarter of
an hour that some of the glass cases contained swords
and epaulettes of ancient colonels and generals;
medals and orders once pinned over hearts that had
long since ceased to beat; snuff-boxes bestowed on
ministers and envoys; copies of works presented, with
inscriptions, by authors now classic. At bottom of it
all for him was the sense of her rare unlikeness to the
women he had known. This sense had grown, since
the day before, the more he recalled her, and had been
above all singularly fed by his talk with Chad in the
morning. Everything in fine made her immeasurably
new, and nothing so new as the old house and the old
objects. There were books, two or three, on a small
table near his chair, but they had n't the lemon-
coloured covers with which his eye had begun to dally
from the hour of his arrival and to the opportunity of
a further acquaintance with which he had for a fortnight now altogether succumbed. On another table,
across the room, he made out the great *Revue;* but
even that familiar face, conspicuous in Mrs. Newsome's parlours, scarce counted here as a modern

note. He was sure on the spot — and he afterwards knew he was right — that this was a touch of Chad's own hand. What would Mrs. Newsome say to the circumstance that Chad's interested "influence" kept her paper-knife in the *Revue?* The interested influence at any rate had, as we say, gone straight to the point — had in fact soon left it quite behind.

She was seated, near the fire, on a small stuffed and fringed chair, one of the few modern articles in the room; and she leaned back in it with her hands clasped in her lap and no movement, in all her person, but the fine prompt play of her deep young face. The fire, under the low white marble, undraped and academic, had burnt down to the silver ashes of light wood; one of the windows, at a distance, stood open to the mildness and stillness, out of which, in the short pauses, came the faint sound, pleasant and homely, almost rustic, of a plash and a clatter of *sabots* from some coach-house on the other side of the court. Madame de Vionnet, while Strether sat there, was n't to shift her posture by an inch. "I don't think you seriously believe in what you 're doing," she said; "but all the same, you know, I 'm going to treat you quite as if I did."

"By which you mean," Strether directly replied, "quite as if you did n't! I assure you it won't make the least difference with me how you treat me."

"Well," she said, taking that menace bravely and philosophically enough, "the only thing that really matters is that you shall get on with me."

"Ah but I don't!" he immediately returned.

It gave her another pause; which, however, she

happily enough shook off. "Will you consent to go on with me a little — provisionally — as if you did?"

Then it was that he saw how she had decidedly come all the way; and there accompanied it an extraordinary sense of her raising from somewhere below him her beautiful suppliant eyes. He might have been perched at his door-step or at his window and she standing in the road. For a moment he let her stand and could n't moreover have spoken. It had been sad, of a sudden, with a sadness that was like a cold breath in his face. "What can I do," he finally asked, "but listen to you as I promised Chadwick?"

"Ah but what I'm asking you," she quickly said, "is n't what Mr. Newsome had in mind." She spoke at present, he saw, as if to take courageously *all* her risk. "This is my own idea and a different thing."

It gave poor Strether in truth — uneasy as it made him too — something of the thrill of a bold perception justified. "Well," he answered kindly enough, "I was sure a moment since that some idea of your own had come to you."

She seemed still to look up at him, but now more serenely. "I made out you were sure — and that helped it to come. So you see," she continued, "we do get on."

"Oh but it appears to me I don't at all meet your request. How can I when I don't understand it?"

"It is n't at all necessary you should understand; it will do quite well enough if you simply remember it. Only feel I trust you — and for nothing so tremendous after all. Just," she said with a wonderful smile, "for common civility."

BOOK SIXTH

Strether had a long pause while they sat again face to face, as they had sat, scarce less conscious, before the poor lady had crossed the stream. She was the poor lady for Strether now because clearly she had some trouble, and her appeal to him could only mean that her trouble was deep. He could n't help it; it was n't his fault; he had done nothing; but by a turn of the hand she had somehow made their encounter a relation. And the relation profited by a mass of things that were not strictly in it or of it; by the very air in which they sat, by the high cold delicate room, by the world outside and the little plash in the court, by the First Empire and the relics in the stiff cabinets, by matters as far off as those and by others as near as the unbroken clasp of her hands in her lap and the look her expression had of being most natural when her eyes were most fixed. "You count upon me of course for something really much greater than it sounds."

"Oh it sounds great enough too!" she laughed at this.

He found himself in time on the point of telling her that she was, as Miss Barrace called it, wonderful; but, catching himself up, he said something else instead. "What was it Chad's idea then that you should say to me?"

"Ah his idea was simply what a man's idea always is — to put every effort off on the woman."

"The 'woman' — ?" Strether slowly echoed.

"The woman he likes — and just in proportion as he likes her. In proportion too — for shifting the trouble — as she likes *him*."

Strether followed it; then with an abruptness of his own: "How much do you like Chad?"

"Just as much as *that* — to take all, with you, on myself." But she got at once again away from this. "I've been trembling as if we were to stand or fall by what you may think of me; and I'm even now," she went on wonderfully, "drawing a long breath — and, yes, truly taking a great courage — from the hope that I don't in fact strike you as impossible."

"That's at all events, clearly," he observed after an instant, "the way I don't strike *you*."

"Well," she so far assented, "as you haven't yet said you *won't* have the little patience with me I ask for —"

"You draw splendid conclusions? Perfectly. But I don't understand them," Strether pursued. "You seem to me to ask for much more than you need. What, at the worst for you, what at the best for myself, can I after all do? I can use no pressure that I haven't used. You come really late with your request. I've already done all that for myself the case admits of. I've said my say, and here I am."

"Yes, here you are, fortunately!" Madame de Vionnet laughed. "Mrs. Newsome," she added in another tone, "didn't think you can do so little."

He had an hesitation, but he brought the words out. "Well, she thinks so now."

"Do you mean by that —?" But she also hung fire.

"Do I mean what?"

She still rather faltered. "Pardon me if I touch on it, but if I'm saying extraordinary things, why, per-

haps, may n't I ? Besides, does n't it properly concern
us to know ?"

"To know what ?" he insisted as after thus beating
about the bush she had again dropped.

She made the effort. "Has she given you up ?"

He was amazed afterwards to think how simply and
quietly he had met it. "Not yet." It was almost as
if he were a trifle disappointed — had expected still
more of her freedom. But he went straight on. "Is
that what Chad has told you will happen to me ?"

She was evidently charmed with the way he took it.
"If you mean if we 've talked of it — most certainly.
And the question 's not what has had least to do with
my wishing to see you."

"To judge if I 'm the sort of man a woman
can — ?"

"Precisely," she exclaimed — "you wonderful gentleman! I do judge — I *have* judged. A woman
can't. You 're safe — with every right to be. You 'd
be much happier if you 'd only believe it."

Strether was silent a little; then he found himself
speaking with a cynicism of confidence of which even
at the moment the sources were strange to him. "I
try to believe it. But it 's a marvel," he exclaimed,
"how *you* already get at it!"

Oh she was able to say. "Remember how much
I was on the way to it through Mr. Newsome
—before I saw you. He thinks everything of your
strength."

"Well, I can bear almost anything!" our friend
briskly interrupted. Deep and beautiful on this her
smile came back, and with the effect of making him

hear what he had said just as she had heard it. He easily enough felt that it gave him away, but what in truth had everything done but that? It had been all very well to think at moments that he was holding her nose down and that he had coerced her: what had he by this time done but let her practically see that he accepted their relation? What was their relation moreover—though light and brief enough in form as yet—but whatever she might choose to make it? Nothing could prevent her—certainly he could n't—from making it pleasant. At the back of his head, behind everything, was the sense that she was—there, before him, close to him, in vivid imperative form—one of the rare women he had so often heard of, read of, thought of, but never met, whose very presence, look, voice, the mere contemporaneous *fact* of whom, from the moment it was at all presented, made a relation of mere recognition. That was not the kind of woman he had ever found Mrs. Newsome, a contemporaneous fact who had been distinctly slow to establish herself; and at present, confronted with Madame de Vionnet, he felt the simplicity of his original impression of Miss Gostrey. She certainly had been a fact of rapid growth; but the world was wide, each day was more and more a new lesson. There were at any rate even among the stranger ones relations and relations. "Of course I suit Chad's grand way," he quickly added. "He has n't had much difficulty in working me in."

She seemed to deny a little, on the young man's behalf, by the rise of her eyebrows, an intention of any process at all inconsiderate. "You must know how grieved he'd be if you were to lose anything. He believes you can keep his mother patient."

Strether wondered with his eyes on her. "I see. *That's* then what you really want of me. And how am I to do it? Perhaps you'll tell me that."

"Simply tell her the truth."

"And what do you call the truth?"

"Well, *any* truth — about us all — that you see yourself. I leave it to you."

"Thank you very much. I like," Strether laughed with a slight harshness, "the way you leave things!"

But she insisted kindly, gently, as if it was n't so bad. "Be perfectly honest. Tell her all."

"All?" he oddly echoed.

"Tell her the simple truth," Madame de Vionnet again pleaded.

"But what *is* the simple truth? The simple truth is exactly what I'm trying to discover."

She looked about a while, but presently she came back to him. "Tell her, fully and clearly, about *us*."

Strether meanwhile had been staring. "You and your daughter?"

"Yes — little Jeanne and me. Tell her," she just slightly quavered, "you like us."

"And what good will that do me? Or rather" — he caught himself up — "what good will it do *you?*"

She looked graver. "None, you believe, really?"

Strether debated. "She did n't send me out to 'like' you."

"Oh," she charmingly contended, "she sent you out to face the facts."

He admitted after an instant that there was something in that. "But how can I face them till I know what they are? Do you want him," he then braced himself to ask, "to marry your daughter?"

She gave a headshake as noble as it was prompt. "No — not that."

"And he really does n't want to himself?"

She repeated the movement, but now with a strange light in her face. "He likes her too much."

Strether wondered. "To be willing to consider, you mean, the question of taking her to America?"

"To be willing to do anything with her but be immensely kind and nice —really tender of her. We watch over her, and you must help us. You must see her again."

Strether felt awkward. "Ah with pleasure — she's so remarkably attractive."

The mother's eagerness with which Madame de Vionnet jumped at this was to come back to him later as beautiful in its grace. "The dear thing *did* please you?" Then as he met it with the largest "Oh!" of enthusiasm: "She's perfect. She's my joy."

"Well, I'm sure that — if one were near her and saw more of her — she'd be mine."

"Then," said Madame de Vionnet, "tell Mrs. Newsome that!"

He wondered the more. "What good will that do you?" As she appeared unable at once to say, however, he brought out something else. "Is your daughter in love with our friend?"

"Ah," she rather startlingly answered, "I wish you'd find out!"

He showed his surprise. "I? A stranger?"

254

BOOK SIXTH

"Oh you won't be a stranger — presently. You shall see her quite, I assure you, as if you were n't."

It remained for him none the less an extraordinary notion. "It seems to me surely that if her mother can't —"

"Ah little girls and their mothers to-day!" she rather inconsequently broke in. But she checked herself with something she seemed to give out as after all more to the point. "Tell her I've been good for him. Don't you think I have?"

It had its effect on him — more than at the moment he quite measured. Yet he was consciously enough touched. "Oh if it's all *you* —!"

"Well, it may not be 'all,'" she interrupted, "but it's to a great extent. Really and truly," she added in a tone that was to take its place with him among things remembered.

"Then it's very wonderful." He smiled at her from a face that he felt as strained, and her own face for a moment kept him so. At last she also got up. "Well, don't you think that for that —"

"I ought to save you?" So it was that the way to meet her — and the way, as well, in a manner, to get off — came over him. He heard himself use the exorbitant word, the very sound of which helped to determine his flight. "I'll save you if I can."

II

In Chad's lovely home, however, one evening ten days later, he felt himself present at the collapse of the question of Jeanne de Vionnet's shy secret. He had been dining there in the company of that young lady and her mother, as well as of other persons, and he had gone into the *petit salon*, at Chad's request, on purpose to talk with her. The young man had put this to him as a favour — "I should like so awfully to know what you think of her. It will really be a chance for you," he had said, "to see the *jeune fille* — I mean the type — as she actually is, and I don't think that, as an observer of manners, it's a thing you ought to miss. It will be an impression that — whatever else you take — you can carry home with you, where you'll find again so much to compare it with."

Strether knew well enough with what Chad wished him to compare it, and though he entirely assented he had n't yet somehow been so deeply reminded that he was being, as he constantly though mutely expressed it, used. He was as far as ever from making out exactly to what end; but he was none the less constantly accompanied by a sense of the service he rendered. He conceived only that this service was highly agreeable to those who profited by it; and he was indeed still waiting for the moment at which he should catch it in the act of proving disagreeable, proving in some degree intolerable, to himself. He failed quite to

see how his situation could clear up at all logically
except by some turn of events that would give him the
pretext of disgust. He was building from day to day
on the possibility of disgust, but each day brought
forth meanwhile a new and more engaging bend of
the road. That possibility was now ever so much
further from sight than on the eve of his arrival, and
he perfectly felt that, should it come at all, it would
have to be at best inconsequent and violent. He
struck himself as a little nearer to it only when he
asked himself what service, in such a life of utility,
he was after all rendering Mrs. Newsome. When he
wished to help himself to believe that he was still all
right he reflected — and in fact with wonder — on
the unimpaired frequency of their correspondence;
in relation to which what was after all more natural
than that it should become more frequent just in proportion as their problem became more complicated?

Certain it is at any rate that he now often brought
himself balm by the question, with the rich consciousness of yesterday's letter, "Well, what can I do more
than that — what can I do more than tell her everything?" To persuade himself that he did tell her, had
told her, everything, he used to try to think of particular things he had n't told her. When at rare moments and in the watches of the night he pounced on
one it generally showed itself to be — to a deeper
scrutiny — not quite truly of the essence. When anything new struck him as coming up, or anything
already noted as reappearing, he always immediately
wrote, as if for fear that if he did n't he would miss
something; and also that he might be able to say to

himself from time to time "She knows it *now* — even
while I worry." It was a great comfort to him in general not to have left past things to be dragged to light
and explained; not to have to produce at so late a
stage anything not produced, or anything even veiled
and attenuated, at the moment. She knew it now:
that was what he said to himself to-night in relation to
the fresh fact of Chad's acquaintance with the two
ladies — not to speak of the fresher one of his own.
Mrs. Newsome knew in other words that very night
at Woollett that he himself knew Madame de Vionnet
and that he had conscientiously been to see her; also
that he had found her remarkably attractive and that
there would probably be a good deal more to tell. But
she further knew, or would know very soon, that,
again conscientiously, he had n't repeated his visit;
and that when Chad had asked him on the Countess's
behalf — Strether made her out vividly, with a thought
at the back of his head, a Countess — if he would n't
name a day for dining with her, he had replied lucidly:
"Thank you very much — impossible." He had
begged the young man would present his excuses and
had trusted him to understand that it could n't really
strike one as quite the straight thing. He had n't
reported to Mrs. Newsome that he had promised to
"save" Madame de Vionnet; but, so far as he was
concerned with that reminiscence, he had n't at any
rate promised to haunt her house. What Chad had
understood could only, in truth, be inferred from
Chad's behaviour, which had been in this connexion
as easy as in every other. He was easy, always, when
he understood; he was easier still, if possible, when he

did n't; he had replied that he would make it all right; and he had proceeded to do this by substituting the present occasion — as he was ready to substitute others — for any, for every occasion as to which his old friend should have a funny scruple.

"Oh but I'm not a little foreign girl; I'm just as English as I can be," Jeanne de Vionnet had said to him as soon as, in the *petit salon*, he sank, shyly enough on his own side, into the place near her vacated by Madame Gloriani at his approach. Madame Gloriani, who was in black velvet, with white lace and powdered hair, and whose somewhat massive majesty melted, at any contact, into the graciousness of some incomprehensible tongue, moved away to make room for the vague gentleman, after benevolent greetings to him which embodied, as he believed, in baffling accents, some recognition of his face from a couple of Sundays before. Then he had remarked — making the most of the advantage of his years — that it frightened him quite enough to find himself dedicated to the entertainment of a little foreign girl. There were girls he was n't afraid of — he was quite bold with little Americans. Thus it was that she had defended herself to the end — "Oh but I'm almost American too. That's what mamma has wanted me to be — I mean *like* that; for she has wanted me to have lots of freedom. She has known such good results from it."

She was fairly beautiful to him — a faint pastel in an oval frame: he thought of her already as of some lurking image in a long gallery, the portrait of a small old-time princess of whom nothing was known but that she had died young. Little Jeanne was n't, doubtless, to die young, but one could n't, all the same, bear on her lightly enough. It was bearing hard, it was bearing as *he*, in any case, would n't bear, to concern himself, in relation to her, with the question of a young man. Odious really the question of a young man; one did n't treat such a person as a maidservant suspected of a "follower." And then young men, young men —well, the thing was their business simply, or was at all events hers. She was fluttered, fairly fevered — to the point of a little glitter that came and went in her eyes and a pair of pink spots that stayed in her cheeks — with the great adventure of dining out and with the greater one still, possibly, of finding a gentleman whom she must think of as very, very old, a gentleman with eye-glasses, wrinkles, a long grizzled moustache. She spoke the prettiest English, our friend thought, that he had ever heard spoken, just as he had believed her a few minutes before to be speaking the prettiest French. He wondered almost wistfully if such a sweep of the lyre did n't react on the spirit itself; and his fancy had in fact, before he knew it, begun so to stray and embroider that he finally found himself, absent and extravagant, sitting with the child in a friendly silence. Only by this time he felt her flutter to have fortunately dropped and that she was more at her ease. She trusted him, liked him, and it was to come back to him afterwards that she had told him things. She had dipped into the waiting medium at last and found neither surge nor chill — nothing but the small splash she could herself make in the pleasant warmth, nothing but the safety of dipping and dipping again. At the end of the ten

minutes he was to spend with her his impression
— with all it had thrown off and all it had taken
in — was complete. She had been free, as she knew
freedom, partly to show him that, unlike other little
persons she knew, she had imbibed that ideal. She
was delightfully quaint about herself, but the vision
of what she had imbibed was what most held him. It
really consisted, he was soon enough to feel, in just
one great little matter, the fact that, whatever her
nature, she was thoroughly — he had to cast about for
the word, but it came — bred. He could n't of course
on so short an acquaintance speak for her nature, but
the idea of breeding was what she had meanwhile
dropped into his mind. He had never yet known it so
sharply presented. Her mother gave it, no doubt; but
her mother, to make that less sensible, gave so much
else besides, and on neither of the two previous occasions, extraordinary woman, Strether felt, anything
like what she was giving to-night. Little Jeanne was
a case, an exquisite case of education; whereas the
Countess, whom it so amused him to think of by that
denomination, was a case, also exquisite, of — well,
he did n't know what.

"He has wonderful taste, *notre jeune homme*": this
was what Gloriani said to him on turning away from
the inspection of a small picture suspended near the
door of the room. The high celebrity in question had
just come in, apparently in search of Mademoiselle
de Vionnet, but while Strether had got up from beside
her their fellow guest, with his eye sharply caught, had
paused for a long look. The thing was a landscape, of
no size, but of the French school, as our friend was

glad to feel he knew, and also of a quality — which he liked to think he should also have guessed; its frame was large out of proportion to the canvas, and he had never seen a person look at anything, he thought, just as Gloriani, with his nose very near and quick movements of the head from side to side and bottom to top, examined this feature of Chad's collection. The artist used that word the next moment, smiling courteously, wiping his nippers and looking round him further — paying the place in short by the very manner of his presence and by something Strether fancied he could make out in this particular glance, such a tribute as, to the latter's sense, settled many things once for all. Strether was conscious at this instant, for that matter, as he had n't yet been, of how, round about him, quite without him, they *were* consistently settled. Gloriani's smile, deeply Italian, he considered, and finely inscrutable, had had for him, during dinner, at which they were not neighbours, an indefinite greeting; but the quality in it was gone that had appeared on the other occasion to turn him inside out; it was as if even the momentary link supplied by the doubt between them had snapped. He was conscious now of the final reality, which was that there was n't so much a doubt as a difference altogether; all the more that over the difference the famous sculptor seemed to signal almost condolingly, yet oh how vacantly! as across some great flat sheet of water. He threw out the bridge of a charming hollow civility on which Strether would n't have trusted his own full weight a moment. That idea, even though but transient and perhaps belated, had performed the office of putting Strether more at his

ease, and the blurred picture had already dropped —
dropped with the sound of something else said and
with his becoming aware, by another quick turn, that
Gloriani was now on the sofa talking with Jeanne,
while he himself had in his ears again the familiar
friendliness and the elusive meaning of the "Oh, oh,
oh!" that had made him, a fortnight before, challenge
Miss Barrace in vain. She had always the air, this
picturesque and original lady, who struck him, so
oddly, as both antique and modern — she had always
the air of taking up some joke that one had already
had out with her. The point itself, no doubt, was what
was antique, and the use she made of it what was
modern. He felt just now that her good-natured irony
did bear on something, and it troubled him a little
that she would n't be more explicit, only assuring him,
with the pleasure of observation so visible in her, that
she would n't tell him more for the world. He could
take refuge but in asking her what she had done with
Waymarsh, though it must be added that he felt himself a little on the way to a clue after she had answered
that this personage was, in the other room, engaged
in conversation with Madame de Vionnet. He stared
a moment at the image of such a conjunction; then,
for Miss Barrace's benefit, he wondered. "Is she too
then under the charm —?"

"No, not a bit" — Miss Barrace was prompt.
"She makes nothing of him. She 's bored. She won't
help you with him."

"Oh," Strether laughed, "she can't do everything."

"Of course not — wonderful as she is. Besides, he

makes nothing of *her*. She won't take him from me — though she would n't, no doubt, having other affairs in hand, even if she could. I've never," said Miss Barrace, "seen her fail with any one before. And to-night, when she's so magnificent, it would seem to her strange — if she minded. So at any rate I have him all. *Je suis tranquille!*"

Strether understood, so far as that went; but he was feeling for his clue. "She strikes you to-night as particularly magnificent?"

"Surely. Almost as I've never seen her. Does n't she you? Why it's *for* you."

He persisted in his candour. "'For' me — ?"

"Oh, oh, oh!" cried Miss Barrace, who persisted in the opposite of that quality.

"Well," he acutely admitted, "she *is* different. She's gay."

"She's gay!" Miss Barrace laughed. "And she has beautiful shoulders — though there's nothing different in that."

"No," said Strether, "one was sure of her shoulders. It is n't her shoulders."

His companion, with renewed mirth and the finest sense, between the puffs of her cigarette, of the drollery of things, appeared to find their conversation highly delightful. "Yes, it is n't her shoulders."

"What then is it?" Strether earnestly enquired.

"Why, it's *she* — simply. It's her mood. It's her charm."

"Of course it's her charm, but we're speaking of the difference."

"Well," Miss Barrace explained, "she's just briliant, as we used to say. That's all. She's various. She's fifty women."

"Ah but only one" — Strether kept it clear — "at a time."

"Perhaps. But in fifty times —!"

"Oh we shan't come to that," our friend declared; and the next moment he had moved in another direction. "Will you answer me a plain question? Will she ever divorce?"

Miss Barrace looked at him through all her tortoise-shell. "Why should she?"

It was n't what he had asked for, he signified; but he met it well enough. "To marry Chad."

"Why should she marry Chad?"

"Because I'm convinced she's very fond of him. She has done wonders for him."

"Well then, how could she do more? Marrying a man, or a woman either," Miss Barrace sagely went on, "is never the wonder, for any Jack and Jill can bring *that* off. The wonder is their doing such things without marrying."

Strether considered a moment this proposition. "You mean it's so beautiful for our friends simply to go on so?"

But whatever he said made her laugh. "Beautiful."

He nevertheless insisted. "And *that* because it's disinterested?"

She was now, however, suddenly tired of the question. "Yes, then — call it that. Besides, she'll never divorce. Don't, moreover," she added, "believe everything you hear about her husband."

"He's not then," Strether asked, "a wretch?"

"Oh yes. But charming."

"Do you know him?"

"I've met him. He's *bien aimable*."

"To every one but his wife?"

"Oh for all I know, to her too — to any, to every woman. I hope you at any rate," she pursued with a quick change, "appreciate the care I take of Mr. Waymarsh."

"Oh immensely." But Strether was not yet in line. "At all events," he roundly brought out, "the attachment's an innocent one."

"Mine and his? Ah," she laughed, "don't rob it of *all* interest!"

"I mean our friend's here — to the lady we've been speaking of." That was what he had settled to as an indirect but none the less closely involved consequence of his impression of Jeanne. That was where he meant to stay. "It's innocent," he repeated — "I see the whole thing."

Mystified by his abrupt declaration, she had glanced over at Gloriani as at the unnamed subject of his allusion, but the next moment she had understood; though indeed not before Strether had noticed her momentary mistake and wondered what might possibly be behind that too. He already knew that the sculptor admired Madame de Vionnet; but did this admiration also represent an attachment of which the innocence was discussable? He was moving verily in a strange air and on ground not of the firmest. He looked hard for an instant at Miss Barrace, but she had already gone on. "All right with Mr. Newsome? Why of course she is!" — and she got gaily back to the question of her own good friend. "I dare say you're surprised that I'm not worn out with all I see — it being so much! — of Sitting Bull. But I'm not, you know — I don't mind him; I bear up, and we get on beautifully. I'm very strange; I'm like that; and often I can't explain. There are people who are supposed interesting or remarkable or whatever, and who bore me to death; and then there are others as to whom nobody can understand what anybody sees in them — in whom I see no end of things." Then after she had smoked a moment, "He's touching, you know," she said.

"'Know'?" Strether echoed — "don't I, indeed? We must move you almost to tears."

"Oh but I don't mean *you!*" she laughed.

"You ought to then, for the worst sign of all — as I must have it for you — is that you can't help me. That's when a woman pities."

"Ah but I do help you!" she cheerfully insisted.

Again he looked at her hard, and then after a pause: "No you don't!"

Her tortoise-shell, on its long chain, rattled down. "I help you with Sitting Bull. That's a good deal."

"Oh that, yes." But Strether hesitated. "Do you mean he talks of me?"

"So that I have to defend you? No, never."

"I see," Strether mused. "It's too deep."

"That's his only fault," she returned — "that everything, with him, is too deep. He has depths of silence — which he breaks only at the longest intervals by a remark. And when the remark comes it's always something he has seen or felt for himself —

267

never a bit banal. *That* would be what one might have feared and what would kill me. But never." She smoked again as she thus, with amused complacency, appreciated her acquisition. "And never about you. We keep clear of you. We're wonderful. But I'll tell you what he does do," she continued: "he tries to make me presents."

"Presents?" poor Strether echoed, conscious with a pang that *he* had n't yet tried that in any quarter.

"Why you see," she explained, "he's as fine as ever in the victoria; so that when I leave him, as I often do almost for hours — he likes it so — at the doors of shops, the sight of him there helps me, when I come out, to know my carriage away off in the rank. But sometimes, for a change, he goes with me into the shops, and then I've all I can do to prevent his buying me things."

"He wants to 'treat' you?" Strether almost gasped at all he himself had n't thought of. He had a sense of admiration. "Oh he's much more in the real tradition than I. Yes," he mused; "it's the sacred rage."

"The sacred rage, exactly!" — and Miss Barrace, who had n't before heard this term applied, recognised its bearing with a clap of her gemmed hands. "Now I do know why he's not banal. But I do prevent him all the same — and if you saw what he sometimes selects — from buying. I save him hundreds and hundreds. I only take flowers."

"Flowers?" Strether echoed again with a rueful reflexion. How many nosegays had her present converser sent?

"Innocent flowers," she pursued, "as much as he

268

likes. And he sends me splendours; he knows all the best places — he has found them for himself; he's wonderful."

"He has n't told them to *me*," her friend smiled; "he has a life of his own." But Strether had swung back to the consciousness that for himself after all it never would have done. Waymarsh had n't Mrs. Waymarsh in the least to consider, whereas Lambert Strether had constantly, in the inmost honour of his thoughts, to consider Mrs. Newsome. He liked moreover to feel how much his friend was in the real tradition. Yet he had his conclusion. "*What* a rage it is!" He had worked it out. "It's an opposition."

She followed, but at a distance. "That's what I feel. Yet to what?"

"Well, he thinks, you know, that *I've* a life of my own. And I have n't!"

"You have n't?" She showed doubt, and her laugh confirmed it. "Oh, oh, oh!"

"No — not for myself. I seem to have a life only for other people."

"Ah for them and *with* them! Just now for instance with — "

"Well, with whom?" he asked before she had had time to say.

His tone had the effect of making her hesitate and even, as he guessed, speak with a difference. "Say with Miss Gostrey. What do you do for *her?*"

It really made him wonder. "Nothing at all!"

III

MADAME DE VIONNET, having meanwhile come in, was at present close to them, and Miss Barrace hereupon, instead of risking a rejoinder, became again with a look that measured her from top to toe all mere long-handled appreciative tortoise-shell. She had struck our friend, from the first of her appearing, as dressed for a great occasion, and she met still more than on either of the others the conception reawakened in him at their garden-party, the idea of the *femme du monde* in her habit as she lived. Her bare shoulders and arms were white and beautiful; the materials of her dress, a mixture, as he supposed, of silk and crape, were of a silvery grey so artfully composed as to give an impression of warm splendour; and round her neck she wore a collar of large old emeralds, the green note of which was more dimly repeated, at other points of her apparel, in embroidery, in enamel, in satin, in substances and textures vaguely rich. Her head, extremely fair and exquisitely festal, was like a happy fancy, a notion of the antique, on an old precious medal, some silver coin of the Renaissance; while her slim lightness and brightness, her gaiety, her expression, her decision, contributed to an effect that might have been felt by a poet as half mythological and half conventional. He could have compared her to a goddess still partly engaged in a morning cloud, or to a sea-nymph waist-high in the summer surge. Above all she suggested to him the reflexion that the *femme du monde* — in these finest developments of the type — was, like Cleopatra in the play, indeed various and multifold. She had aspects, characters, days, nights — or had them at least, showed them by a mysterious law of her own, when in addition to everything she happened also to be a woman of genius. She was an obscure person, a muffled person one day, and a showy person, an uncovered person the next. He thought of Madame de Vionnet to-night as showy and uncovered, though he felt the formula rough, because, thanks to one of the short-cuts of genius, she had taken all his categories by surprise. Twice during dinner he had met Chad's eyes in a longish look; but these communications had in truth only stirred up again old ambiguities — so little was it clear from them whether they were an appeal or an admonition. "You see how I'm fixed," was what they appeared to convey; yet how he was fixed was exactly what Strether did n't see. However, perhaps he should see now.

"Are you capable of the very great kindness of going to relieve Newsome, for a few minutes, of the rather crushing responsibility of Madame Gloriani, while I say a word, if he'll allow me, to Mr. Strether, of whom I've a question to ask? Our host ought to talk a bit to those other ladies, and I'll come back in a minute to your rescue." She made this proposal to Miss Barrace as if her consciousness of a special duty had just flickered up, but that lady's recognition of Strether's little start at it — as at a betrayal on the speaker's part of a domesticated state — was as mute as his own comment; and after an instant, when their fellow guest had good-naturedly left them, he had been given something else to think of. "Why has Maria so suddenly gone? Do you know?" That was the question Madame de Vionnet had brought with her.

"I'm afraid I've no reason to give you but the simple reason I've had from her in a note — the sudden obligation to join in the south a sick friend who has got worse."

"Ah then she has been writing you?"

"Not since she went — I had only a brief explanatory word before she started. I went to see her," Strether explained — "it was the day after I called on you — but she was already on her way, and her concierge told me that in case of my coming I was to be informed she had written to me. I found her note when I got home."

Madame de Vionnet listened with interest and with her eyes on Strether's face; then her delicately decorated head had a small melancholy motion. "She didn't write to *me*. I went to see her," she added, "almost immediately after I had seen you, and as I assured her I would do when I met her at Gloriani's. She hadn't then told me she was to be absent, and I felt at her door as if I understood. She's absent — with all respect to her sick friend, though I know indeed she has plenty — so that I may not see her. She doesn't want to meet me again. Well," she continued with a beautiful conscious mildness, "I liked and admired her beyond every one in the old time, and she knew it — perhaps that's precisely what has made her go — and I dare say I haven't lost her

for ever." Strether still said nothing; he had a horror,
as he now thought of himself, of being in question
between women — was in fact already quite enough
on his way to that; and there was moreover, as it
came to him, perceptibly, something behind these
allusions and professions that, should he take it in,
would square but ill with his present resolve to simplify. It was as if, for him, all the same, her softness
and sadness were sincere. He felt that not less when
she soon went on : " I 'm extremely glad of her happiness." But it also left him mute — sharp and fine
though the imputation it conveyed. What it conveyed
was that *he* was Maria Gostrey's happiness, and for
the least little instant he had the impulse to challenge
the thought. He could have done so however only
by saying "What then do you suppose to be between
us ?" and he was wonderfully glad a moment later not
to have spoken. He would rather seem stupid any
day than fatuous, and he drew back as well, with a
smothered inward shudder, from the consideration of
what women — of highly-developed type in particular
— might think of each other. Whatever he had come
out for he had n't come to go into that; so that he
absolutely took up nothing his interlocutress had now
let drop. Yet, though he had kept away from her for
days, had laid wholly on herself the burden of their
meeting again, she had n't a gleam of irritation to
show him. "Well, about Jeanne now ?" she smiled
— it had the gaiety with which she had originally come
in. He felt it on the instant to represent her motive
and real errand. But he had been schooling her of a
truth to say much in proportion to his little. "*Do* you

make out that she has a sentiment? I mean for Mr. Newsome."

Almost resentful, Strether could at last be prompt. "How can I make out such things?"

She remained perfectly good-natured. "Ah but they're beautiful little things, and you make out — don't pretend! — everything in the world. Have n't you," she asked, "been talking with her?"

"Yes, but not about Chad. At least not much."

"Oh you don't require 'much'!" she reassuringly declared. But she immediately changed her ground. "I hope you remember your promise of the other day."

"To 'save' you, as you called it?"

"I call it so still. You *will?*" she insisted. "You have n't repented?"

He wondered. "No — but I've been thinking what I meant."

She kept it up. "And not, a little, what *I* did?"

"No — that's not necessary. It will be enough if I know what I meant myself."

"And don't you know," she asked, "by this time?"

Again he had a pause. "I think you ought to leave it to me. But how long," he added, "do you give me?"

"It seems to me much more a question of how long you give *me*. Does n't our friend here himself, at any rate," she went on, "perpetually make me present to you?"

"Not," Strether replied, "by ever speaking of you to me."

"He never does that?"

"Never."

She considered, and, if the fact was disconcerting

to her, effectually concealed it. The next minute indeed she had recovered. "No, he would n't. But do
you *need* that?"

Her emphasis was wonderful, and though his eyes
had been wandering he looked at her longer now.
"I see what you mean."

"Of course you see what I mean."

Her triumph was gentle, and she really had tones
to make justice weep. "I've before me what he owes
you."

"Admit then that that's something," she said, yet
still with the same discretion in her pride.

He took in this note but went straight on. "You've
made of him what I see, but what I don't see is how
in the world you've done it."

"Ah that's another question!" she smiled. "The
point is of what use is your declining to know me when
to know Mr. Newsome — as you do me the honour
to find him — *is* just to know me."

"I see," he mused, still with his eyes on her. "I
should n't have met you to-night."

She raised and dropped her linked hands. "It
does n't matter. If I trust you why can't you a little
trust me too? And why can't you also," she asked in
another tone, "trust yourself?" But she gave him
no time to reply. "Oh I shall be so easy for you!
And I'm glad at any rate you've seen my child."

"I'm glad too," he said; "but she does you no
good."

"No good?" —Madame de Vionnet had a clear
stare. "Why she's an angel of light."

"That's precisely the reason. Leave her alone.

Don't try to find out. I mean," he explained, "about what you spoke to me of — the way she feels."

His companion wondered. "Because one really won't?"

"Well, because I ask you, as a favour to myself, not to. She's the most charming creature I've ever seen. Therefore don't touch her. Don't know — don't want to know. And moreover — yes — you *won't*."

It was an appeal, of a sudden, and she took it in. "As a favour to you?"

"Well — since you ask me."

"Anything, everything you ask," she smiled. "I shan't know then — never. Thank you," she added with peculiar gentleness as she turned away.

The sound of it lingered with him, making him fairly feel as if he had been tripped up and had a fall. In the very act of arranging with her for his independence he had, under pressure from a particular perception, inconsistently, quite stupidly, committed himself, and, with her subtlety sensitive on the spot to an advantage, she had driven in by a single word a little golden nail, the sharp intention of which he signally felt. He had n't detached, he had more closely connected himself, and his eyes, as he considered with some intensity this circumstance, met another pair which had just come within their range and which struck him as reflecting his sense of what he had done. He recognised them at the same moment as those of little Bilham, who had apparently drawn near on purpose to speak to him, and little Bilham was n't, in the conditions, the person to whom his heart would be most closed. They were seated

BOOK SIXTH

together a minute later at the angle of the room obliquely opposite the corner in which Gloriani was still engaged with Jeanne de Vionnet, to whom at first and in silence their attention had been benevolently given. "I can't see for my life," Strether had then observed, "how a young fellow of any spirit — such a one as you for instance — can be admitted to the sight of that young lady without being hard hit. Why don't you go in, little Bilham?" He remembered the tone into which he had been betrayed on the garden-bench at the sculptor's reception, and this might make up for that by being much more the right sort of thing to say to a young man worthy of any advice at all. "There *would* be some reason."

"Some reason for what?"

"Why for hanging on here."

"To offer my hand and fortune to Mademoiselle de Vionnet?"

"Well," Strether asked, "to what lovelier apparition *could* you offer them? She's the sweetest little thing I've ever seen."

"She's certainly immense. I mean she's the real thing. I believe the pale pink petals are folded up there for some wondrous efflorescence in time; to open, that is, to some great golden sun. *I'm* unfortunately but a small farthing candle. What chance in such a field for a poor little painter-man?"

"Oh you're good enough," Strether threw out.

"Certainly I'm good enough. We're good enough, I consider, *nous autres*, for anything. But she's *too* good. There's the difference. They would n't look at me."

Strether, lounging on his divan and still charmed by the young girl, whose eyes had consciously strayed to him, he fancied, with a vague smile — Strether, enjoying the whole occasion as with dormant pulses at last awake and in spite of new material thrust upon him, thought over his companion's words. "Whom do you mean by 'they'? She and her mother?"

"She and her mother. And she has a father too, who, whatever else he may be, certainly can't be indifferent to the possibilities she represents. Besides, there's Chad."

Strether was silent a little. "Ah but he does n't care for her — not, I mean, it appears, after all, in the sense I'm speaking of. He's *not* in love with her."

"No — but he's her best friend; after her mother. He's very fond of her. He has his ideas about what can be done for her."

"Well, it's very strange!" Strether presently remarked with a sighing sense of fulness.

"Very strange indeed. That's just the beauty of it. Is n't it very much the kind of beauty you had in mind," little Bilham went on, "when you were so wonderful and so inspiring to me the other day? Did n't you adjure me, in accents I shall never forget, to see, while I've a chance, everything I can? — and *really* to see, for it must have been that only you meant. Well, you did me no end of good, and I'm doing my best. I *do* make it out a situation."

"So do I!" Strether went on after a moment. But he had the next minute an inconsequent question. "How comes Chad so mixed up, anyway?"

BOOK SIXTH

"Ah, ah, ah!"—and little Bilham fell back on his cushions.

It reminded our friend of Miss Barrace, and he felt again the brush of his sense of moving in a maze of mystic closed allusions. Yet he kept hold of his thread. "Of course I understand really; only the general transformation makes me occasionally gasp. Chad with such a voice in the settlement of the future of a little countess — no," he declared, "it takes more time! You say moreover," he resumed, "that we're inevitably, people like you and me, out of the running. The curious fact remains that Chad himself isn't. The situation doesn't make for it, but in a different one he could have her if he would."

"Yes, but that's only because he's rich and because there's a possibility of his being richer. They won't think of anything but a great name or a great fortune."

"Well," said Strether, "he'll have no great fortune on *these* lines. He must stir his stumps."

"Is that," little Bilham enquired, "what you were saying fo Madame de Vionnet?"

"No—I don't say much to her. Of course, however," Strether continued, "he can make sacrifices if he likes."

Little Bilham had a pause. "Oh he's not keen for sacrifices; or thinks, that is, possibly, that he has made enough."

"Well, it *is* virtuous," his companion observed with some decision.

"That's exactly," the young man dropped after a moment, "what I mean."

It kept Strether himself silent a little. "I've made

it out for myself," he then went on; "I 've really, within the last half-hour, got hold of it. I understand it in short at last; which at first — when you originally spoke to me — I did n't. Nor when Chad originally spoke to me either."

"Oh," said little Bilham, "I don't think that at that time you believed me."

"Yes — I did; and I believed Chad too. It would have been odious and unmannerly — as well as quite perverse — if I had n't. What interest have you in deceiving me?"

The young man cast about. "What interest have *I*?"

"Yes. Chad *might* have. But you?"

"Ah, ah, ah!" little Bilham exclaimed.

It might, on repetition, as a mystification, have irritated our friend a little; but he knew, once more, as we have seen, where he was, and his being proof against everything was only another attestation that he meant to stay there. "I could n't, without my own impression, realise. She's a tremendously clever brilliant capable woman, and with an extraordinary charm on top of it all — the charm we surely all of us this evening know what to think of. It is n't every clever brilliant capable woman that has it. In fact it 's rare with any woman. So there you are," Strether proceeded as if not for little Bilham's benefit alone. "I understand what a relation with such a woman — what such a high fine friendship — may be. It can't be vulgar or coarse, anyway — and that 's the point."

"Yes, that 's the point," said little Bilham. "It can't be vulgar or coarse. And, bless us and save us,

it *is n't!* It's, upon my word, the very finest thing
I ever saw in my life, and the most distinguished."

Strether, from beside him and leaning back with
him as he leaned, dropped on him a momentary look
which filled a short interval and of which he took no
notice. He only gazed before him with intent participation. "Of course what it has done for him,"
Strether at all events presently pursued, "of course
what it has done for him — that is as to *how* it has
so wonderfully worked — is n't a thing I pretend
to understand. I've to take it as I find it. There
he is."

"There he is!" little Bilham echoed. "And it's
really and truly she. I don't understand either, even
with my longer and closer opportunity. But I'm like
you," he added; "I can admire and rejoice even when
I'm a little in the dark. You see I've watched it for
some three years, and especially for this last. He
was n't so bad before it as I seem to have made out
that you think —"

"Oh I don't think anything now!" Strether impatiently broke in: "that is but what I *do* think! I mean
that originally, for her to have cared for him —"

"There must have been stuff in him? Oh yes, there
was stuff indeed, and much more of it than ever
showed, I dare say, at home. Still, you know," the
young man in all fairness developed, "there was room
for her, and that's where she came in. She saw her
chance and took it. That's what strikes me as having
been so fine. But of course," he wound up, "he liked
her first."

"Naturally," said Strether.

281

"I mean that they first met somehow and somewhere — I believe in some American house — and
she, without in the least then intending it, made her
impression. Then with time and opportunity he made
his; and after *that* she was as bad as he."

Strether vaguely took it up. "As 'bad'?"

"She began, that is, to care — to care very much.
Alone, and in her horrid position, she found it, when
once she had started, an interest. It was, it is, an interest; and it did — it continues to do — a lot for herself as well. So she still cares. She cares in fact," said
little Bilham thoughtfully, "more."

Strether's theory that it was none of his business
was somehow not damaged by the way he took this.
"More, you mean, than he?" On which his companion looked round at him, and now for an instant
their eyes met. "More than he?" he repeated.

Little Bilham, for as long, hung fire. "Will you
never tell any one?"

Strether thought. "Whom should I tell?"

"Why I supposed you reported regularly —"

"To people at home?" — Strether took him up.
"Well, I won't tell them this."

The young man at last looked away. "Then she
does now care more than he."

"Oh!" Strether oddly exclaimed.

But his companion immediately met it. "Have n't
you after all had your impression of it? That's how
you 've got hold of him."

"Ah but I have n't got hold of him!"

"Oh I say!" But it was all little Bilham said.

"It's at any rate none of my business. I mean,"

BOOK SIXTH

Strether explained, "nothing else than getting hold of him is." It appeared, however, to strike him as his business to add: "The fact remains nevertheless that she has saved him."

Little Bilham just waited. "I thought that was what *you* were to do."

But Strether had his answer ready. "I'm speaking — in connexion with her — of his manners and morals, his character and life. I'm speaking of him as a person to deal with and talk with and live with — speaking of him as a social animal."

"And is n't it as a social animal that you also want him?"

"Certainly; so that it's as if she had saved him *for* us."

"It strikes you accordingly then," the young man threw out, "as for you all to save *her?*"

"Oh for us 'all' —!" Strether could but laugh at that. It brought him back, however, to the point he had really wished to make. "They 've accepted their situation — hard as it is. They 're not free — at least she 's not; but they take what 's left to them. It's a friendship, of a beautiful sort; and that's what makes them so strong. They 're straight, they feel; and they keep each other up. It's doubtless she, however, who, as you yourself have hinted, feels it most."

Little Bilham appeared to wonder what he had hinted. "Feels most that they 're straight?"

"Well, feels that *she* is, and the strength that comes from it. She keeps *him* up — she keeps the whole thing up. When people are able to it 's fine. She's wonderful, wonderful, as Miss Barrace says; and he is, in his way, too; however, as a mere man, he may sometimes rebel and not feel that he finds his account in it. She has simply given him an immense moral lift, and what that can explain is prodigious. That's why I speak of it as a situation. It *is* one, if there ever was." And Strether, with his head back and his eyes on the ceiling, seemed to lose himself in the vision of it.

His companion attended deeply. "You state it much better than I could."

"Oh you see it does n't concern you."

Little Bilham considered. "I thought you said just now that it does n't concern you either."

"Well, it does n't a bit as Madame de Vionnet's affair. But as we were again saying just now, what did I come out for but to save him?"

"Yes — to remove him."

"To save him *by* removal; to win him over to *himself* thinking it best he shall take up business — thinking he must immediately do therefore what's necessary to that end."

"Well," said little Bilham after a moment, "you *have* won him over. He does think it best. He has within a day or two again said to me as much."

"And that," Strether asked, "is why you consider that he cares less than she?"

"Cares less for her than she for him? Yes, that's one of the reasons. But other things too have given me the impression. A man, don't you think?" little Bilham presently pursued, "*can't*, in such conditions, care so much as a woman. It takes different conditions to make him, and then perhaps he cares more.

Chad," he wound up, "has his possible future before him."

"Are you speaking of his business future?"

"No — on the contrary; of the other, the future of what you so justly call their situation. M. de Vionnet may live for ever."

"So that they can't marry?"

The young man waited a moment. "Not being able to marry is all they've with any confidence to look forward to. A woman — a particular woman — may stand that strain. But can a man?" he propounded.

Strether's answer was as prompt as if he had already, for himself, worked it out. "Not without a very high ideal of conduct. But that's just what we're attributing to Chad. And how, for that matter," he mused, "does his going to America diminish the particular strain? Would n't it seem rather to add to it?"

"Out of sight out of mind!" his companion laughed. Then more bravely: "Would n't distance lessen the torment?" But before Strether could reply, "The thing is, you see, Chad ought to marry!" he wound up.

Strether, for a little, appeared to think of it. "If you talk of torments you don't diminish mine!" he then broke out. The next moment he was on his feet with a question. "He ought to marry whom?"

Little Bilham rose more slowly. "Well, some one he *can* — some thoroughly nice girl."

Strether's eyes, as they stood together, turned again to Jeanne. "Do you mean *her?*"

His friend made a sudden strange face. "After being in love with her mother? No."

"But is n't it exactly your idea that he *is n't* in love with her mother?"

His friend once more had a pause. "Well, he is n't at any rate in love with Jeanne."

"I dare say not."

"How *can* he be with any other woman?"

"Oh that I admit. But being in love is n't, you know, here"—little Bilham spoke in friendly reminder —"thought necessary, in strictness, for marriage."

"And what torment—to call a torment—can there ever possibly be with a woman like that?" As if from the interest of his own question Strether had gone on without hearing. "Is it for her to have turned a man out so wonderfully, too, only for somebody else?" He appeared to make a point of this, and little Bilham looked at him now. "When it's for each other that people give things up they don't miss them." Then he threw off as with an extravagance of which he was conscious: "Let them face the future together!"

Little Bilham looked at him indeed. "You mean that after all he should n't go back?"

"I mean that if he gives her up —!"

"Yes?"

"Well, he ought to be ashamed of himself." But Strether spoke with a sound that might have passed for a laugh.

END OF VOLUME I